The Pursuit of

WITHDRAWN

D0775653

APR 11 2018

The Pursuit of

Lady Harriett

RACHAEL ANDERSON

HEA Publishing

Cover image credit: Lee Avison/Trevillion images

ISBN: 978-1-941363-20-1

Published by HEA Publishing

Oh, what a tangled web we weave
When first we practise to deceive!
—Sir Walter Scott, *Marmion*

"HOW DREADFUL IT WOULD be to live on one's own permanently," Lady Harriett Cavendish said to no one in particular as she walked through a thick grove of pines in Askern, Yorkshire. Most of the landscape surrounding Tanglewood Manor appeared barren and lifeless, still dormant from a chilly winter, but this particular area of evergreens felt alive with the promise of spring. Despite the light drizzle and overcast skies, a bird chirped from somewhere overhead, and Harriett smiled at the happy sound.

The current owners of Tanglewood, Lord and Lady Jonathan Ludlow, had departed a week prior on their wedding trip, leaving Harriett in the capable hands of their staff. When she had bid her friends farewell, Harriett had envisioned a grand foray into the glittering world of independence. But now that a week had come and gone with no one but servants to speak with, she found herself developing a severe case of the blue devils.

Harriett missed participating in lively conversations, or any conversations for that matter. She wanted to discuss, tease, be teased, and laugh heartily. She wanted something to think about beyond her own insipid contemplations.

The rain had not helped matters in the least. For three days it had poured down on Askern, confining her indoors with the hollow sounds of servants' footsteps, hushed voices, and silence. How odd that a warm, cozy, and welcoming home could now feel so . . . oppressive. Out of desperation, Harriett had chosen a random book from the library and had become better acquainted with a process called the Norfolk Four-Course Farming Method. The fact that she had found the information interesting was further proof of how wretched she had become.

It was with great relief that she had awakened to a warmer, late-February day with nothing more than a light, misty rain. She had wasted no time donning her pelisse and making her escape to the damp outdoors. The muddy ground squished beneath her boots, but Harriett paid it no mind. She strode into the woods with determination, filling her lungs with fresh, invigorating air.

Yes, this was precisely what she had needed. She could already feel her spirits rise.

After a time, Harriett came to a road riddled with puddles and muck. She sighed and lifted her gaze, smiling when she spotted a rainbow arching across the sky. It wasn't the brightest one she'd ever seen, but that did not matter. Even in its muted state, Harriett decided it was a sign of something beautiful coming her way.

The sound of pounding hooves met her ears, and she squinted down the road to see a horse and rider approaching at a fast clip. As the man neared, Harriett raised her arm in greeting, but the rider showed no signs of slowing. His gaze remained fixed on the road ahead of him as his sleek chestnut galloped through the puddles, both of them taking the bumps and lurches of the uneven ground with ease and grace.

You ride beautifully, Harriett thought as he galloped towards her without a flicker of a glance her way. The horse's hooves landed in a puddle nearby, and a spray of muddy water splattered across her lovely, deep-green pelisse. A few errant specks of mud even reached her face.

Shocked and open-mouthed, Harriett stared down at her clothes before glaring after the rider. Any admiration she'd felt for his skill floated away in the steam seething from her nostrils. How dare he be so unaware of his surroundings! What sort of man did not notice a woman at the side of a road? Or *had* he seen her and chosen not to acknowledge her?

The cad.

Harriett bit her lip in consternation as she wiped the moisture from her cheeks. When it came to men, she had always drawn their notice, whether or not she sought it. During her first London season, she'd never lacked for dance partners, suitors, or even offers of marriage and had lost count of how many times she had been proclaimed a picture of loveliness. Mr. Thomas Chant once rewrote Wordsworth's "The World is Too Much with Us" in her honor, comparing Harriett's fair skin to the petals of a flower and calling her blue eyes captivating.

At first, such declarations had been amusing and even flattering, but Harriett quickly tired of superficial compliments that did not extend beyond her appearance. Someday, her looks would fade as everyone's did, and she felt a great desire to be admired on a deeper level.

After she'd declined an offer of marriage from the eligible, handsome, and excessively wealthy Lord Castlebury, her mother, the dowager Countess of Drayson, had asked, "What is it you seek, Harriett? Of all your suitors, I would have thought Lord Castlebury a prime candidate."

Not entirely sure herself, Harriett had given the matter some thought. "I cannot say for certain, Mother. I only know that I could never love a man who does not see the real me. Lord Castlebury was interested in obtaining an adornment, not a wife, and I could never be content with such a marriage. That, and he does not make me laugh."

Her mother responded with a fond smile and a squeeze. "How very wise you have become, my dear. I would not wish anything less than happiness for you, and I'm sure it is only a matter of time before the right sort of man comes along."

Harriett had once been comforted by the words, but as the days had passed and the season came to an end, she began to wonder at the possibility—or impossibility—of it. Did a man exist who could find something within her to love, or would she only ever be noticed for her beauty? Or worse, not be noticed at all, as had been the case with the man on the road just now.

Reminded of her ruined pelisse, Harriett lifted her gaze and frowned at the diminishing rainbow. "Something beautiful was supposed to come my way, not a care-for-nothing rogue on a horse," she accused. But the rainbow didn't seem the least bit remorseful. Rather, it appeared to perk up a bit as though laughing at her.

Feeling suddenly out of sorts with the day, Harriett lifted her skirts, turned her back on the rainbow, and began the long walk back to Tanglewood.

Harriett's boots were heavy with mud as she emerged through the trees near the western side of the manor house. She debated briefly about whether or not to enter through the servant's entrance or the front door, but it seemed worse to tromp through the kitchen while food was being prepared, so the great hall it would be. She circled around to the front of the house, only to stop abruptly and hide behind some shrubbery when she spotted a man standing next to a muddied chestnut horse. He was speaking with Charlie, one of the stablehands, and although his back was to her, Harriett recognized him as the reckless rider who had sped past her only thirty minutes prior. He wore the same dark jacket, tan trousers, and black beaver hat. And that was definitely the same horse.

Why was he here?

She studied him for a moment before an unhappy realization struck. *Oh, no. He couldn't possibly be Lieutenant Christopher Jamison, could he?*

Harriett closed her eyes in dismay. Who else could he be? The man carried himself with an arrogant air of command, and hadn't Jonathan warned her that his friend was a gentleman in only the loosest of terms? Of course it was him. No true gentleman would fail to notice a woman at the side of the road or leave her coated in mud.

But why had he taken so long to arrive? Jonathan had received word from Lieutenant Jamison on his wedding day, saying his friend was already en route. Harriett had assumed he would arrive in a day or two at most—not a week. When the fourth day had come and gone, she had happily concluded he must have changed his plans and she would no longer be required to receive him after all.

But here he was, several days overdue and catching her by surprise for the second time that morning.

"I am glad to hear I have come to the right estate at last," the man said to Charlie. "The innkeeper's directions were not at all clear, and I found myself visiting a place called

Knotting Tree before a kindly butler redirected me here. But you say your master is away at present?"

"Aye, sir. On 'is weddin' trip."

The man muttered an oath that further convinced Harriett he was far from being a gentleman—that, and his slight West Country burr denoted a less-than-exacting education. Who was this man and how had he come to know Jonathan—not that Harriett really cared to know. As quietly as she could, she backed around the side of the house, staying out of sight. With any luck, he would come to the conclusion that his journey had been in vain and would return to London directly. Perhaps he would even be good enough to take his leave with Charlie now so that Harriett would not be required to speak with him at all. How fortuitous would that be?

"Beggin' your pardon, sir," Charlie said. "But might you be Lieutenant Jamison?"

"Yes. I take it Ludlow received my letter before he left?"

"That 'e did, sir. Left instructions with the staff that Lady 'Arriett's ter receive you."

Did you have to reveal that information, Charlie? Harriett thought as she rolled her eyes, wishing the stable-hand had kept his tongue in check.

"Lady . . . Harriett, you say?" Apparently the lieutenant had never heard of her before, which was not at all surprising. They obviously ran in vastly different circles.

"She's a friend of milady's," Charlie explained. "Stayin' 'ere whilst the honeymooners are away."

"Ah," said the lieutenant, his tone brightening. "Then I shall inquire within immediately and speak to Lady Harriett. In the meantime, would you be so kind as to see to Wicked's needs?"

Harriett peeked around the corner to see Charlie

grinning at the horse as he took the reins. "Wicked, eh? Beggin' your pardon, but 'e don't look at'll wicked ter me, sir. A fine specimen 'e is."

"Don't let him fool you, lad. The animal is the devil himself. He can escape any confine he wishes and will undoubtedly cause a great deal of mischief whenever your back is turned. It's the reason we get on so well, you see. We're of like minds."

Charlie laughed as though it was a great joke, but Harriett could only gape at the man. What sort of person was this lieutenant, and why had Jonathan thought it appropriate for Harriett to receive him? Surely the butler would have been a better choice—not an innocent young lady.

The lieutenant started up the steps, only to be halted by Charlie's voice. "Lady 'Arriett ain't inside, sir. Spotted 'er out walkin' a bit ago."

The man hesitated only a moment before shrugging. "I don't mind waiting. I'm certain the butler will show me to a room where I can cool my heels."

"Aye, sir. Watts'll look after you good and proper."

He planned to wait for her?

Harriett clenched her jaw, realizing there would be no avoiding a confrontation now. Perhaps if she intercepted him before he reached the door, he wouldn't find it necessary to remain for tea. Wicked was still saddled, after all. A brief conversation, and he could be well on his way.

Harriett strode forward, raising her voice to be heard by both Charlie and the lieutenant. "Good morning, Charlie," she called as she nodded at the horse. "Who is this beautiful creature?"

Charlie eyed the animal with pride. "This 'ere's Wicked, milady. Belongs to Lieutenant Jamison."

"Oh, has he finally arrived?" Harriett feigned surprise

and glanced up the steps, pretending to notice the lieutenant for the first time. He had stopped and turned around, but did he descend to meet her as a proper gentleman would? Of course not. He remained exactly where he was, perched several steps above so that she had to crane her neck to meet his gaze.

His very attractive gaze.

Harriett was loath to admit it, but striking was the only way to describe the man. Tall and lean, his strong and broad shoulders supported a sturdy neck, and his eyes were the color of stormy gray skies. He parted his dark blonde hair down the middle, letting it rise and fall to each side like waves cresting and crashing in an unruly manner. It was an unusual hairstyle for a man, but it seemed to suit him. His closely-shaved mustache only added to his rugged masculinity. She could easily envision him as an intimidating naval lieutenant—not that she had any intention of allowing him to intimidate *her*. He had an air of self-importance about his person that she could not like at all.

The corners of his eyes crinkled in a mild show of amusement. "Lady Harriett, I presume?" Rather than look at her with appreciation as most men did, he appeared amused.

At her nod, he tucked his hands behind his back, remaining on the stairs. "I am Lieutenant Christopher Jamison, an old friend of Jonathan's."

"I was expecting you days ago," she answered. "Lord Jonathan charged me with the unhappy task of informing you he and his new bride are currently away on their wedding trip. He is sorry he cannot be here to meet with you and has asked that I relay his apologies."

"May I inquire as to how long they will be away?" he asked.

No, you may not, she wanted to say. Her neck was

beginning to ache from looking up at him, but she forced her gaze to remain steady. "They expected to be gone a fortnight, sir."

"And they have been gone how long, exactly?"

She felt an unaccountable hesitancy to tell him. "A week."

"Ah." He sounded disappointed but seemed to take the news in stride, glancing at Charlie as though wondering whether he ought to retrieve his horse or not. Harriett prayed that he would.

When his gaze strayed back to her, he took the unwelcome, and *ungentlemanly*, liberty of perusing her figure. When his eyes met hers again, his lips twitched into a slight smile. "Forgive me, my lady, but you appear to have had a run-in with a mud puddle and lost."

How kind of him to point that out. Harriett kept her hands at her side rather than attempt to brush the dirt from her face and pelisse yet again. The damage was done, and no amount of brushing or shaking would remove the muck. What she needed was a hot bath and a change of clothes.

"Actually, sir, I was merely an innocent bystander."

"Indeed?"

She picked up her skirts and ascended the steps, stopping on the stair above him so that she was eye level with him. "Are you always such a reckless rider, sir? Do you not pay heed to your surroundings?"

"Of course I do."

"If you had, you would have seen me standing at the side of the road and, I would hope, thought to slow your animal down so as to not splash mud all over my pelisse."

Her chilly set down did not have the desired effect. He did not appear the least bit repentant. Rather, he looked ready to burst into laughter. "And your face, apparently." He leaned forward and squinted. "If I'm not mistaken, there is a splash or two of mud on your bonnet as well."

Harriett glared at him. "How observant you are, Lieutenant Jamison. One can only wonder why you didn't put that skill to good use earlier. If you had, perhaps my pelisse, face, *and* bonnet would still be clean."

"I am always observant, my lady," he said. "But might I suggest that if you would like to be noticed at the side of the road, you should wear a color that does not blend so perfectly with your surroundings. That particular shade of green looks quite lovely on you, but only someone with the eyes of an eagle would have spotted you in front of a landscape of evergreens."

Harriett opened her mouth to respond, but no words were forthcoming. The man did not even *attempt* to behave like a gentleman. How could he be so . . . so . . .

"Have you no apology to offer, sir?" she finally spluttered.

"Oh, did I not apologize? Forgive me."

"For what? Forgetting to apologize or for not doing so in the first place?"

He tucked his hands behind his back and looked at the ground as though attempting not to laugh. When he spared a glance at her again, his eyes danced merrily. "You seem to be a woman of strong opinions, Lady Harriett. Perhaps you should tell me which you'd prefer. Or would you like me to beg your forgiveness on both counts?"

Obviously, Lieutenant Jamison could not be prevailed upon to behave properly, and Harriett refused to provide him with further amusement at her expense.

She took another step up and peered down her nose at him. "I will not detain you any longer, sir. Now that you have been made aware that your friend is away from home, I'm certain you would like to be on your way. London is a far cry from Askern, after all."

Rather than bid her farewell, he glanced past her at the house. "Actually, I was hoping you would offer me a cup of tea and perhaps a bite or two of something to eat. I confess to feeling quite famished."

Of course you are, Harriett thought in frustration, knowing she could not send him packing no matter how much she would like to do so. She was but a guest at Tangle-wood and had no business turning away an old friend of Jonathan's.

She mustered as polite an expression as she could. "Of course, Lieutenant. How thoughtless of me not to offer you some refreshment. If you would care to follow me inside, I will see that you get something to eat. But you must forgive me for not joining you. As you have already noted, I am unfit for the parlor in my current state."

"Of course." He gestured for her to precede him, the only gentlemanly thing he'd done thus far, so she picked up her skirts and led him into the house.

As soon as they entered the great hall, Watts emerged from the kitchen, and his large, square body created a welcoming picture. He took one look at Harriett, and his bushy gray eyebrows creased in concern. "My lady, are you all right? You appear to have taken a fall."

Harriett could have hugged the man for his thoughtfulness. "How kind of you to care about my well-being, Watts," she said. "But other than my untidy appearance, I am quite all right. This, er . . . gentleman"—she had to force herself to say the word—"is Lord Jonathan's friend, Lieutenant Christopher Jamison. Will you show him into the parlor and ask that Sally bring him some tea and refreshment? And please let Tabby know that I am in need of her assistance as well."

"Of course, my lady. Right this way, sir."

The lieutenant did not immediately follow. Instead, he offered Harriett a casual bow. "It was a delight to make your acquaintance, Lady Harriett."

"And I, yours," she lied. "Good day to you."

She turned and ascended the steps, anxious to be away from the man's unnerving gaze. Once she reached the safety of her bedchamber, she allowed herself a sigh of relief. She had done her duty. She had received the lieutenant, relayed Jonathan's message, and had even offered him some refreshment. Now she was free to relax and rid her mind of all disagreeable thoughts concerning the arrogant man. He would be long gone by the time she had bathed and dressed, and she would not be required to speak to him ever again.

NEARLY TWO HOURS LATER, a bark of masculine laughter met Harriett's ears as she descended the staircase. It came from the direction of the parlor and caused her to stiffen and strain to hear more. *Oh no. Surely that man was not still here, was he?*

"I don't believe I have ever been called dimwitted before, ma'am." came that West Country burr, much to Harriett's frustration.

For goodness' sake, why was he still here? And to whom was he speaking? Harriett had been at Tanglewood for a week with no visitors at all—not one. But only two hours after Lieutenant Jamison's arrival, a caller happens by? Had the woman come to see him? Was he now playing host when he ought to be riding his wicked horse back to London?

Lieutenant Jamison was like a burr caught in her stockings, snagging, pulling, and poking in the most irritating way.

"You're twisting my words, sir," said the woman. "I was not calling *you* dimwitted, only your plans. Surely you cannot mean to return to London without seeing Lord Jonathan.

He will be most disappointed to come home and find his friend long gone."

There was no mistaking that rich, authoritative voice. Apparently, Mrs. Bidding had not forgotten about Harriett after all. At the wedding breakfast, she'd promised to call on Harriett and invite her to dinner, but a week had come and gone without a word from the woman—until now, that is, when her timing could not have been more inopportune. Could Mrs. Bidding not have waited to call until after the lieutenant had departed?

"Lady Harriett," boomed Watts's voice from behind, startling her. "You are looking much improved."

His loud timbre had undoubtedly alerted those gathered in the parlor to her presence, making Harriett think unkind thoughts about the butler's timing as well. Resigned that she would be required to speak to the lieutenant once more, she sighed. "Thank you, Watts. I *feel* much improved."

"Mr. and Mrs. Bidding have only just arrived. I took the liberty of showing them into the parlor and introducing Lieutenant Jamison."

"Oh. How . . . delightful." If the Biddings had only just arrived, why was the lieutenant still here? Had he taken up a book and made himself cozy by the fire? Did he plan to settle in for the day and stay through supper as well?

That man!

"Now that you have come down," added Watts, "I shall have Mrs. Caddy brew a fresh pot of tea for you."

Tea sounded heavenly at the moment. "Thank you."

As the butler's footsteps faded away, Harriett drew in a fortifying breath and forced her legs to carry her across the great hall. The parlor was a small room with only two chairs and a settee. As Mr. and Mrs. Bidding occupied the settee, only the chair next to the lieutenant's remained empty.

She pasted a welcoming smile on her lips. "Why, Mr. and Mrs. Bidding, how good of you to come."

Mr. Bidding stood immediately, as any gentleman would, but the lieutenant seemed to take his cue from the older man, standing a second or two later. Harriett briefly wondered if he would have bothered to stand at all if Mr. Bidding had not shown him how he ought to behave when a lady entered the room.

Harriett gracefully took a seat and clasped her fingers neatly in her lap. Ignoring the lieutenant, she directed a smile at the Biddings, who happened to be the oddest couple she had ever met. Where Mrs. Bidding was tall and willowy, with almost masculine features, Mr. Bidding was short, portly, and bald.

"We must apologize for leaving you alone at Tanglewood for so long," said Mrs. Bidding. "I'm sure you've felt quite abandoned this week, what with the Shepherds gone to see their new grandson and the Ludlows away. We had every intention of visiting daily and inviting you to dine, but our roof sprang a leak and we were forced to realign our priorities."

"How dreadful," said Harriett. "Of course you must attend to your house. Please do not fret on my account. I assure you I have been perfectly comfortable. How is your roof? Have you been able to make the necessary repairs?"

"Yes, thank heavens. But with all the rain we've had, it took much longer than we'd hoped."

"I'm glad it is in working order once more," said Harriett, casting a glance at the lieutenant. Good manners dictated that she include him in the conversation, but she rather liked hearing silence from that quarter. He did not offend when he did not speak.

Mrs. Bidding didn't seem to share that opinion.

15

"Lieutenant Jamison has been telling us that he is to return to London on the morrow and will miss seeing Lord Jonathan. Is that not a tragedy?"

Harriett managed a sympathetic smile even though she did not think it tragic in the least. "Indeed. It would be frustrating to embark on such a long and arduous journey, only to have it prove fruitless."

"I would not call it fruitless, my lady," the lieutenant said. "Along the way I met with friends and potential business associates, and now I have had the great pleasure of making your and the Biddings' acquaintance as well. That alone has made the trip worthwhile."

"You are too kind, sir," said a very pleased Mrs. Bidding.

Harriett, on the other hand, was not fooled. The lieutenant's words lacked sincerity, and it bothered her greatly that he suddenly found it in his best interests to be polite. Apparently he thought the Biddings more deserving of courtesy.

"I would happily remain in Askern to await Jonathan's return," Lieutenant Jamison said, "had I not already promised to meet my parents in London at the end of the week. Family obligations, unfortunately, must take precedence over a visit with an old friend, wouldn't you agree, Mrs. Bidding?"

"Certainly. That is to say, unless your obligations could be waylaid a week or so without any harm. It seems a shame to take your leave prematurely when you have come all this way. Surely your parents would understand."

He shrugged and smoothed his hands over the arms of the chair. "Perhaps they would, but in all honesty, I have no wish to settle in at the inn and twiddle my thumbs for a week while I await Jonathan's return. I'm afraid a visit with him will have to be postponed until the conclusion of the season."

"But you will not be staying at the inn," pronounced Mrs. Bidding. "You shall stay with us, of course."

A flicker of surprise and perhaps panic appeared in the lieutenant's expression before he schooled his features and shook his head. "It is good of you to offer, madam, but I could never impose upon the kindness of strangers."

"Nonsense," she said. "We are strangers no more, sir, and any friend of Lord Jonathan's is a friend of ours, especially a military man. Isn't that right, dearest?" She patted her husband's knee as though prompting him in the correct response.

"Yes, yes. Quite right," he said.

"You would not guess as much," Mrs. Bidding added, "but Mr. Bidding was an officer back in his day. His experiences have given us a great deal of respect for any and all soldiers, and it would be an honor to welcome you into our home, sir."

Mr. Bidding nodded agreeably. "An honor indeed to host a fellow comrade in arms."

Harriett couldn't have been more surprised by the news. Mr. Bidding had been an officer? He certainly did not have the air of command that the lieutenant, or even his wife, had. Perhaps when they had married, he'd passed all of his command along to her.

The lieutenant seemed to squirm a bit in his chair at the Biddings' persistence, and Harriett held back a smile. With anyone else, she would have come to his aid, but the man inspired no sympathy in her whatsoever. In fact, she rather liked seeing him squirm. Mrs. Bidding was a difficult woman to deflect, and Harriett looked forward to seeing how the lieutenant would extricate himself from the situation. Perhaps his earlier rudeness would emerge for all to see.

"How lucky you are, Lieutenant," said Harriett, yielding

to a wicked urge to increase his discomfort. "I'm certain the Biddings don't welcome just anyone into their home. It is an honor, indeed, to be offered such a rare treat."

She awaited his response with amusement, half expecting him to leap from his chair and make a hasty retreat. But he did no such thing. Instead, his eyes met hers in what appeared to be some sort of assessment. After a moment, the discomfort faded from his expression as he settled back in his seat and clasped his fingers over his waist.

He smiled warmly at the Biddings. "Lady Harriett is quite right. I would be a fool to pass on your offer. If you are certain I would not be an inconvenience, I would love nothing more than to await my friend's return as your guest."

"Wonderful." Mrs. Bidding clapped her hands in a show of delight. "And Lady Harriett, of course you will be included in all of our plans as well, beginning with dinner this evening. Do say you will join us."

Harriett blinked, dumfounded. What had just happened? She had been so certain Lieutenant Jamison had no wish to stay, but now he'd agreed to do exactly that for at least a week and possibly even longer? How could that be? He was a former lieutenant in the navy, for goodness' sake. Where was the man's fortitude—his ability to hold strong despite the pressures surrounding him?

One glance in his direction, and Harriett had her answer. The amused triumph lurking in his eyes said it all. It was as though he had just made a highly calculated move and called out, *Check.*

She had to clench her jaw to keep it from falling open in astonishment. Did he truly mean to punish himself so that he could punish her as well? Was the man so wretched as that? Apparently. He'd professed to be of a wicked nature, after all.

"Lady Harriett," said Mrs. Bidding. "Are you attending? I asked if you are able to dine with us this evening."

The lieutenant leaned forward in his chair to look at Harriett, his smile far too satisfied. "You have just been offered a rare treat, my lady. I'm quite certain the Biddings do not invite just anyone to sup with them. Surely you will not deny us the pleasure of your company."

Harriett attempted not to scowl but couldn't be sure if she'd succeeded or not. Her plans had gone dreadfully awry, and she had no one to blame but herself. She had known the lieutenant's true nature and should have expected his response. Why could she not have left well enough alone—or better yet, helped to extricate him from the Biddings' invitation? If so, he would soon be on his way back to London.

Instead, she had no choice but to acquiesce. With tight lips, she said, "I would be delighted to join you for dinner, Mr. and Mrs. Bidding."

"Wonderful."

With that settled, the Biddings and the lieutenant took their leave. As Mr. Bidding helped his wife with her pelisse, Harriett snuck a glare at the lieutenant. He responded with a smirk and even had the temerity to tip his hat in her direction as he walked outside.

Harriett seethed as she closed the door behind them, thinking unladylike thoughts about retaliation. She had been taught many times that revenge did not answer, and for the most part, she had always agreed with such wisdom. But as the lieutenant strode confidently down the steps, she decided that sometimes it was all right to exact a little revenge, and this happened to be one of those times.

SOMETIME DURING THE AFTERNOON, the skies finally cleared and the sun made a long overdue appearance. The lovely change in weather inspired the Biddings to push back dinner half an hour so the foursome could take a stroll through the still-dormant gardens. Although Harriett always enjoyed an invigorating walk, especially on a glorious evening such as this, she did not appreciate the narrowness of the pathways, nor the fact that Mr. and Mrs. Bidding had moved ahead and were now absorbed by the antics of their pampered Yorkshire terrier, leaving Harriett to entertain Lieutenant Jamison on her own.

"It's a lovely evening, is it not?" he said.

Harriett almost laughed. Already he was commenting on the weather? Goodness, this conversation was certainly doomed to failure.

"Yes," she answered, running her palm across the tips of some tall, brown grasses that they passed. The gardens were beautifully organized, with stone-lined pathways meandering through the various arrangements of leafless hedges and plants. But at this time of year, it appeared like a tangle of stems and branches.

Lieutenant Jamison clasped his hands behind his back, and after a few moments of strained silence, tried again. "Poor Mr. Bidding. To be compelled to lead about such a feminine-looking dog. How unmanly he must feel at the moment."

Harriett eyed the couple ahead of them. The terrier was small as all terriers were, with short legs and a round middle. Its white, brown, and black hair had been left to grow long enough to brush into soft, straight lines. Harriett couldn't deny that Mr. Bidding *did* look rather silly doting over such a dog, but she would never admit as much to the lieutenant. And besides, the Biddings were a little odd, so it suited them.

The terrier stopped to sniff at something, and Mr. Bidding paused as well, turning back to look at the animal with an expression one could only describe as indulgent.

"He doesn't seem to mind the task so very much," commented Harriett. "In fact, he appears enamored of the creature, and who can blame him? The dog is adorable."

"Adorable for a woman, perhaps. Utterly ridiculous for a man. Mr. Bidding really ought to acquire a foxhound or a mastiff—a man's dog."

Harriett cocked her head at him. "You dare to call your host ridiculous, sir?"

"Of course not. I only said he has the appearance of it when he's leading that dog about. The animal has a pink bow in its hair for pity's sake."

Harriett barely stopped herself from laughing. "Heaven forbid a man show an interest in anything so darling. I wonder, sir, should you ever have a little girl with a bow in her hair, will you shy away from her? Or perhaps you would dress her up as a boy so that she would not have such a negative effect on your masculinity."

He smiled a little. "Dress a daughter up as a boy? Don't be absurd."

"I believe it is you who are being absurd."

"I am not the one comparing a canine to a little girl."

Harriett rolled her eyes. Speaking with the lieutenant was like trying to have a conversation with a stubborn child. She swished her rose skirts away from a prickly bush, refusing to continue such a silly conversation.

"Tell me, Lady Harriett, where do you hail from?" Apparently he did not prefer to walk in silence as she did.

"Heaven, of course," Harriett quipped, causing him to chuckle. It was a nice sound—deep and rich and perfectly melodious, as though he had taken lessons on how to laugh in the most pleasing way. How irritating.

"What about you, sir? Do you come from Heaven as well, or . . . someplace else?"

He laughed again, and Harriett felt her traitorous cheeks warm. Why on earth was she reacting to that sound? She certainly did not wish to. It ought to grate on her nerves as the lieutenant did.

"I suppose I could say Heaven as well, since I come from Cornwall," he answered.

Having never been so far south, Harriett was curious. "Is it heavenly there?" she asked. With the exception of London and Yorkshire and wherever the road had carried her in between, she hadn't been much of anywhere. Perhaps if she didn't despise riding in a carriage for hours on end she'd be more inclined to travel.

"It is," he answered, sounding wistful. "Beautifully white, sandy beaches, rugged green hills, and the most breathtaking turquoise waters. I take it you are not from Cornwall."

"No." Though Harriett suddenly wished to go there very much.

"Devon, perhaps?"

She shook her head, noticing that the Biddings were no longer in sight. Apparently they'd allowed their dog to set the pace and had forgotten about their guests. Harriett hoped they would realize their lapse sooner than later and pause to wait.

"Somerset?" the lieutenant inquired, persevering in his quest to discover the location of her family home. What did he intend to do, rattle off each and every county until her answer changed to the affirmative?

And she had thought a discussion about the weather would be dull.

He must have taken Harriett's silence as a no because he continued on. "Dorset?"

She sighed impatiently. "I come from Danbury in Essex, sir."

"Ah," he grinned triumphantly—a look she was growing very tired of seeing. "That was not so difficult to reveal, was it? Though I must say that Essex is quite a ways from here."

"Not as far as Cornwall."

"No, but as I was most recently in London, my journey did not take as long as yours. Did you come for the wedding?"

The man brimmed with questions, didn't he? Harriett was beginning to feel quite harassed. "Yes."

"But the wedding has come and gone and still you are here."

Which was *her* concern, not his. She glanced up at him. "My, you are observant when you choose to be, Lieutenant. Did you learn that skill in the navy?"

"No, actually. It is a talent I have always possessed. As a lad, I would climb various trees on our property and . . . well, observe, I suppose you could say. I found it most interesting and enlightening. The apple trees were a particular favorite as they had the best branches for climbing."

Harriett found this aspect of his character surprising. "Pray forgive me, sir, but I cannot picture you doing anything as reflective as pondering over various observations."

"No?" he asked. "What can you picture me doing?"

Harriett searched the path ahead, wondering where the Biddings had run off to, and shrugged. "I don't know. Picking apples and lobbing them at unsuspecting passersby, perhaps?"

He threw back his head and laughed. The sound warmed Harriett's body clear through, pleasing and vexing her simultaneously. *Good heavens.* Why could she not be immune to this one and only charm he possessed? She ought to be plotting her retaliation on him, not blushing like a silly, impressionable girl. This would not do at all.

"I may or may not have lobbed an apple a time or two in my life," he said, "but I will never say for certain."

They walked under a stone archway to find a happily situated meadow stretching out before them. The Biddings waited on a bench under a willow with leafless branches draping charmingly over the top of them. Their small terrier played at their feet, sniffing, scurrying, and straying only so far as its leash would allow.

The lieutenant slowed his steps and touched Harriett's arm lightly, just above her elbow. A smattering of goose bumps sprinkled across her arm, and she had to fight the instinct to jerk away.

"You are not still upset about the mud incident, are you?" he asked. "I assure you I did not splatter you on purpose, and I did apologize."

"You did no such thing. You merely apologized for not apologizing, which is entirely different. You seem to take great delight in needling me, sir, and I cannot understand why."

"Can you not?" His mustache tightened as he smiled, and his eyes glimmered with humor. "Perhaps it's because you are entirely too fun to tease, Lady Harriett. But if it will appease your sensibilities, pray forgive me for racing down the lane with such abandon, for not seeing your lovely face amidst all the pines, and for causing you to suffer as a result."

It was a pretty apology, Harriett had to concede, but it lacked sincerity. "When one must extract an apology, sir, it most certainly does *not* appease. I cannot fathom how you might think it would."

He studied her for a moment. "Tell me, Lady Harriett, how am I to earn your forgiveness if you will not accept belated apologies?"

"Perhaps you should have thought about that before now."

He glanced down at his boots and smiled, only to lift his gaze to hers a moment later. "'To err is human; to forgive, divine,' wouldn't you agree?" he asked, quoting Alexander Pope.

Years ago, when Harriett had first read those words, they had moved her. Now, they did not budge her in the least. The lieutenant was merely making excuses for his bad behavior and attempting to guilt her into overlooking them.

"I have never claimed to be divine, sir, nor do I hold out any hope of reaching such a state of perfection in my lifetime."

He chuckled again. "Did you not just claim to come from Heaven?"

Harriett had no answer to this, other than to clamp her mouth shut and scowl. The man was impossible. However did he and Jonathan come to be friends?

"I must say, Lady Harriett, that I have never met anyone quite so . . . interesting as you."

Interesting? Harriett frowned, wondering at his meaning. One might say the Biddings were an "interesting" couple or that Lady Monroe threw the most "interesting" parties. If that was the way he meant the word, Harriett had to disagree. She was not at all interesting. She was annoyed. Again. How many more days did he plan to stay?

"Sir, are you certain you wish to keep your parents waiting in London? They must be missing you dreadfully."

The lowering sun reflected in his eyes, lightening them to an almost sky blue mixed with darker hues. Harriett had never seen such color in a person's eyes before, and she found the sight captivating.

"How kind of you to be concerned for my parents' welfare, but I can assure you that they will survive my absence for another fortnight."

"Fortnight?" she blurted.

"Or longer," he added, dusting off one sleeve as though oblivious to the upset he had just caused.

Harriett pierced him with a sharp look—not that he noticed it as he was still concerned with the state of his sleeve. "Exactly how long do you plan to remain in Askern, Lieutenant Jamison?"

His attention finally returned to her, and he leaned in close enough that she felt his breath on her cheek. "As long as it takes for me to gain your forgiveness."

She bristled. "That could take forever, sir."

"Hence the reason I said 'or longer.'" He grinned and she frowned. Then he peered over her head to a spot in the distance and added, "Mrs. Bidding is watching us with great interest. Perhaps we should continue this conversation at a later date."

Without waiting for a response or even offering her his arm, he clasped his hands behind his back and began sauntering towards the Biddings, no doubt expecting her to rush to catch up. Harriett stayed exactly where she was and watched him go, not surprised by such behavior. He was Lieutenant Jamison, after all, a man who'd already tried her patience more than any other man had ever done. She drew in a deep breath and admired the views on either side of her before meandering along a sedate pace, noting that he'd finally stopped to wait for her.

How thoughtful of him, she thought sourly. They walked the remaining few steps to the Biddings in silence.

"I hope you enjoyed your stroll," said Mrs. Bidding.

"Yes, it was most . . . *enlightening,*" said Harriett, more than ready for a little comeuppance. "I learned that Lieutenant Jamison is vastly fond of terriers and that yours has quite captured his heart. He was even hoping you might allow him to take it for a jaunt about the yard. He finds the sweet creature so very entertaining, you see, not to mention adorable with that darling bow in her hair."

Mr. Bidding smiled like a proud parent and held the leash out to the lieutenant. "Of course you may take Pippin for a turn about the meadow. She has far too healthy an appetite, and if you hadn't already noticed, her middle is growing very round indeed. You would be doing us a favor by exercising her further, sir, and we are happy to oblige."

It was the most Harriett had ever heard Mr. Bidding speak. She would have stared at him in astonishment if not for her desire to see the lieutenant's reaction.

He looked at the leash as though it were a maggot, and Harriett had to stifle a burst of laughter. After a moment, he lowered his pride enough to accept the offering.

"How kind you are, Mr. Bidding. I assume you would like to join me, Lady Harriett, as you are vastly fond of Pippin as well?"

Harriett sank down on a bench next to Mrs. Bidding and waved her hand in a dismissive fashion. "You go ahead, sir. After this morning's long walk, I find myself quite exhausted."

His jaw clenched momentarily, but ever the gentleman around the Biddings, he nodded and walked slowly away, pulling the dog along behind him. Harriett delighted in the sight, though she wished the lieutenant was not quite so handsome. Her eyes lingered on his broad shoulders and the masculine lines of his arms and legs. She could not help but admire the snug fit of his coat or the confident way he carried himself.

Mrs. Bidding leaned towards Harriett and lowered her voice slightly. "Lieutenant Jamison reminds me of Mr. Bidding back in the day. He was once just as dashing and quite stole my heart." She patted her husband's knee. "Isn't that right, my love?"

"Quite so." Mr. Bidding didn't seem to hear his wife's praise. He was smiling at Pippin's antics, looking every inch the indulgent parent. Harriett found him almost as amusing as the lieutenant.

She couldn't help but wonder if the Biddings would continue to sing Lieutenant Jamison's praises once they discovered he did not adore their dog at all. Had they noticed the tightness in his jaw, the stiff set to his shoulders, and his obvious displeasure at being made to carry out such a feminine chore? Harriett certainly had. She noticed all of it, including the glare the lieutenant cast in her direction.

A genuine smile lifted her lips. Darling, darling Pippin. What a wonderful, accommodating creature. Harriett had always been fond of animals, but little Pippin was quickly earning a special place in her heart.

"I do so admire military men," Mrs. Bidding said, eyeing Harriett with a look that could only be described as knowing. "I believe you are of the same mind, are you not? I can see it in your eyes that you find the lieutenant charming. Did you enjoy your tête-à-tête? I had hoped that if Mr. Bidding and I allowed you some time to converse privately, you'd become as thick as thieves in no time."

Harriett's amusement dwindled in an instant. Mrs. Bidding believed her to be charmed? How was that even possible? Either Harriett had marvelous acting skills, which was certainly not the case, or her hostess was in dire need of a pair of spectacles. How else could she mistake expressions of annoyance, frustration, and displeasure for adoration?

Mrs. Bidding patted Harriett's knee in a comforting gesture. "Not to worry, my dear. I shall never let on that I know. A woman must be allowed her secrets, hmm?"

Harriett blinked at Mrs. Bidding in surprise. According to Colin and Lucy, the woman was quite the stickler for propriety and frowned on any and all scandalous behavior. Surely, she would never intentionally leave Harriett alone with such a man as Lieutenant Jamison?

Yet she'd done precisely that.

Harriett swallowed, choosing her words carefully. "I must say, Mrs. Bidding, that you do not strike me as the matchmaking sort."

The woman smiled as though she knew something Harriett didn't. "I do not usually condone meddling, my dear, but I could not help but notice how well suited the two of you seem."

Well suited? Certainly not! Colin and Lucy were well suited, as were Jonathan and Cora. Harriett and the lieutenant, on the other hand, were very much *ill* suited. How was that not obvious?

Mrs. Bidding persevered. "Come now, Lady Harriett, and confess. You think him quite captivating."

At a loss as to how to respond, Harriett clamped her mouth shut. Something told her that Mrs. Bidding would not appreciate being informed that her judgment of the lieutenant was far from sound, but Harriett could not pretend to agree that she thought him captivating either. But how to nip such matchmaking attempts in the bud without injuring the woman's pride?

Harriett finally settled on, "I'm afraid I don't know the lieutenant well enough to comment on whether or not he is deserving of such admiration."

Mrs. Bidding gave Harriett's knee another pat. "Never fear, my dear. I will be sure to arrange more opportunities for you to further your acquaintance with the good lieutenant. If the weather is as pleasing tomorrow, I was thinking a picnic would be just the thing."

Harriett gave a slight nod, all the while wondering what plans Mrs. Bidding had in store for her and Lieutenant Jamison. Did she intend to place Harriett in one compromising situation after another until the man had no choice but to offer for her? Not that he ever would as that would require him to behave as a gentleman.

What was Mrs. Bidding thinking to encourage such a match? Perhaps military men cast some sort of enchantment over her. It was the only explanation.

Harriett nearly sighed in relief when the lieutenant started back in their direction with Pippin in tow. As she watched him approach, she again wondered what the Biddings would think of the lieutenant if they knew he was not fond of their precious dog. Would Mrs. Bidding continue to play the matchmaker, or would such a revelation dissuade her?

Hmm . . .

As Lieutenant Jamison handed Pippin's leash back to Mr. Bidding, Harriett eyed her hostess. "I agree that a picnic would be just the thing, Mrs. Bidding, but you really ought to bring Pippin along for the lieutenant's sake. He would undoubtedly be saddened if his new little admirer was left behind, don't you think?"

"Of course we'll bring Pippin," inserted Mr. Bidding as though the matter had already been decided. "She must get her exercise."

"Yes," agreed his wife. "It goes without saying that wherever we go, Pippin goes."

Wonderful, thought Harriett, leaning forward to give the creature a gentle rub. Perhaps if Pippin continued to accompany them, Lieutenant Jamison's dislike of the creature would be made obvious, his true colors shown, and Mrs. Bidding would come to the realization on her own that this particular military man was not nearly as charming or dashing as her husband had been.

Harriett pulled herself up and looked at the lieutenant. "Did you enjoy your walk, sir?"

He took a seat on the bench beside her and, in a diplomatic fashion, answered, "Not nearly as much as I enjoyed my walk with you, Lady Harriett."

His words seemed to please Mrs. Bidding immensely, much to Harriett's displeasure.

"Lady Harriett and I were only just discussing the enchantments of picnics, sir," said Mrs. Bidding. "Do say that you will come with us on the morrow."

"Yes, do," added Harriett. "Only think of how fun it will be to escort Pippin around."

Lieutenant Jamison's eyes narrowed for a brief spell before he mustered a smile. "Of course I will come, Mrs. Bidding. A picnic with Pippin sounds . . . delightful."

From the corner of her eye, Harriett watched the Biddings to gauge their reaction. Surely they detected the sarcasm in his answer. It was impossible to miss. But Mr. Bidding was once again occupied with his beloved dog while his wife continued to appear as pleased as punch.

Good heavens. Whatever enchantment Lieutenant Jamison had cast over the woman was strong indeed. But no matter. With Pippin's help, it was only a matter of time before any and all enchantments wore off.

MUCH TO HARRIETT'S DELIGHT, she awoke to sunny skies, chirping birds, and the luscious smell of dew-kissed earth. With a smile on her lips, she sipped her chocolate, ate a bite of toast, and turned herself over to the ministrations of her maid, Tabby.

The two women were similar in age, height, and build, but where Harriett had fair skin and dark curls, Tabby had a great many freckles and hair so blonde it almost looked white. The maid obviously spent a great deal of time out of doors without a bonnet. Most would consider her complexion shockingly neglected, but Harriett found it refreshing. Tabby had been blessed with a sunny disposition, and it was apparent that she placed greater importance on living a joyful life than attempting perfection. It was an enviable perspective, to be sure, not that Harriett was ready to give up her bonnets just yet.

"Aren't you in a chipper mood, this mornin', milady," commented Tabby as she arranged Harriett's hair in a lovely knot on the crown of her head. Her quick smile never failed to lift Harriett's spirits on the rare occasions they dipped low, such as this past week. Too many days of solitude would have landed her squarely in the doldrums if not for Tabby's cheerfulness.

"Yes," agreed Harriett. "I believe the change in weather has done me good."

Through the looking glass, Tabby grinned coyly. "From what's bein' said below stairs, I would've thought a certain lieutenant was the reason."

Harriett suddenly felt much less chipper. "What, exactly, is being said below stairs?"

Not easily cowed, Tabby replied pertly, "Nothin' to wipe that smile from your face, milady. Only that an 'andsome lieutenant came callin' yesterday, and if an 'andsome man were ter call on me, I'd be a sight more chipper too."

Harriett didn't think it possible that her maid could get any more cheerful, but she couldn't deny that Tabby was correct in a way. Harriett's reflection in the mirror did look happier. Her eyes sparkled brighter, her complexion appeared more radiant, and her countenance glowed with increased energy. Tabby would have to be blind not to notice the change, although she'd given credit to the wrong source.

"'Tis only the sunny skies, Tabby. Nothing more."

"Aye, Miss." Tabby's eyes continued to dance merrily as though she did not believe a word Harriett said. The maid was a romantic at heart, and if she wanted to believe a handsome lieutenant had come to sweep her mistress off her feet, she would believe it despite Harriett's claims to the contrary. Besides, the lieutenant *was* responsible for her elevated spirits in a way. She very much looked forward to watching him take a turn about the park with a certain small dog on a leash. Perhaps she should commission a sweater to be made for Pippin—a pink one to match its bow. Wouldn't the lieutenant enjoy that.

Harriett's grin returned, and she found herself wishing

she'd applied herself more to her drawing lessons. Some happy hours could be spent sketching out a scene of a toplofty man walking a sweet little dog. How she'd love to gift such a picture to Lieutenant Jamison and enjoy his expression when he saw it.

Unfortunately, Harriett lacked the skill to draw anything resembling her subjects. She could outline an apple or make a valiant attempt at sketching the veins in a leaf, but if an image required more detail, texture, or dimension, the poor thing would come away looking haggard and misshapen. Such a work of art would inspire the lieutenant's laughter, not his chagrin, and Harriett most certainly did not want that. So instead of drawing, she would simply have to commit the scene to memory so that she would be able to share it in glorious detail with her dear friend, Cora, once she returned from her wedding trip.

Her mind thus engaged, Harriett's chipper mood remained throughout the morning, and when the Biddings arrived to collect her for the picnic, she happily climbed into the carriage. But as she settled in next to the lieutenant and looked around, her smile faltered when she saw no sign of sweet, little Pippin. The dog was not on anyone's lap, not on the floor, and certainly not with the coachman. Mr. Bidding would never allow that, would he?

Whatever happened to Mrs. Bidding's declaration that wherever they went, Pippin went?

Harriett made a show of arranging her skirts and attempted to sound casual as she asked, "Where's Pippin?"

Mr. Bidding sighed and peered out the window, his forehead crinkled with worry. "Still at home with our housekeeper, I'm afraid. Lieutenant Jamison pointed out to us this morning that the roundness of her middle might not be the result of a healthy appetite after all. He seems to think our dear Pippin is increasing."

Increasing? Harriett tried to mask her annoyance. *What fustian.* Surely the man could have come up with a better Banbury tale than that.

"How very *observant* you are, Lieutenant," Harriett said wryly.

His mustache twitched with amusement. He appeared not to have shaved this morning, and the stubble along his jaw made him look even more ruggedly dashing.

Drat the man.

Mrs. Bidding nodded solemnly, though there was a delighted twinkle in her eyes. "The lieutenant could be in the right of it, I think. Pippin has been acting more lethargic of late. We will send for a cow-leech this afternoon to confirm the diagnosis, but until we know for certain, we thought it best to leave her at home. Lieutenant Jamison, the compassionate man that he is, pointed out that too much excitement could be harmful for her."

Harriett barely refrained from rolling her eyes. "Observant *and* compassionate. My, how blessed the Biddings are to have you as their guest, sir."

He seemed to mold his face into an impassive expression. "I could never forgive myself if Pippin endangered her health or the health of her puppies on my account."

"No, I'm sure you could not," said Harriett tightly. She turned her gaze towards the window and noticed that the outside world suddenly seemed dimmer than it had before, as though the sun had taken refuge behind a cloud. She blamed the lieutenant entirely. He'd outmaneuvered her, and it rankled. But it was only a matter of time before the cow-leech confirmed that Pippin was *not* increasing, so the picnic was nothing more than a minor setback. By dinner this evening, all would be set to rights and Harriett would once again be at liberty to promote an unwanted attachment between Lieutenant Jamison and the dog.

In the meantime, she would simply have to make the best of things.

A few turns in the road later, the coachman stopped near a pleasant spot on a hilltop overlooking a beautiful valley. In another month, the leaves would sprout and the entire countryside would be bursting with vibrant shades of green. Harriett enjoyed the scenery while two footmen spread out a rug and carried over a large basket filled with food. They settled down for a cozy picnic, and Harriett filled her plate with a delicious assortment of bread, meats, and cheeses, thinking that perhaps the afternoon was not entirely spoiled.

It was in that peaceful moment that the lieutenant chose to pull out a book from a knapsack he carried. Harriett peered closer, furrowing her brows in confusion. What on earth did the lieutenant plan to do with a Bible? He was certainly not the sort of man to ever read such a book, was he? Surely he was not considering entering the church. That would be altogether too laughable.

Much to her surprise, he announced, "I thought a biblical passage would be just the thing for an inspirational day such as this."

Beneath the brim of a wide-brimmed bonnet, Mrs. Bidding nodded politely, murmuring her approval. "I have always loved a nice reading, Lieutenant, and what could be more inspiring than scripture from the Good Book? Let us hear your passage, sir."

Mr. Bidding nodded as well. "Yes, do carry on."

Thus encouraged, Lieutenant Jamison wasted no time in opening to a section that appeared to have been previously marked. "These particular verses of scripture come from the fifth chapter of Matthew and struck me as wise counsel." He cleared his throat, and a slight smile teased his lips as he glanced briefly at Harriett before continuing. "'Ye have heard that it hath been said, An eye for an eye, and a tooth for a tooth: But I say unto you, That ye resist not evil: but whosoever shall smite thee on thy right cheek, turn to him the other also.'"

He continued to read a few more verses before concluding with, "'Ye have heard that it hath been said, Thou shalt love thy neighbour, and hate thine enemy. But I say unto you, Love your enemies, bless them that curse you, do good to them that hate you, and pray for them which despitefully use you, and persecute you;'"

Even with his slight burr, his deep voice sounded powerful and even regal. If Harriett had not found the subject matter so irritating, she could have imagined him standing at a pulpit before a captivated congregation.

But he hadn't been standing at a pulpit or speaking to a congregation. He'd been speaking to *her*—or rather, *preaching*.

The cad.

Sure enough, he closed the book and studied her. "What are your thoughts on that message, my lady?"

That you are a hypocritical boor, thought Harriett, feeling extremely unchristian at the moment. She took a bite of cheese to keep from saying something she'd likely regret.

"It is a wonderful sentiment," interjected Mrs. Bidding. "I only wish it would inspire more people. Only think of how pleasant this world would be if such an attitude existed in the hearts of every soul."

"I couldn't have put it better myself," said the lieutenant good-naturedly, bestowing a triumphant smile upon Harriett.

Unfortunately, she could think of no rejoinder to this, at least not one that could be spoken in the presence of the

Biddings. "Tell me, Lieutenant," she said instead. "Have you forgiven all who have done *you* harm?"

He set the Bible aside and picked up his plate once more. "In all honesty, I cannot say that I have, only that I try my best. Carrying a grudge is a heavy burden that I'd rather not shoulder if I can help it."

Harriett pressed her lips together, not sure what to make of his words. He seemed the sort who was rarely serious, yet he'd sounded as though he truly did try to forgive all. But did he, or was his opinion merely part of his scheme to prod her into forgiving him? What sort of man was Lieutenant Jamison?

She brushed a few crumbs from her lap before responding. "I do think that grudges are burdens that I'd prefer not to carry. But I am also human, sir, and as such I find it very difficult to, er . . . excuse certain people, especially when they are often in my company. Sometimes I find it necessary to distance myself from them so that I can truly forgive—or at the very least, forget."

He laughed, and once again the sound wormed its way into Harriett's emotions, confusing and unsettling her. Her appetite gone, she set her plate aside, wondering how long the picnic would last. Was it too soon to plead a headache? Or perhaps Pippin could come to her aid after all.

"Mr. and Mrs. Bidding," said Harriett. "I'm certain you are both worried about the health of Pippin. Shall we end the picnic a little early so that you might see to her needs and put your minds at ease?"

Mr. Bidding appeared hopeful, but his wife waved Harriett's concerns aside with an elegant flip of her wrist. "And waste this beautiful afternoon? Certainly not. If Pippin is indeed breeding, she will still be breeding when we arrive home. A few hours will not change matters in the least."

Hmm . . . It seemed Pippin would not come to Harriett's aid at all today, the little scamp.

Lieutenant Jamison finished off the last of his luncheon and set his plate aside. He brushed his hands together and jumped to his feet before extending a hand to Harriett. "Would you do me the honor of taking a walk with me, my lady?"

Before Harriett could think of an excuse, Mrs. Bidding clapped her hands. "What a wonderful notion. Of course you young people ought to enjoy yourselves with a lovely stroll. Mr. Bidding and I can chaperone adequately from here." She wagged a playful finger at the lieutenant. "Just promise that you will not stray too far."

"You have my word that we will not, madam," he answered, always eager to please everyone but Harriett.

Knowing she had no other choice but to graciously accept, she placed her gloved fingers in his and allowed him to assist her to her feet. As soon as she could, she released his hand and clasped her fingers behind her back, determined to keep her distance.

They began descending the small rise, and as soon as they were out of earshot of their hosts, Lieutenant Jamison leaned in close, brushing his shoulder against hers. Harriett tried her best not to notice the touch, but the rush of heat that infused her body was impossible to ignore.

"Pippin *is* increasing, you know," he said. "I did not falsify that information."

"Fiddlesticks," said Harriett. "That dog is no more carrying puppies than I am."

He lifted an eyebrow in challenge. "Would you care to place a wager on that, my lady?"

"Yes, as a matter of fact, I would." She gave the matter a little thought before presenting him with her terms.

"According to the Bible, which you obviously hold in high esteem, a good son would honor his parents' wishes and not keep them waiting. It's one of the ten commandments, you know. So if I am right, I think you ought to consider shortening your stay in Askern."

He chuckled softly. "Do you find my company so intolerable, Lady Harriett?"

She didn't answer right away because she wasn't sure how. The truth was that sometimes she did and sometimes she didn't. But that was the problem, wasn't it? A person should never feel so befuddled by another. It was most unnatural, and she had no intention of allowing it to continue if she could help it.

Rather than answer his question, she posed one of her own. "What are *your* terms, sir, should you win?"

He sauntered along for a few more steps before answering. "If I should win, then if the weather permits, I'd like you to either ride or drive with me every afternoon until Jonathan returns. If the weather does not permit, I propose a game of cards or charades and some lively conversation. You see, Lady Harriett, you might find my company intolerable, but I am growing rather fond of yours."

Stunned into silence, Harriett continued to place one foot in front of the other. Under normal circumstances, such pretty words would have pleased her immensely, but she did not trust them anymore than she trusted him. The almost glint of humor in his eyes and his constant desire to tease planted far too many doubts in her mind. She was simply a lark to him—an entertaining way to pass the time until he returned to London.

Certain that Pippin was not increasing, Harriett lifted her chin. "Very well, sir, I agree to your terms and look forward to . . . possibly forgiving you one day."

"Once I am no longer in your company, you mean." He chuckled again, making Harriett wish she could stuff a stocking into his mouth. His laughter and words tricked and confused her emotions, attempting to lure her into liking him.

It didn't help when he gently clasped her upper arm to steer her around a small puddle, furthering her confusion. She felt his touch keenly, liking and disliking it at the same time. Why was he behaving so gentlemanly all of a sudden? Nothing about the man made sense.

Harriett turned her thoughts back to the day she'd met him, when he'd found her distress so amusing. She needed to remember *that* Lieutenant Jamison and not fall victim to this newer version of him.

"Did you not wish to stomp in that puddle, sir?" she said. "My pelisse is still clean, after all. I'm certain you are itching to muddy it."

"Why would I wish to do such a thing when it would also muddy my boots and breeches? Besides, it is Wicked who enjoys that particular pastime, not I."

"Are you certain, Lieutenant?" Harriett asked. "Because I recall overhearing you tell Charlie that you and your horse are of like minds. So, which is it? *Are* you a wicked person by nature, or do you immerse yourself in the Bible and strive to be respectable? You cannot be both at the same time."

He grinned and winked at her in a devilish way. "When a wicked person is making a valiant attempt to become *un*wicked, then he *can* be both."

"You expect me to believe that when you take great delight in vexing me?"

"I did not say it was an easy feat. Merely an attempted one. As you stated earlier, we are but humans, are we not?"

"Exactly," she quipped. "Which is why I shan't be

44

forgiving you anytime soon, or any wicked person for that matter."

The lieutenant laughed yet again. Why he'd felt the need, she couldn't say. She'd said nothing at all amusing. Perhaps he'd perceived that the sound of his laughter had a weakening effect on her defenses, and so he laughed as often as he could, hoping to cripple her.

Distracted by such thoughts, Harriett took no notice of the bird perching in a tree above, at least not until the creature dropped a large white bead of goo down the arm of her deep-blue pelisse. Her eyes widened first in astonishment and then disgust. First Wicked, then Pippin, and now that wretched bird! Was every creature in the world against her? Could nothing go right for her of late?

Openmouthed, she looked to the lieutenant for help, but did he offer her a handkerchief or express his outrage that a bird would behave so abominably? Of course not. Instead, he laughed. He laughed with so much fervor that he had to bend over and clutch his knees for support.

This time, that particular sound did not warm Harriett's insides or confuse her emotions in the least. It caused her blood to boil and her temper to flare. She was tired of sacrificing her pride to such a man.

"I'm sorry," he finally managed to say as he drew himself up and wiped at his eyes. "I could not help it. But you had only just said that your pelisse was still clean, and now—" He chuckled again, and when she did not appear amused, added, "Oh, come now, Lady Harriett, surely you can find the humor in such an unlucky coincidence. Even if you cannot, why are you glaring at me and not the bird? You must know that I had nothing at all to do with that."

His speech served to infuriate Harriett further, loosening her tongue to the point where she could keep silent no longer. "You are no gentleman, sir," she blurted. "I can see now why you are so fond of my company. My misfortunes provide you with endless amounts of amusement, isn't that right?"

He stopped chuckling, but that dratted smile remained on his lips as he squinted through the sunlight at her. "Is this not a case of the pot calling the kettle black, my lady? Only yesterday you placed me in a predicament that gave you a reason to laugh at *my* expense, so are we not both at fault?"

"I was merely trying to even the score, Lieutenant, which is only fair. But will you allow such a thing to occur? Of course not. You are determined to retain the upper hand."

"How, exactly, have I retained the upper hand? That bird dropping was not of my doing."

"No, but didn't you read that passage from the Bible for my particular benefit—or rather, *yours*?"

He pressed his lips together to keep from either smiling or laughing, she didn't know which. She only knew that she felt the greatest urge to slap him.

At long last, he seemed to gain control over his mirth. "What would you say to a truce, my lady?"

She eyed him with distrust. "What sort of truce?"

"If you promise to cease inflicting Pippin on me, I will promise to cease preaching. We can even do away with our wager so you will not feel obligated to keep company with me when you have no wish to do so. Although I must confess, I would miss our repartee greatly. You have a liveliness about you that I cannot help but like."

Amusement glittered in his eyes, along with a challenge and possibly even a hint of sincerity. Why did he say such things? And for what purpose? His words fed an insecure part of Harriett's soul—to be liked for something deeper than her appearance—but she did not believe he truly meant it. How could he when she'd been nothing but cold to him?

This had to be another of his tricks—a calculated attempt to put an end to a wager he knew he'd lose. But why would it matter to him if he *did* lose? Had Mrs. Bidding not pressured him into staying when he had no wish to do so? Would he not be glad for an excuse to return to London? Or was he so competitively driven that he felt compelled to stay until Harriett admitted defeat?

Her head began to throb with all the questions pounding through it. Nothing about the lieutenant made sense. He was a riddle, and she wearied of trying to figure him out. She wanted him out of her head and out of her life, which was precisely why she would not agree to a truce. She would win the wager and thus the war, bid farewell to Lieutenant Jamison, and finally feel at peace once more.

Lifting her chin, she met the lieutenant's gaze un-flinchingly. "I will admit that I have underestimated you, Lieutenant, and have allowed you to outwit me today. But you will not do so again. I have complete confidence that Pippin has merely been overfed and under-exercised, so I will not renege on our wager or admit defeat."

Her words seemed to please him because a slow smile stretched across his lips, spreading his mustache. "I confess, I am relieved to hear it. I can now look forward to many more lively conversations to come."

"We shall see," she answered as she turned around, more than ready to rejoin the Biddings.

When Harriett arrived at the Biddings for dinner later that evening, the smug expression on the lieutenant's face had an immediate lowering effect on her hopes. It didn't take long for Mr. Bidding to confirm her fears.

"Lieutenant Jamison was correct," he said, his chest puffed out with pride. "According to the cow-leech, Pippin is indeed increasing. Isn't it wonderful?"

With all eyes on her, Harriett managed a nod even though she did not find the news wonderful in the least. She found it upsetting and . . . aggravating. Why did that dratted man have to be right? Why did she have to be wrong? Why did the whole world seem to be against her?

Harriett sank down in her chair, attempting to keep her expression somewhat pleased as Mrs. Bidding prattled on about how darling the puppies were sure to be. There was even speculation about who the father was. Mr. Bidding and the lieutenant seemed quite determined to uncover the naughty creature so they might know what sort of puppies to expect.

Harriett didn't pay much attention to the discussion. Her posture rigid and her thoughts full of self-pity, she merely counted down the minutes of what was bound to be a very long night. How could a day that had begun with such promise fail to deliver anything of the kind? It seemed vastly unfair. In fact, she wouldn't be at all surprised if, when the time came for her to depart, the clouds converged and the skies began to quake, tremble, and pour rain down upon her head.

Her dark-orange pelisse was still clean and dry, after all.

WHEN LIEUTENANT JAMISON AND the Biddings called upon her the very next morning to invite her for a drive, Harriett learned very quickly that he had every intention of collecting on their wager. As soon as they'd settled into the open landau, he made a grand production of gifting her with a lovely peach parasol to better protect her pelisses from dirt and bird droppings. From Mrs. Bidding's pleased expression, the woman thought the gesture charming and romantic, but Harriett saw the gift for what it really was—a source of amusement for the lieutenant.

"How thoughtful you are, sir," she said.

"Think nothing of it, my lady."

I won't, thought Harriett, forced to accept the parasol and use it during their sunny drive. But every time a bird chirped or flew by overhead, and the lieutenant said, "Have a care, Lady Harriett, here comes another one," she felt like poking him in the ribs with it.

As soon as she returned home, she sentenced the lovely creation to the back of her wardrobe, never to be used in the lieutenant's presence again.

The following day it rained, and when the Biddings and

the lieutenant came to call, Harriett invited them to pass the time at Tanglewood. The lieutenant proposed a game of whist and asked Mrs. Bidding to be his partner. Harriett was happy to play opposite him, having an aptitude for cards, and looked forward to putting him in his place. Less than an hour later, however, after the lieutenant and Mrs. Bidding had beaten her and Mr. Bidding soundly for the fifth time, Harriett decided she did not like whist any longer and suggested a game of loo or piquet instead. But it did not matter which game they played or how the cards were dealt. The lieutenant was almost always on the winning team.

Drat the man.

The following day, when he challenged Harriett to an archery tournament and trounced her yet again, she decided that Lieutenant Jamison remained in Askern and sought her company for one purpose and one purpose only—to torment her.

"May I offer some suggestions, my lady?" he finally asked when another one of her arrows strayed to the right of the target.

With the Biddings seated not far away, ever the observant chaperones, Harriett could not decline the offer without appearing petty. Keeping hold of the upper limb, she set the bow on the ground and turned to face him. "What suggestions do you have for me, sir?"

He retrieved an arrow and walked over to her, taking the bow from her hands. "If you position your back foot perpendicular to the target, you'll find the arrow is more likely to travel the direction you aim it." With deft movements, he put the arrow in place, lifted the bow, and pulled back on the necking point of the string, saying, "And if you anchor the string against your chin, like so, your arrow will be less likely to . . . wander."

Harriett hadn't known either of those things. She'd attempted archery only a handful of times and had never cared for the sport overly much, probably because she'd never known how to do it properly. But if she were to learn how to hit a target regularly, that might change things. In fact, it could be a diverting way to pass the time—without the lieutenant of course, as his arrows found the center of the target every blasted time.

"Thank you, Lieutenant," said Harriett as she accepted the bow once more, making sure to line up her back foot as he'd suggested. She tucked the arrow against the necking point and pulled on the string, lifting the bow out in front of her and bringing the string to her chin as the lieutenant had done.

She almost flinched when his gloved fingers touched the tender part of her elbow. He turned it slightly out, and his breath tickled her ear as he explained, "This way the string will not hit your arm when you release it."

She didn't trust herself to respond. Her voice would no doubt sound breathless, as his close proximity caused her heart to pound in a ridiculous fashion, so she quickly released the arrow just to be rid of him. Much to her frustration, it veered away from the target and bounced across the grass before plowing into a barren shrub.

So much for the lieutenant's suggestions, she thought with a frown.

"You dropped the bow too quickly after you released the arrow," he said. "If you remain still and count to three, you will have better luck."

Harriett handed the bow back to him, ready for the lesson to be over. Did the man have to be good at everything? "Perhaps I'll give it a try another day. My arms could use a rest."

He smiled knowingly as though he saw right through her excuse. "Another day then."

Yes, Harriett thought, *once you have gone back to London.*

In addition to losing at cards and archery, the lieutenant continued to favor the group with more "inspiring passages" from the Bible each night following dinner. Harriett was required to endure all sorts of counsel on the subjects of forgiveness, humility, and loving one's neighbor. Though she would never admit it out loud, not that it mattered as God was privy to one's thoughts, she was coming to despise the Bible almost as much as cards. She even went so far as to conjure a headache to avoid attending services on the Sabbath.

Unfortunately, that plan went awry when the Biddings and the lieutenant arrived at Tanglewood bearing a draught guaranteed to cure any headache. The lieutenant insisted that she drink it straightaway, such was his concern for her welfare, and Harriett had never tasted anything so vile in her life.

She choked down the concoction before handing the bottle back to him with a grimace. "It seems I am in your debt, Lieutenant. Someday, I hope to repay the kind service you have done for me today."

"I'm sure you would love nothing more," he said with a grin. "But I shall hope for the opposite. I detest headaches."

"You must rest now, my dear," said Mrs. Bidding in a motherly way. "With any luck, the draught will relieve the pain in your head, and we shall still see you tonight at dinner."

Harriett nodded, thanked the woman, mustered a smile for the lieutenant, and gratefully watched them descend the steps to the waiting carriage. As she closed the door and leaned her back against it, Harriett sighed in relief. At least she would have one afternoon free from the lieutenant's knowing looks, triumphant grins, and the constant reminders of her many deficiencies and shortcomings.

If only she could best him at *something*.

Rather than retire to her bedchamber, Harriett sought refuge in the library. Having recently discovered a fondness for reading—the knowledge she gained acted as a balm to her bruised ego—the dark and spacious room had become somewhat of a sanctuary to her. Perhaps she would be able to learn something that Lieutenant Jamison did not already know.

As the hour approached dinner, Harriett was in no mood to dine with anyone, least of all the lieutenant, so she sent a note to the Biddings, crying off. It was a cowardly thing to do, which did nothing to improve her disposition, and by the time morning arrived, Harriett was certain that Tabby would not think her the least bit chipper.

Sure enough, Tabby's brow furrowed as she studied her mistress through the looking glass. "Is your 'ead still achin', milady?"

Even if it was, Harriett would never admit to it. News would somehow reach Lieutenant Jamison's ears, and he would undoubtedly feel the need to bring her more of his dreadful tonic.

"I'm only tired, is all."

"Are you fit to go drivin' with the lieutenant this mornin', milady? You don't seem in good spirits, and there's no sense in spoilin' 'is day if you're needin' a bit more rest. 'Appen you could go out drivin' later, once you're feeling a mite better."

Tabby spoke as though it would be a bad thing to spoil the lieutenant's day, but that was exactly what Harriett wished to do. How many of her days had *he* spoiled? Plenty. It was only fair that she be given the opportunity to return that particular favor, was it not? Especially when it would lift her spirits like no rest could ever do.

With that thought, Harriett sat up straighter, her mind suddenly whirling. Of course. Why hadn't she considered that before? The lieutenant had made no secret that he was fond of her liveliness, but what would happen if he arrived to collect her for their drive and found a changed Harriett—one who was not lively *or* interesting? Would he at last tire of her and decide that London would be more to his liking? It was possible. There was nothing worse than tedious conversation, after all, and with the Biddings not accompanying them this morning, Harriett could be as dull or ridiculous as she pleased.

Tabby tucked in the last hairpin, and Harriett jumped to her feet, clasping her maid by the shoulders. "Tabby, you are brilliant."

The girl blinked in surprise. "I can't think why you'd say so, milady, but I'm glad ter see you smilin' again. Are you feelin' better then?"

"I feel transformed. You have given me the most wonderful idea, and I shall put it to work straightaway. Please inform me the moment Lieutenant Jamison arrives."

Tabby left the room in a state of cheerful confusion while Harriett began to plot and plan. She even retrieved the parasol the lieutenant had gifted her days earlier and twirled it around, thinking that she could put it to good use after all.

As the gig stumbled along beneath partly cloudy skies with a groom stationed at the back, Harriett peeked at the lieutenant from the corner of her eye. Blue suited him, as did most everything he wore. Several shades darker than the color of the sky, his coat fit him well, and with his hat tilted at a rakish angle, he appeared a handsome and charming gentleman. His jaw was smooth, his mustache neatly trimmed, and his eyes appeared lighter than usual.

It was a good thing Harriett had already determined not to like him or she might be tempted to fall under his spell.

Harriett twirled the peach parasol, gushed over every sight she saw, and simpered at every word the lieutenant uttered.

"La, Lieutenant, is that flower not the loveliest creation you have ever seen?"

He arched his eyebrow quizzically. "Most would consider a dandelion to be a weed and not a flower."

"I think it as charming as this charming day, don't you?"

Another quizzical glance accompanied his answer. "Yes, the day *is* quite charming."

"As are you, Lieutenant Jamison. Quite charming indeed." She batted her lashes, smiled flirtatiously, and began rambling on about the new pelisse she would commission the moment she arrived in London.

"I believe I shall choose the color yellow to remind me of this charming and sunny day. Or perhaps blue as a reminder of the charming skies." She leaned over and smiled flirtatiously. "Your eyes are also a charming blue as well. Did you know that, Lieutenant? Quite charming indeed." She hoped her overuse of the word "charming" would irritate him as it did her.

Lieutenant Jamison nodded, a small smile touching his lips. "You are in a lively mood this morning, Lady Harriett. I find it most energizing and find myself wondering what your housekeeper put in your tea this morning."

Harriett looked away so that he would not see the annoyed expression on her face. He still thought her lively? Truly? Well, perhaps she *had* been lively, but not in a good, energizing sort of way. In an irritating and draining way that ought to have brought on a headache. Why on earth was the lieutenant smiling?

Perhaps she needed to rethink her plan and strive to say as little as possible.

Lieutenant Jamison began peppering her with questions, wanting to know all about her family, how her friendship with Lady Jonathan had come about, and if she'd enjoyed her first season in London. Harriett tried to keep her answers as brief and dry as possible, doing her best to play the part of a proper young lady wholly lacking in personality. But he did not seem to notice the change or be bothered by it.

"I don't understand," he said at one point. "If your sister is currently in London, why do you remain in Askern? Why not go to London now?"

Harriett folded her hands in her lap and stared straight ahead, wondering how to answer the question in a placid, nondescript way. Unfortunately, there was no boring way of admitting that she could not go to town yet because the majority of the ton had not arrived. This was her second season, and if she was to make any splash at all, she would need to appear on the scene fashionably late.

But of course she could not say as much to the lieutenant. Such information would give him reason to goad and tease her, and she would be required to rise to the occasion in order to defend her position. Within minutes, an engaging discussion would take over, and once again, the man would come away champion.

Goodness, it was difficult to mask one's personality.

Harriett finally settled on, "The weather and quality of the air is finer in Askern than London."

"Then why go to London at all?"

If her mother, Cora, or Lucy had asked her such a question, Harriett would have said that she'd enjoyed her first season immensely. The balls, parties, musicales, and outings had made her feel adventurous and alive. It had been fun to dress in lovely creations, flirt outrageously, and be termed an Original.

But once again, that was too interesting of an answer to suit her objectives, and so Harriett redirected the conversation instead.

"Did you learn your interrogation skills in the navy, sir? Or do they stem from the time you spent observing your surroundings in your favorite apple tree?"

The moment his lips pulled into another smile, Harriett berated herself. Why had she said such a thing? The question had not been the least bit insipid or dull. It was a good thing she did not need to make a living on the stage. She was dreadful at playing the part of someone else.

"Not from the treetops, though I did attempt to interrogate a bird at one point when I discovered a partially eaten red apple. But alas, I could not decipher its tweeting and never did get to the bottom of it."

Harriett could actually picture him having such a conversation with the bird. It almost made her smile.

"Enough about birds, though," the lieutenant said. "I am much more interested in the real reasons you remain at Tanglewood. Correct me if I'm wrong, but I'm guessing that you do not wish to go to town as of yet because you prefer to be the last one to the party, so to speak. You want the ton to question your absence so that your arrival will cause a stir, am I right? You see, Lady Harriett, I have not been gone so long that I have forgotten the silly games society likes to play."

Harriett found nothing to like in that particular observation, or how he so easily condemned the ways of society. Was he not one of the ton himself? Did he not now sit in a gig scheming and plotting and playing his own "silly games?"

"They are not games, sir."

"What would you call them?"

"Calculations," she replied, wondering how she might explain it so that he would understand. "I believe that the season is similar to the war in many ways. Everyone approaches it with some sort of goal. The husbands go to appease their wives, the mothers to find a suitable match for their daughter or son, and the daughter or son—well, they are more like pawns or soldiers, required to bend to the will of their superiors, are they not?"

"Something tells me, my lady, that you have never bent to anyone's will."

"Only because I have been blessed with a doting mother who believes that I will benefit more from making my own choices. Most young ladies are not as lucky as I, but that is beside the point. As I was saying, everyone comes to London for a reason, and if left strictly to chance, what is the probability that their desired outcome will come about on its own? Far less than if one is proactive, don't you think? Surely you, of all people, can understand that."

He pulled the horses to a stop and shifted in his seat to study her. "When it comes to war, yes. When it comes to love and relationships . . . well, let's just say that I think chance ought to play a greater role."

Harriett furrowed her brow, not agreeing at all. "In other words, when it comes to the future of our country, you would not consider leaving it to chance, but in the case of your own happiness, you would? That makes little sense, Lieutenant."

He shook his head and scooted closer, making Harriett keenly aware of his knee touching hers. "You misunderstand me, my lady. I only meant that victory in war is very different than victory in love. War has a clear objective—to defeat one's enemy while protecting and securing the rights of your country and people. That never changes. It is the nature of war. Love, on the other hand, is much less clear. I can research every debutante coming to town this season and deduce which woman I'd like to pursue based on her beauty, wealth, accomplishments, and grace. But in the end, if I cannot also love or desire her, all my deductions and plans have been for naught and my goal must change. Otherwise, I would end up unhappily married, and how sensible is that?"

Harriett did not answer right away. His words had touched a tender place in her heart and she found herself drawn to Lieutenant Jamison in an unexpected way. She also yearned for more than a sensible match. She wanted a match based on compatibility, respect, admiration, and desire. It was the reason she had not accepted any of the offers she'd received the previous season. But was love truly a possibility for everyone, or only the lucky few?

Harriett swallowed and allowed her gaze to drop to where her knee touched the lieutenant's. She shifted it away and cleared her throat. "Most fashionable people would disagree with you, Lieutenant. They'd say it is far better for one's head to rule one's heart and not the other way around."

"Is that what you believe, Lady Harriett?"

"I . . ." Her words trailed off as she realized her faux pas. She had joined the lieutenant this morning for the specific purpose of irritating and boring him to tears, yet here they were, discussing love and war, hopes, and possibly even dreams. How had such a conversation come to pass?

Apparently, she lacked the ability to remain focused on one particular goal for an extended period of time. Either that or the lieutenant was highly proficient in the art of distraction. It was probably a combination of the two.

In an effort to refocus, Harriett turned her attention to the countryside, noticing a newly plowed field in the distance. If she could not get the lieutenant to think of her as irritating or dull, perhaps she could put him off by becoming an unfashionable bluestocking. Or better yet, tell him something that he did not already know.

She nodded towards the field. "Do you think the farmer intends to grow wheat, sir? I hope so. According to the Norfolk Four-Course Method, planting wheat is the wisest thing to do, unless, of course, he planted wheat last year. In which case, he ought to plant turnips instead."

The comment seemed to catch him off guard, and rightfully so. He blinked a few times before shaking his head in confusion. "I beg your pardon?"

"Have you not heard of the Four-Course System, Lieutenant?" asked Harriett, prepared to barrage him with a myriad of tedious facts about the benefits of growing wheat, turnips, and barley in successive years and even shock him by mentioning the merits of enriching the soil with animal waste from turnip-fed cattle.

But the wretched man didn't look at all bored or even surprised. He looked amused. "I *have* heard of it, as a matter of fact. What I'm wondering is how you know about it. Are you a bluestocking in disguise, Lady Harriett? Because that would be delightful."

Good grief, thought Harriett, very nearly throwing up her hands in frustration. Delightful?

Apparently, no matter what she said or how she behaved, Lieutenant Jamison was determined to think well of her. Was this another of his many attributes—to find something "delightful" in everyone no matter their intelligence or personality? *How very Christian of him,* she thought sourly. Perhaps the man truly *did* read from the Bible often.

But how was it that a former lieutenant in the navy was familiar with a lesser-known method of farming? Or *was* it lesser known? The book in Jonathan's library had looked to be in newer condition and had made the technique sound revolutionary, but Harriett hadn't checked the date of publication, so she couldn't say for certain. Perhaps it was old news now.

Once again, the lieutenant had outwitted her, and once again, it rankled.

Drat the man! Drat his parents for not being more persuasive, the Biddings for being too persuasive, and this beautiful day for not looking more questionable. She frowned at the smattering of white, fluffy clouds that moved ever so slowly across the wide expanse of the sky, hiding the sun every now and again like an irritating game of peek-a-boo.

"It looks as though it might rain soon," she remarked. "Perhaps we should return."

He chuckled and shook his head. "If those clouds produce even one raindrop, I will send you a pretty posy every day for an entire year."

Harriett tilted her face upwards and closed her eyes. Surely God would be merciful enough to grant her this one small victory over the lieutenant. *One little raindrop is all I need,* she pled. *Preferably placed squarely on the dratted man's nose.*

Instead of a raindrop, the sun moved from behind a cloud, bathing her in light and warmth.

Drat the heavens as well.

"Why do I get the feeling that you are upset with me?" asked Lieutenant Jamison.

Harriett turned her frown on him. "Must you always triumph over me? Can you not concede even one small battle, sir?"

His eyebrows creased together in confusion. "Are we battling, my lady? I was not aware."

"Of course we are battling! We are *always* battling and you are *always* winning. It is incredibly vexing."

"Pray enlighten me. How, exactly, have I bested you today?" he asked, appearing both confused and entertained. "It was my understanding that we were simply enjoying some interesting conversation on a beautiful day."

"But don't you see?" said Harriett. "It was not supposed to be interesting. It was supposed to be tedious."

He stared at her for a moment before his mouth began to tremble and twitch. "I'm not sure I'm understanding you correctly. Are you saying that if I had found your companionship tiring, you would have won some sort of battle?"

"Possibly even the war," said Harriett.

"How? I must be a slowtop this morning because I cannot make sense of it."

"Don't you see?" she said. "If you did not find our daily outings lively or interesting, you would no longer wish to spend time with me and would renege on our wager. You might also come to the conclusion that the amusements in town are much more to your liking and make a hasty retreat, which, of course, would make me the victor at last."

It wasn't until Harriett voiced her thoughts aloud that

she realized how ridiculous and juvenile they sounded—like a plan concocted by an imaginative child. *Or a desperate woman,* she thought, feeling as though she belonged in Bedlam. Perhaps a few months of confinement would restore her good sense.

The lieutenant must have thought the same because he began to laugh and laugh and laugh. At one point he even clutched his stomach and slapped his knee.

Humiliation and defeat settled around Harriett, enclosing her in a bubble of misery. She might have raised a white flag in surrender if she'd had one, but she didn't. She didn't have anything anymore, not even her pride.

As though sensing her drooping spirits, the lieutenant at last quieted and scooted closer, touching his shoulder to hers in a playful nudge. With that rich, perfect timbre, he said, "Lady Harriett, attempting to be tedious, dull, or even bird-witted will not serve—not when I already know you are none of those things."

His words soothed and comforted, causing her further frustration. How did he manage to flatter her while triumphing at the same time? It made her feel weak and feeble, as though what remained of her defenses—if anything at all—could be broken down with a prettily-worded compliment.

Lieutenant Jamison picked up the ribbons, called out to the horses, and began circling the beasts around and back in the direction of Tanglewood. As the gig bounced along, Harriett remained silent and contemplative, thinking over the events of the past week and how she'd managed to land herself at this point. What was it about Lieutenant Jamison that unnerved her so? Why had she felt the need to battle with him and prove that she could outwit him? Why did it matter when she didn't care about him at all?

As they journeyed up the carriage path leading to Tanglewood, a blessed sight met her eyes. Not far ahead stood a pristine, black carriage with four matching bays. Two footmen were unloading a trunk to be carried inside.

"They're back!" Harriett exclaimed, feeling as though a raindrop had finally fallen in the guise of her dear friends, Lord and Lady Jonathan Ludlow. She closed her eyes and sent a silent "Thank you" to the heavens, feeling at peace with God once more.

Her friend could not have arrived at a more needful time.

"Ah," said the lieutenant. "They've returned a day earlier than expected. How fortuitous for the both of us, I imagine."

Harriett had no reply to this. She waited for the lieutenant to stop the gig before scrambling down on her own.

"Good day to you, Lieutenant," Harriett called over her shoulder as she hurried toward the house. She did not care that she was behaving in an unladylike manner. She only cared about getting away from an unsettling man and seeing her dear friend once again.

HARRIETT CHARGED INTO THE house, plowing into Lord Jonathan's solid back. He removed his hat as he turned around, revealing a mop of unruly, light-brown hair.

"Pray forgive me, Jonathan," she said as she stepped around him, brightening when she spied her friend conversing with the butler.

"Oh, hello, Harr—" Jonathan began.

"Cora!" Harriett exclaimed, belatedly realizing how dramatic she sounded. Had she truly just interrupted Jonathan? Goodness, what had come over her? Ladies did not jump unassisted from a gig, they did not flee their companions, they did not interrupt friends or even strangers, and they did not behave as though it had been ages since they had last seen a friend when it had not yet been a fortnight.

I really have gone mad.

Cora nodded at Watts before holding her arms out to Harriett with a smile. "How wonderful it is to see you, Harriett." She gave her friend a quick hug before pulling back. "I was so worried that you would find Tanglewood a dreadful bore without the Shepherds to keep you company. But Watts was only just telling us that the Biddings and

Lieutenant Jamison have been frequent visitors. He mentioned you had gone driving with the lieutenant only this morning, in fact, and I feared it would be hours before I would get to speak with you. But here you are." Her eyes narrowed as she studied her friend. "Are you quite well? You look a bit flushed."

Harriett did not find the news surprising in the least. She had just run from the lieutenant, after all. Of course she appeared flushed. She probably looked frazzled, disheveled, and cowardly as well. That's what happened to a person when she allowed her emotions to seize control.

Harriett waved Cora's concerns aside and struggled for a light-hearted tone. "I am perfectly well, thank you. I simply could not wait to, er . . . ask about your wedding trip. It seems an age since I have seen you last."

Truth be told, in her wretched state, Harriett had no wish to hear about a blissful wedding trip. And it had been blissful. The joy radiating from Cora attested to it. Dressed in a stylish deep-green traveling dress and matching bonnet, she had a glow about her that could not be dimmed. Her auburn hair shone with more vibrancy, her blue eyes sparkled, and her smile stretched far and wide.

What would it be like to have someone to cherish and be equally cherished in return? Harriett had no idea and probably never would. Bedlam likely discouraged courtship.

"We had a marvelous time, didn't we, my love?" Cora said. "We took long walks along the coast, saw the most exquisite sunsets I've ever beheld, ate lobster and the most decadent—" She stopped, pausing to scrutinize Harriett once again. "Are you quite certain that you're all right? Perhaps we should adjourn to the drawing room and call for some tea. You look as though you could use some refreshment."

Harriett panicked. She didn't wish to adjourn to the

drawing room where the lieutenant would come upon them once he'd seen to the gig and horses. Rather, she wanted to retire to her bedchamber with only Cora as company so that she might lay all of her troubles at her friend's door. Cora appeared of sound mind at the moment. Surely she could prod Harriett back to seeing reason.

"Perhaps later," Harriett said, silently imploring Jonathan to give her a few moments alone with his wife.

As though correctly interpreting her plea, Jonathan cleared his throat. "Is Jamison still about?"

A knock sounded on the door, much to Harriett's annoyance, and Jonathan was quick to open it, revealing a grinning Lieutenant Jamison on the other side. Harriett immediately dropped her gaze to the floor, refusing to look into those laughing eyes another moment.

"Jono, old chap," said the lieutenant.

Three hearty raps were heard—no doubt the men slapping each other on their backs in greeting—before Jonathan replied. "Christopher, you spineless jellyfish, how have you been?"

"Spineless?" the lieutenant answered. "I'm afraid that nickname will no longer suffice, my friend. Have you not heard that I'm a great war hero now?"

"Only from you, which makes it rather suspect. And war hero or not, I shall never forget the sight of you running away with an angry duck on your heels."

"You would have fled as well had you been in my position. The creature's bite hurt like the devil."

"I never would have been in your position," said Jonathan. "Attempting to steal one of its ducklings was a barbaric thing to do, and I'm most certainly not barbaric."

"Borrow," the lieutenant insisted. "I only meant to borrow it for a time, as you well know. After foisting Letty

Lagerfield on me for the supper dance, my sister deserved to find a duckling floating in her wash basin."

Jonathan chuckled. "If only you could have explained as much to its mother. I'm certain she would have let you borrow her offspring without protest."

The lieutenant laughed, and the sound rumbled through the great hall, prodding Harriett to lift her gaze at last. Why did he always have to be so dratted cheerful and collected?

"It's good to see you unchanged, my friend," said the lieutenant.

"*Au contraire.*" Jonathan reached a hand out to his wife and pulled her to his side. "As you can see, I am very much changed. Not only have I become remarkably responsible, but I've somehow managed to snare this beautiful woman. Lieutenant Christopher Jamison, meet my wife, Lady Jonathan Ludlow."

The lieutenant bowed low over her hand. "Jonathan is lucky indeed, my lady."

"Please, you must call me Cora."

"Cora it is, then."

Harriett rolled her eyes. Where was this version of the lieutenant when Harriett had first met him? *He's laying it on thick,* she wanted to tell Cora. *Don't you dare fall victim to his flattery.*

But Harriett knew it was only a matter of time before Cora did exactly that. With the exception of Harriett, everyone seemed to adore the man. The Biddings, Jonathan, the stablehands, and Tabby. Even Pippin had chosen to rest at his feet the other evening—the little traitor.

"Tell me, Cora," the lieutenant's voice pulled Harriett back to the conversation at hand. "Now that my friend has become so very responsible, is he a dreadful bore?"

"A bore? No, I cannot say that he is." She eyed her

husband with a playful look. "But I *have* learned that he prefers salt only in small doses, believes paintings should be devoid of people, and despises it when chickens escape their coop."

"Ah." The lieutenant grinned. "He's become a curmudgeon then. Tell me, does he rant and rage about?"

"Only before Cora reformed me," said Jonathan, wrapping an arm around his wife. "Now I'm much more placid and on my way to becoming very dull indeed. I wouldn't be surprised if you grew tired of me within the hour, Christopher."

Lieutenant Jamison looked past his friend to catch Harriett's eye. "In that case, perhaps you can give Lady Harriett some lessons. I have it on good authority that she would like to become a dreadful bore as well."

Harriett glared at him, not appreciating the reminder of her earlier humiliation.

Cora studied her friend with open curiosity. "I'm not sure why you would wish to become such a thing, Harriett, but I must say that you could never pass yourself off as dull anymore than Jonathan could. You are both far too intelligent, witty, and interesting."

Jonathan chuckled and placed a kiss on his wife's temple. "My wife's only weakness is that she's far too kind. Cora cannot speak ill of anyone no matter how much he or she might deserve it."

"I would call that a strength, not a weakness." Lieutenant Jamison bestowed upon Cora a look of genuine admiration, and Harriett felt a stab of jealousy at the sight. Why, she couldn't say. If anyone deserved high praise and admiration, it was Cora. But the lieutenant had never looked at Harriett in that manner, and she found herself wishing he would.

"Being able to overlook the bad in people is a fine quality," said the lieutenant, "and one that will come in very handy when associating with the likes of me. You see, Cora, according to Lady Harriett, I'm hopelessly flawed."

Harriett's jaw clenched as she stared daggers at the man. What sort of person said such things in polite company with her standing right there? The lieutenant, that's who, and she refused to put up with his teasing any longer.

"I have said no such thing, sir."

"Perhaps not in those precise words, but I'm certain you've referred to me as a cad."

"I have not." Harriett thought back over all their conversations, not recalling one instance when she'd called him that. She may have *thought* it once or twice, but she had not spoken it.

"Oh, that's right," he said. "You called me a bounder, not a cad."

He was needling her yet again, and Harriett felt her hackles rise. "You must have mistaken me for someone else, sir. I have never called you either of those things."

"Loose screw then?" he continued, relentless.

"Loose cannon, more like," said Jonathan, putting an end to the ribbing. Harriett barely refrained from adding, *And a wicked rogue who delights in taunting and teasing vulnerable young women—or rather, a* certain *vulnerable young woman.* Harriett was beginning to feel increasingly singled out and could not understand why he'd fixed a target solely on her.

Probably because you fixed one on him, came an inner voice of reason, one that Harriett quickly dismissed.

Lieutenant Jamison laughed. "I can't deny I've been called a loose cannon before. That particular endearment seems to follow me wherever I go."

Harriett rolled her eyes and looked away, knowing further comment would only encourage him. She needed to get away from him and soon.

"I'm feeling a bit tired all of a sudden," said Harriett. "I think I shall retire to my room."

Cora shot her friend a worried and quizzical glance. Then she turned to her husband and rested a hand on his arm. "I'm certain you two gentlemen have much to discuss, and I am rather tired after our journey as well. If it's agreeable with you, I shall go up with Harriett."

"Of course, my dear. Whatever you wish."

"It was a pleasure to meet you, Cora," added the lieutenant in a rare show of sincerity. Harriett felt another pang of jealousy, accompanied by a small dose of hurt. Would the lieutenant ever find something to admire in *her*— other than her "lively" spirit, that is? Would he ever be able to say, in all honesty, that it had been a pleasure to meet Harriett as well?

Probably not.

Cora threaded her arm through Harriett's and prodded her towards the stairs. Nothing more was said until they were safely ensconced in her bedchamber with the door closed.

"Harriett, whatever is the matter?" Cora removed her bonnet and set it on a chair, all the while staring at her friend in bewilderment. "I have never seen you in such a state."

Harriett dropped down on her bed, cast her own bonnet aside, and leaned forward, letting her head fall into her hands. "I do not know. It's the lieutenant. He has . . . well, I don't know what he's done, exactly. I only know that I've never felt more at odds with another person in my life."

Cora sat down and laid a hand on Harriett's shoulder. "Has he been unkind to you?"

"No, not really. He has only teased, tried, and tested me,

probably finding me wanting at every turn. Tell me, Cora, do I possess any talents at all? Any strengths that you can think of? You, for example, are always so kind and level-headed and have an unerring sense of fashion. And Lucy has a knack for creating such beautiful things—from floral arrangements to improvements around the estate. And now that my brother has encouraged her in horsemanship, she rides with even greater skill than I, and I have been riding my entire life. How is it possible that every woman I know seems to excel in various things, whereas I am only able to become average at best?"

"What in the world are you talking about?" said Cora. "An unerring sense of fashion? Me? Honestly, Harriett. You are the most fashionable woman I know."

Harriett sighed. "Only because Mother has engaged the services of Madame Bissonette. It is she who has taught me that the colors blue, peach, gold, and deep green suit me best. I could never have drawn such conclusions on my own. I once picked out a beautiful violet silk, and Madame looked at me as though I'd gone daft. That is the only reason I know that violet does not suit me at all. And do you remember that bonnet we spied on display in the milliner's when we first met? I thought it looked interesting in an unusual sort of way, but I did not know whether it was unusual good or unusual bad—at least not until you found something to admire in it. Only then did I know that it was a good sort of unusual. Don't you see, Cora? My appearance is merely a product of others' good tastes. If left to my own devices, I would look ridiculous."

"Fiddlesticks," said Cora. "Everyone turns to their modistes, friends, mothers, and maids for advice."

"Advice, yes," agreed Harriett. "Complete dependence, no."

"You give yourself far too little credit," said Cora, "not that it really matters one way or the other. Having good fashion sense is nothing compared to having a good character—and that you have in spades, Harriett. A kinder friend I could never find. Do you not remember how you befriended me even though I was far beneath you? And who jumped to my aid when I needed it most? Who plotted and arranged for me to come to Askern, traveled all this way to be present at my wedding, and even managed to convince my parents to attend? Heavens, you are kindness itself. I owe all my current happiness to you."

Harriett could not deny she had done those things, although her motives were perhaps not as altruistic as her friend seemed to think. The only reason she'd befriended Cora was because Harriett had been in desperate need of a friend and she'd taken an instant liking to Cora. And although Harriett *had* helped with the arrangements to transport Cora to Askern, she'd been most unhappy about it.

The fact of the matter was that if anyone were to compare Harriett with Cora in a question of who was the kindest, Cora would win by leaps and bounds. Kindness was one of her greatest strengths, which led Harriett back to the question she'd posed moments before. What, exactly were *her* greatest strengths?

Harriett frowned, unable to think of a single one.

Looking down at her kid boots peeking out from beneath her skirts, Harriett thought that she was rather like her shoes—shiny and unblemished on the outside, due to the talents of others, and wholly lacking substance within. It was an insecurity that had begun to emerge during her first London season, but Harriett had always been able to push it aside. Until now.

"Harriett," said Cora, her voice soft and gentle. "I don't

understand. What has Lieutenant Jamison done or said to make you so uncertain of yourself?"

Harriett shrugged and gave the only answer she could give. "He's winning the war."

A moment of silence descended before Cora spoke again. "To what war are you referring?"

With a sigh, Harriett lay back on the bed and tucked her hands behind her head. Her eyes traced the gold-leafing designs on the ceiling while her mind traveled back almost a week.

In a tone devoid of emotion, she began telling Cora about a man who'd raced past her on the road, leaving Harriett wet and seething. After that came the Biddings untimely arrival, the lieutenant's decision to stay, the sweet, but unhelpful dog, the card games lost, the horrid archery lesson, the lessons from the Bible, and Harriett's latest failed attempt to bore the lieutenant back to London.

"He is constantly laughing at me—not *with* me, mind you, *at* me. No matter how hard I try, Cora, I cannot find one weakness within him, other than his aggravating behavior, that is. And all of my attempts to uncover something have fallen short of the mark. Can you not see the sorry predicament I'm in?"

Harriett glanced at her friend, only to see Cora biting her lip in an effort to keep from smiling. It made Harriett scowl and think that Cora and Lieutenant Jamison would get along famously.

"And now *you're* laughing at me as well," Harriett accused. "Honestly, Cora, if you side with the lieutenant on this, I shall take back my praise of your kindness."

Cora was quick to school her features into something resembling sympathy, but humor still lurked in her eyes. "Of course I will not side with Lieutenant Jamison, Harriett. You have every right to be upset with him. A gentleman ought to allow a lady to win at least a few battles."

Harriett had said much the same thing to the lieutenant, but hearing it from Cora's lips made it sound petulant and silly.

She frowned. "I would prefer to earn a win instead of be handed one, as though I am a child in need of coddling. But that is precisely my point, Cora. Despite my best efforts, I cannot outwit the man."

"I see." Cora nodded slowly, as though seriously considering the problem.

Harriett returned her gaze to the ceiling, wondering how she might avoid Lieutenant Jamison from now on. She could feign an illness and keep to her room, she could go to London earlier than planned, or she could suffer through the five-day journey back to her family's estate in Danbury. Were those her only options? Why couldn't the lieutenant be the one to depart? His parents were expecting him, after all. Surely he should feel some obligation towards them.

"Tell me what you know about Lieutenant Jamison," Cora's voice intruded.

Harriett opened her mouth to respond, only to frown when nothing came immediately to mind. What *did* she know about the man? "He's a former lieutenant in the navy."

Cora nodded. "Yes, I had gathered as much."

Harriett shrugged. "He calls his horse Wicked, rides the beast recklessly, despises small dogs, and is unnaturally good at cards, archery, and everything else, it seems."

Cora shook her head as though Harriett's answer didn't suffice. "No one is good at everything. Now tell me something I don't already know."

Harriett blew out the side of her mouth in an unladylike fashion, thinking back to all the times she had spent in his company. "He comes from Cornwall and likes to observe people from apple trees."

Cora blinked a few times before shaking her head. "In other words, you know very little about him."

"I do not wish to know the man. I only wish to outwit him."

Cora laughed and shook her head, probably thinking Harriett a peagoose. She seemed to choose her next words carefully. "How can you expect to outwit your opponent if you do not know him? Don't you think it would benefit your cause to learn about his strengths and weaknesses?"

"He has no weaknesses."

Cora chuckled again. "You only think that because you don't truly know him. *Everyone* has weaknesses. In a way, it's what makes life worth living, don't you think? If we were all perfect individuals, there would be no room for growth, learning, or joy when we finally do overcome. I'm quite certain that Lieutenant Jamison still has a great deal to learn. We all do."

Harriett's mouth opened then closed when she realized she had no reply to that. Slowly, she lifted herself up, giving the matter some more thought. Cora's words made a great deal of sense. The lieutenant had to have *some* weaknesses. Surely she could discover a few of them if she put her mind to it. But did she dare give it one more try? Could her pride handle another loss if she failed again?

Cora grabbed Harriett's hand and gave it a squeeze. "Harriett, you are a beautiful, talented, intelligent, and confident woman. Don't ever forget that."

The words warmed Harriett's heart, breathing vigor and peace into her soul. If everyone had weaknesses, it must follow that everyone had strengths as well. She simply needed to figure out what hers were and stop allowing the lieutenant to make her doubt their existence.

Harriett straightened her spine and lifted her chin a notch. "You are absolutely right."

"Of course I am," said Cora. "Now, I want you to put all thoughts of battles, wits, and wagers out of your mind and focus instead on getting to know the lieutenant the way you would any other gentleman."

"He is no gentleman," Harriett felt the need to insert.

"Perhaps not," said Cora carefully. "But if you can get past that, I'm certain you can show him the beautiful, talented, confident woman you are."

Harriett smiled a little. "You forgot intelligent."

"That goes without saying."

Harriett grinned and hugged her friend, feeling some of her confidence return. She may have been wrong about a great many things, but in one thing she had been correct. Cora had indeed been an answer from Heaven.

CHRISTOPHER WAVED OFF JONATHAN'S offer of a drink and relaxed against the back of the large wingback chair in the study. A small smile touched his lips as he recalled the image of Lady Harriett climbing down from the buggy on her own and rushing away in a flurry of peach muslin, her chin high, her back straight, and her bonnet slightly askew.

"What are you smiling about?" Jonathan asked as he draped his elbow over the corner of the fireplace mantle, looking very much the same as he had years before. Other than a few additional lines around his eyes and mouth, he still sported the same ramshackle hairstyle, the same lean body, and the same dignified stance. Only now he had an air of wisdom and maturity that had been absent before.

Christopher understood the change well. When life had its way with a person, one had to either give up or grow up.

They'd both grown up.

Christopher's gaze travelled to the painting of Cora that hung above the mantle, next to where his friend stood. He studied it a moment before commenting. "It's a good likeness. The artist has captured her beauty and goodness."

Jonathan glanced at the piece and chuckled before taking a seat in the matching wingback chair across from Christopher, stretching his legs out before him. "Cora has disliked every picture I have placed there and this one most of all. She only agreed to sit for the artist because I begged her to, but she detested every moment of it, insisting that portraits should only be hung after a person died. I told her that I would rather look upon her face than anyone else's, but every time she enters this room, she glares first at the painting and then at me."

Christopher laughed. "Did she commission a painting of you to be placed in her sitting room as revenge?"

"Not yet. I'm certain she's hoping I'll eventually come around to her way of thinking, as I often do. But I'm afraid she's doomed to disappointment this time. Her extreme dislike of the painting has only endeared it to me even more."

"You are fortunate she is so patient with you. Lady Harriett would not have been. She would have retaliated straightaway, directing the artist to paint her husband wearing a pink cravat and place a small, ridiculously-pampered Yorkshire terrier atop his lap—with a bow in its hair, no less."

Jonathan raised an amused eyebrow. "Is that so?"

"The woman is stubborn and unforgiving. She cannot let matters rest until she has exacted some sort of revenge."

"Ah. So she is like you in that respect."

Christopher should have expected the quip. The two had always been like brothers, and as such, there had been many competitions between them. It was a well-known fact that Christopher liked to win—and Jonathan too, of course—but Christopher had always cared just a little bit more.

He adopted an air of nonchalance. "I have settled down in my old age."

Jonathan chuckled and shook his head, obviously not believing the claim. "Do not forget to whom you are speaking, my friend. I know you too well."

Too well indeed, thought Christopher. "Perhaps you are right," he conceded. "But I would not call my encounters with Lady Harriett competitions as much as diversions, though she would probably disagree with me. She is so . . ." He did not know how to finish the sentence or even begin to explain his thoughts about the lady. He only knew that the past week had been the most entertaining and mystifying of his life. She kept him on his toes, that much was certain.

"She is so . . .?" Jonathan moved his hand in a circular motion, prodding his friend to finish his thought.

Propping his elbows on the arms of the chair, Christopher threaded his fingers together. "Let us just say that Lady Harriett is a challenge. She's intelligent and confident yet vulnerable at the same time. I don't know why, but I feel a puzzling inclination to understand her better. She, on the other hand, desires only to see my backside retreat to London with as much haste as possible. There are moments when I think we could become great friends, but something shifts and she is at loggerheads with me once more. It's truly perplexing."

Jonathan watched him closely, no doubt perceiving things as only a close friend could. "So it is Lady Harriett who has kept you here."

"Don't be ridiculous. I was awaiting your return."

Jonathan chuckled and shook his head, once again showing his perception. "You are far too impatient to twiddle your thumbs for a week, and you know it."

Christopher couldn't deny it, nor could he deny that

Lady Harriett had piqued his interest enough to waylay him for a time. "As I said before," Christopher allowed, brushing a nonexistent fleck from his trousers, "she has been . . . diverting."

Apparently Jonathan thought he'd prodded his friend enough for one day—either that or he had something of greater importance to discuss—because he let the matter drop. "For what it's worth, I'm glad you remained. It has been too long."

"Agreed," said Christopher, thinking of the letter he'd received from his mother only yesterday. "Unfortunately, I must return to London soon. My parents have unknowingly sided with Lady Harriett in that they are insisting I meet up with them by the week's end."

"You do not wish to go?" Jonathan asked.

"It's complicated." Christopher drew in a deep breath and released it slowly, feeling like too many years of no communication had left him with much to explain. "I gave them my word that I would choose a bride by the end of the season, and they are anxious for me to begin my search."

Other than a slight widening of his eyes, Jonathan showed no reaction. "You don't seem overly pleased by the prospect. Why make such a promise?"

Christopher felt the weight of it bear down on him the way it always did when he allowed himself to dwell on it. Only this morning, he had spoken with such conviction to Lady Harriett that love should be stumbled upon and not sought after. Yet here he was, a man forced to seek after it because of a promise he'd made to his parents. The task daunted him like no war assignment had ever done.

Christopher had come to realize that there were a few ways a man could risk his life. He could raise his sword and charge into battle, putting his mortality on the line, or he could offer for a young lady after only a brief acquaintance, not knowing whether or not the remainder of his life would be spent in misery or joy. At least in battle if things went south, his life would have been taken quickly. Marriage, on the other hand, could easily mean decades of torture. What man would be pleased by such a prospect?

"There is something you're not telling me, my friend," said Jonathan.

"There are a great many things I have not told you and a great many things you already know, such as the fact that my father's pockets are to let."

Jonathan nodded. "The reason you insisted on going to war, I believe."

Christopher rubbed the back of his neck, stretching it from side to side. "That's what I told you and everyone else, but the truth is that I needed to get away. Mother began pressuring me to take on more responsibility, and when she informed me that Father was running the estate into the ground and I was their only hope of salvation, it scared me. For a man, or rather *boy*, who despised any sort of responsibility, it was too much all at once. While at school in Falmouth, I would sneak away from my studies to watch the ships come and go from the wharf, thinking how free the sailors must feel. I began to crave that freedom and eventually joined up, hoping that by the time I came back all would be resolved with Pencarrow." He shook his head. "How stupid I was."

Jonathan said nothing. He only watched and waited, giving Christopher his full attention.

"When Mother learned what I had done, she accused me of caring more about myself than my family. At the time, I thought such claims irrational. I would be earning a living, after all, and what act was less selfish than fighting for one's king and country? But life as a midshipman and war in general was not at all what I had anticipated. The first time I came face-to-face with death, I realized how right she had been. Not long after I left, she wrote me that my father nearly risked our family home in a desperate game of cards. Did you know that? If not for your father's timely interference, he would have lost everything. What would have become of my mother and sisters if I had died at sea? I shudder to think on it."

Even now, Christopher could still remember the chilling sensation he'd experienced when he'd read his mother's letter. He would have left for home immediately if he could have, but he had been bound to the war efforts in the way he was now bound to his familial obligations.

"After the war, I made a promise to myself and my mother that I would never shy away from responsibility again. Now it's time to retire my childhood and become a man—and a married one at that."

Jonathan nodded, his expression contemplative. "Surely you must see yourself settled first. No father would allow you to marry his daughter if you cannot afford to do so."

"I am settled in a way. Our crew became fairly good at taking over enemy ships without too much loss or bloodshed. Every prisoner captured and commodity commandeered resulted in a fair amount of prize money earned—enough that I was able to pay off my father's debts and have a little left over to begin anew. Trouble is, I don't know a blasted thing about managing an estate. And obviously, Father doesn't either."

Jonathan leaned back in his chair and steepled his fingers under his chin, watching Christopher with what could only be described as consideration. "I would begin by dismissing your old land steward and hiring a competent one."

Christopher nodded, having had the presence of mind to take care of that at least. "Already done. Father has also recognized he's made a mess of things and has signed over all estate management to me. Whether or not that was a wise thing for him to do remains to be seen, but I'm certain I cannot do worse than him. Which brings me to the reason I have come, aside from wanting to catch up with an old friend, that is."

Jonathan lifted a questioning brow and waited.

Christopher sighed, hating that he needed help of any kind. He was not easily humbled, but he'd rather his pride take a beating in the privacy of his friend's study than publicly, which was what would happen should he lose his home. "I knew before I even saw Tanglewood that it would be a thriving estate, and so it is. You've always had a head for business and numbers, and . . . well, I would very much like to learn from you."

Jonathan stood and wandered over to a large window, looking out across his property. "It's a work in progress, my friend. Always will be, as will Pencarrow House."

"I realize that, but I would like it to be a work in progress for a long while yet."

Jonathan smiled a little as he turned away from the window. "It will take longer than a few days to teach you what I have learned."

"I didn't intend to get started directly, only to see if you were amenable to the idea. I can return at the end of the season and stay for as long as it takes."

"Won't you have a wedding to plan and attend by then?"

Christopher rubbed the back of his neck again. Life used to be a great deal more fun. Perhaps that's why he enjoyed Lady Harriett's company so much. She distracted him from his concerns and made life interesting once more. "I will have chosen a bride by then. That will be enough. The wedding can wait until after I am better prepared to manage Pencarrow."

Jonathan walked slowly to his chair, pausing to rest his elbows across the back of it. "I have been wanting to repurpose some of my land for an agricultural venture for some time. At one point, I even had some interested investors, but after a harrowing day here at Tanglewood, they decided they would be better off not investing. So I placed my plans on hold for a few months, thinking I would begin my search again after the wedding. Thankfully, I no longer need to do that. Cora recently learned that her father did not cut her off as she thought he would. Rather, he settled quite a large dowry on her, making it possible for me to move forward without needing additional financial assistance. I'm only telling you this because I would be a willing investor should you have an interest in starting a similar venture at Pencarrow."

Christopher straightened, his curiosity piqued. From the time they were young, Jonathan's nose had always been buried in various newspapers or books, reading about the market and current economic trends. Christopher had to use his powers of persuasion to lure him away from such studies, and they'd had a great deal of fun, but when all was said and done, Jonathan would return to his books and his studies.

If only Christopher had been as interested in books and news back in those days.

He was certainly interested now. "Tell me more."

Jonathan walked around the chair and took a seat. "If you truly are interested, I will need you to stay longer than a few days. You can help me work out the final details and perhaps see a field or two drained, plowed, and readied for planting."

In the silence that followed, a clock could be heard ticking down the seconds. Christopher thought of his anxious mother, his vow to find a wife, and the ever-shortening season ahead of him. "How much longer?"

"Another fortnight at least."

Christopher whistled. The season would be well underway by then, and his mother would not countenance that late of an arrival. But Jonathan was practically handing Christopher an opportunity that he would be a fool to let pass by. Besides, what difference would another week or two make? There would still be enough time to find a bride and keep his promise.

"Now that Cora and I are back, of course you're welcome at Tanglewood," Jonathan added.

"What the devil am I going to tell my mother?" Christopher muttered, more to himself than to Jonathan. He could already anticipate her irate response. He'd lost count how many times she'd written to him during the war, saying, *If the unthinkable happens and your imbecile cousin becomes heir, I shall never forgive you.*

And she wouldn't. Christopher knew that with absolute certainty. His mother could carry a grudge to her grave if she wished.

Jonathan grinned. "Tell her you are pursuing a woman here—and a lady to boot."

Christopher had to concede that it would be the perfect solution if it were true. "But I am not."

"Aren't you?" Jonathan asked, a mischievous gleam in his eyes. "There are different reasons to pursue a person, you know, and they don't all end in matrimony. Weren't you in constant pursuit of your enemies during the war?"

Christopher laughed. "If that is the way we are choosing to think of it, then it is Lady Harriett who is in pursuit of me and not the other way around."

"Even better," said Jonathan. "What mother wouldn't love to hear that her son is being pursued by the beautiful and intelligent sister of the Earl of Drayson?"

Christopher couldn't help but chuckle at this reversal of roles. It had always been him who'd concocted the duplicitous schemes and Jonathan who attempted to talk him out of them. "I think I have finally rubbed off on you, my friend. Your plan is most devious. I own myself rather surprised. You've always been so upstanding."

Jonathan chuckled. "My wife has always said that sometimes a person can have a good reason for behaving badly. I think this is one of those times."

Christopher's grin widened. "The more I come to learn about your wife, the more I like her. However did you convince her to marry you?"

"Sometimes a man simply gets lucky."

Christopher couldn't argue with that, considering that luck was also on his side at the moment. After all, if he had not encountered Lady Harriett or the Biddings upon his arrival, he would have returned to London directly and waited until after the season to approach Jonathan. But he *had* encountered them, he'd found a reason to stay, and now his friend was offering to not only teach him a thing or two about estate management, but invest in what could become a lucrative agricultural venture. It felt like an answer to many prayers.

"Very well, my friend." Christopher pushed himself out of his seat and glanced around. "If you have a quill and some Foolscap handy, I shall write to Mother straightaway."

"Will you tell her you are being pursued?" Jonathan teased, opening a drawer in his desk to produce the requested paper.

"It is the truth, is it not?"

Jonathan laughed. "Indeed it is."

Christopher took a seat at the desk and wrote his letter, feeling a return of the excitement that he and Jonathan had often experienced once upon a time, back when life was not as complicated. It was good to have something hopeful to smile about again. When he thought about Lady Harriett and how she'd react when she learned that he would be remaining in Askern a few more weeks—and as a guest at Tanglewood, no less—his grin widened.

Christopher arrived in the drawing room to find Lady Harriett already seated on the sofa, the toes of her slippers bouncing up and down. Other than that small indication of anxiousness, she appeared her usual self—composed, impervious, and beautiful, the light blue of her gown matching the color of her eyes almost exactly. Jonathan and Cora had yet to make an appearance, so Christopher took a seat next to her.

"Can you tell me which Lady Harriett I am addressing tonight?" he asked, attempting to dispel the awkward tension. "Will you attempt to be bird-witted, dull, a blue-stocking, or your charming and headstrong self? I'd prefer to know now so that I might better prepare my defense."

A light blush appeared on her cheeks—the only indication his comment had affected her. "I have decided to cease battling with you, Lieutenant, so let us begin anew, shall we?" She held out her hand. "I am Lady Harriett Cavendish, daughter of the dowager Lady Drayson in Essex."

Christopher wasn't sure what to make of this new approach. What game was she playing at this time? He accepted her hand, taking note of how soft it was. "Are we to disregard everything we already know about each other then?"

"That's just it, Lieutenant." She slipped her hand away. "I don't feel as though I *do* know you—not well, at any rate—and I would like to change that."

This definitely was a new approach and one Christopher would enjoy figuring out, but not before he disclosed something she would likely not want to hear. "It relieves my mind to hear you say that, my lady. I was worried that I would incur your displeasure once you discovered that I am now a guest at Tanglewood and plan to stay for another fortnight."

He watched her closely for signs of distress, but her lips did not pinch, her jaw did not harden, and her eyes did not flash in annoyance. On the contrary, they brightened as though the prospect actually delighted her—something he found very hard to believe.

"Not at all, sir. That is happy news indeed. Only think of how much better we will come to know each other by then."

If Christopher had known her during the war, he would have been tempted to enlist her aid in strategizing. The best attack was to catch one's enemy by surprise, after all, and she certainly had a way of surprising him on a daily basis. But what was she hoping to achieve with this latest endeavor, or did she truly wish to let bygones be bygones? Christopher could scarce believe it, though she appeared in earnest. Or perhaps she only wanted him to *think* she was in earnest. There was no telling with her.

"What—or rather, *who*—has convinced you to stay in Yorkshire, Lieutenant?" she asked, the interested smile still on her face.

Christopher settled more comfortably against the sofa and casually draped his arm across the spine behind her. Her posture stiffened, and she leaned slightly forward, probably to ensure that the exposed skin of her back did not graze his arm. He found it both aggravating and intriguing. If she was that repelled by him, why go to the effort of getting to know him?

"Jonathan wishes to discuss a business proposition with me," he answered.

"Ah," she said. "That sounds . . . interesting. Are you at liberty to share any of the particulars, Lieutenant?"

He eyed her quizzically, wondering what she was about. She couldn't possibly want to converse about such a dull topic.

"Lady Harriett," he suggested, "if we are to become great friends, might we dispense with your title and my rank? I would be honored if you would call me Christopher."

She hesitated only a moment before nodding. "I'd like that, Christopher."

And *he* liked the way his name sounded on her lips. "And I will call you Harry," he teased.

She did not seem to care for that idea at all. "You may call me either Lady Harriett or Harriett, sir, and that is all. I was not blessed with a name that can be shortened."

"'Tis a shame," he said, shaking his head as though saddened by the fact. "If we are to become bosom friends, Chris and Harry has a good ring to it, don't you think?"

She must have thought the comment not worthy of a reply. "Do many people call you Chris? I rather like it."

"No, as a matter of fact. You would be the first, Harry . . . ett." He grinned the moment her eyes narrowed.

She was quick to drop her gaze to her lap and began dusting off her gown with one hand, probably in an attempt to hide her annoyance with him. After a time, she said, "I do love to be the first at things."

Did that mean that she intended to call him Chris from this point forward? Christopher didn't know how he'd take to the shortened version of his name. Every time he had tried it out in his head, it had always sounded feeble, weak, and unsubstantial, but if she began calling him that, he had no one to blame but himself. He'd been the one to plant the idea in her mind, after all.

"What are you two discussing so intently?" Cora's voice broke through his thoughts. Christopher glanced up in surprise as she sank down in a nearby chair while her husband took another not far away.

Hopefully Cora would realize that Christopher had not meant to slight her by not standing at her entrance. His years in the war had made him a little lax when it came to social niceties, and it was taking some time for certain things to become second nature again. "I was simply telling Harriett the good news that I have relocated to Tanglewood and plan to remain for an additional fortnight."

"And I was just telling *Chris*"—Harriett smiled pointedly at him—"that I am delighted to hear it. Only think how cozy our group will be during the upcoming days. That is . . ." She frowned. "What about your parents, Chris? Will they not be angered by your continued absence? I thought they were most insistent that you meet them in London by the end of the week."

Christopher exchanged an amused look with Jonathan before answering. "I wrote to my mother only this morning, informing her of my new . . . plans, and, well, I'm quite certain that once she, er . . . understands the situation, she will agree that it's in my best interests to stay."

Jonathan covered his chuckle with a cough, and when his wife cast him an inquiring glance, he shrugged. Christopher had to resist the urge to smile. It brought back memories of all the good times they had shared over the years. How he'd missed his friend. No one had ever understood him the way Jonathan did.

Judging by the quizzical way Harriett watched him, she must've thought his answer a trifle odd. Christopher thought it best to change the subject before either of the ladies began to question them further.

"Cora," he said. "I hear you recently returned from the coast. Did you see anything of interest while you were there?"

Cora dismissed his inquiry with a wave of her hand. "Nothing worth mentioning, I assure you. I am much more interested to hear about you. Jonathan has told me about a few of your escapades, like the time he lost a wager, and you made him write a poem and recite it in front of a large gathering."

Christopher laughed. He had not thought about that wager in years. "What a dreadful poem it was. If those in attendance had not already known we were close friends, I would have denied any association with the man."

Jonathan nodded. "It *was* dreadful. But I did get the thing to rhyme, so there was that."

"Yes, two whole times if I remember correctly."

"I take it the two of you have been friends for a long time?" asked Harriett.

"We grew up on neighboring estates," explained Jonathan. "We used to spend a great deal of time catching frogs, snakes, lizards, mice, and any other creature we could find. Christopher has five younger sisters, you see, and they were a great deal of fun to tease."

"*Torment*, more like," said Harriett dryly. "Have your sisters ever forgiven you?"

"All but one." Christopher grinned slyly, thinking of his

sister, Penelope, and the string of unladylike words she had cast at him the time he'd given her a bottle of lavender scent for her bath water. Unbeknownst to her, he'd added purple dye as well. She had thought the color of her bath water charming until her skin and hair had taken on a similar hue.

"She has yet to learn that to forgive is divine? Did you not favor her with one of your readings from the Bible?" Harriett said sweetly.

Christopher chuckled and shook his head. Penelope had always been the most ornery of his sisters, always determined to find fault with anyone and anything. "I suppose that gaining her good opinion did not matter as much to me as . . . other's good opinions."

Christopher had meant it as a joke, but as he spoke the words, he realized they were true. He *did* wish for Harriett's good opinion. He also wished for her forgiveness and for her not to stiffen or shrink away from his touch. Something told him that she was fiercely loyal to those she cared about, and he wanted to belong to that exclusive inner circle.

"Did you lob apples at her from your favorite tree?" she asked.

Christopher shook his head again. He knew better than to do that to his sisters. "Only at Jonathan. And the coach-man a time or two." Before he'd knocked the poor man off his seat and broken his arm, that is. For that act of idiocy, Christopher had been sentenced to read the entire book of Psalms and write a paragraph about each one. There was a reason he was so well versed in the Bible. It had been his nursemaid's preferred method of punishment.

"Now that we've established you're a tease and possibly even a brute," said Harriett. "Tell me of a kindness you've done for someone."

Christopher thought back over his youth and frowned

when he couldn't recall anything but the many pranks he'd concocted—none of which had been very kind. It wasn't as though he'd had a sinister nature. He'd merely enjoyed making life more interesting, and a few harmless pranks here and there had always livened things up. But surely he'd done something good somewhere along the way.

Hmm . . .

Did offering his sister a hand after she'd tripped over the twine he'd stretched between two trees count? Probably not, considering he'd tricked her into walking that direction on purpose, telling her he'd found a new shortcut.

Good gads, he had been a troublesome youth, hadn't he?

But that had all happened before the war and before he'd learned a thing or two about the world and people. Since then, he'd done many things he'd consider kind and good, like taking a slug to save a crew member and sharing his last ration with someone worse off than he. But he could never boast of such acts, not even to gain Harriett's good opinion.

"Christopher once saved a kitten from drowning," said Jonathan, coming to his rescue. "He stayed up all night to make sure it didn't come to lasting harm. He also attempted to bake a cake for his family's cook when he learned it was her birthday, though I'm not sure you could call that a kindness as it turned out quite vile. But he did once punch a stableboy for daring to hold hands with his sister. Despite our many pranks, we were both very protective of his sisters."

Christopher nodded, grateful for the reminder that he had done a few redeemable acts during his youth, although the poor stable boy had come away with a bleeding and broken nose.

Harriett didn't look overly impressed by his good deeds, but she pressed on, inquiring about his family, his home in Cornwall, and his years at school, learning about several more of his scrapes in the process.

When dinner was at last announced, Christopher breathed a sigh of relief. He had never been the recipient of so many questions and could only be grateful they had not progressed to the time he'd spent in the navy. Those had been long and difficult years that offered very little in the way of entertainment.

He rose and offered Harriett his arm. "Would you care to accompany me into dinner, my lady?"

After only a slight hesitation, she placed her hand on the crook of his elbow. Christopher chose to think of it as progress. She had never willingly touched him before.

"I thought we were to dispense with titles and ranks," she said. "Or do you regret giving me leave to call you Chris?"

Christopher couldn't say that he did. Each time he heard her say it, he liked it more than the last.

"Oddly enough, I'm growing fond of it."

"Truly?"

"Truly."

He couldn't tell if that pleased or irritated her, but as they walked into dinner in what felt like perfect accord with each other, Christopher had the happy thought that perhaps she'd finally forgiven him—or at least was on her way to doing so.

Miracles did happen, after all.

HARRIETT STARED AT HER reflection in the looking glass while Tabby arranged a knot at the crown of her head. But her mind was not on her appearance or Tabby's ramblings about the recent goings on below stairs. She was thinking about three nights prior, when Lieutenant Jamison had become Chris. They had spent the entire evening conversing, and Harriett had asked him every question she could think to ask, but the only discovery she'd made was that Chris had experienced a childhood very similar to her own, filled with plenty of mischief and mayhem. Only his stories were far more interesting and his pranks more ingenious.

Once again, she had paled in comparison while he had come away conqueror.

Drat the man.

Harriett pressed her lips together, chiding herself for such ridiculous thoughts. But honestly, was it too much to ask to have an affinity for *something*? She'd take anything at this point, even shuttlecock champion. Unfortunately, her brother, Colin, already held that particular title. Her sister, Charlotte, had the loveliest singing voice in all of Essex. And her other brother, James, had always been known as a charmer. His smile and sugary words could turn anyone up sweet, even the crotchety Mrs. Simms from the grocer, as evidenced by the day he returned from town with a pocketful of sweets from the woman. Harriett had never received even one treat from her, let alone an entire pocketful of them.

And then there was Chris, who could probably best Colin at shuttlecock, cast Charlotte in the shade with his rich, melodious voice, and come away from the grocer with *two* pocketfuls of sweets. The man had turned Mrs. Bidding up sweet in only a matter of minutes, after all. Even Harriett had to catch herself from falling under his spell on numerous occasions—like the other night, for example, when he'd nearly captivated her with his charming burr, his rich laughter, and the devilish gleam in his eyes.

Yes, he was certainly difficult to resist.

Since that night, he and Jonathan had been much absent, being consumed with discussions about some sort of farming venture. Locked away in Jonathan's study or surveying the estate with the bailiff, they'd joined the ladies only for dinners, and only briefly at that.

The worst part was that Harriett had actually begun to miss Chris. She found herself glancing up anytime someone strode past, hoping for a glimpse of him, only to decide that the house had far too many servants. And every night after dinner, when the men excused themselves and returned to the library or Jonathan's study, she felt . . . disappointed.

Disappointed? How could that be?

Drat the man.

She had no idea how he'd managed to weasel into a small part of her heart, but somehow he had. It was highly disconcerting.

"Tabby was correct. You really are away with the fairies," said Cora from behind, startling Harriett from her wretched thoughts.

Much to Harriett's surprise, Tabby had not only finished the coiffure, but she'd curled a few tendrils, added a lovely ribbon to Harriett's hair, and was now nowhere to be seen. How was that possible? Tabby always bustled about, prattling on about something. And she had never departed without a cheerful, "Enjoy your day, milady." Had Harriett missed that as well?

Gracious, she really *had* been away with the fairies, hadn't she?

"How long have you been standing there?" Harriett asked, watching her friend through the mirror.

"Long enough to know you have something on your mind," Cora teased. "But I am glad to see that you have returned to us once again. Now that my husband has decided to occupy his every hour with business matters, I'm sure I wouldn't know what to do with myself without you to keep me company."

Harriett rose from the dressing table and turned around. "In that case, thank you for bringing me back to the world in which we live."

Cora sat down on the bed and patted a spot next to her. "Fairies can be much more interesting at times, can they not? What is on your mind, my friend? You are obviously troubled about something."

Not long ago, Cora had been the one to lay her problems at Harriett's door, but now it seemed to be the other way around—a circumstance Harriett did not care for at all. It was dreadful to be on the needy end of things.

Still, Harriett sat by her friend and felt a great temptation to rest her head on Cora's shoulder.

"Is it Christopher? Have you allowed him to steal your confidence again?" Cora asked.

Harriett almost winced at the unhappy reminder that

she had, indeed, allowed him to make her feel quite pathetic. But that was not the cause for her reflections this morning.

"No," Harriett said. "He hasn't been around enough lately to do that, has he?"

"Oh, is that the problem?"

Harriett was about to tell her that no, his absence was definitely *not* the problem, but Cora was quick to add, "Because if it is, I might know of a solution."

Her curiosity piqued, Harriett couldn't help asking, "What sort of solution?"

"Well, I was only just speaking with our cook, Mrs. Caddy, and she happened to mention that the past few nights someone has been helping himself—or herself—to what's left of the dessert after the servants had gone to bed. Normally, I would point the finger at Jonathan, as he is fond of late night snacks, but I know it is not him because he has been with me. And I can't imagine it was you either."

"Definitely not me," said Harriett.

"Which leaves only Christopher as our culprit."

Harriett wondered what that had to do with Cora's so-called solution. Unless . . . She eyed her friend sharply. "You're not suggesting what I think you are, are you?"

Cora shrugged. "I said I *might* know of a solution—not that I *did* know of one."

Harriett gaped at her in astonishment. "Have you gone daft, Cora? A lady does not creep downstairs in the middle of the night with the hope of encountering a certain man."

Rather than appear properly chastised, Cora played with the fabric of her skirts. "Perhaps not, but Jonathan and I shared a midnight snack on more than one occasion, and I will always remember those moments with fondness. There is something about that time of day, whether it's exhaustion or the shielding effects of darkness, that makes people feel more comfortable revealing things they'd never consider discussing over luncheon."

Harriett had to concede the truth in that statement. Her tongue had always been more willing to wag in the evening than the morning. But if she ever did happen upon Chris, would his tongue loosen as well, or would it only be hers? She frowned, knowing it would likely be the latter. Which was precisely why she would never consider hunting down a man in the dead of night—that, and it would be highly improper.

Goodness, she had dwelled on this far too long. It was time to be done with it—all of it—the competing, the contrasting, the comparing, and the always finding herself wanting. What good did it do? None. *Absolutely* none.

Enough was enough. Chris was a man of many talents. Was that so bad? Let him be good at everything. Let Cora be known for her kind-hearted spirit and positive outlook. Let her siblings enjoy their many talents. It was all well and good. Harriett had to *make* it well and good or she would go mad.

The simple fact was that no matter how hard she tried, she could not control her situation. The only thing she could control was her attitude, and starting right now she would strive to be as upbeat and optimistic as her dear friend.

Oh dear. There she went, comparing herself yet again. Would she never learn?

"Harriett?" Cora teased. "Are you away with the fairies again?"

For whatever reason, be it lunacy or Harriett's fierce desire to feel happy once more, she started to laugh, long and hard. When her eyes began shedding tears, she buried her giggles in the pillow and allowed her shoulders to shake them free. She could not help herself. After such a long spell of scheming and fretting to no avail, the feeling of letting everything go intoxicated her. It brightened the room, sent her frustrations scurrying away, and uplifted her heart.

Oh, what a blessed feeling.

As her laughter died down, she rolled onto her back and felt the sunlight streak across her face. Spring was not the time for wretchedness. It was a time for glorying in new beginnings, enjoying flowery scents, and observing the beauty of renewed life. She must remember that.

She *would* remember that.

Cora looked down on her with twinkling eyes and a wide smile. "Most people would have cried, you know."

"I am not most people," said Harriett.

"I am glad to hear you have finally realized that."

Harriett drew herself up and rested her head on Cora's shoulder. "Bless you for being so good to me."

"I could say exactly the same to you, you know. The way I see it, we're now square." Cora patted Harriett's knee. "Now what do you say we drive ourselves to town and spend the remainder of the day increasing our wardrobes and emptying Jonathan's purse? Perhaps that will give him a reason to notice me once more. He watches the books with an eye of an eagle, you know."

Harriett grinned and pushed herself to her feet. "I think it a marvelous plan. Shall we be off?"

"Not until you allow me to tuck your errant hair back into place. I'm afraid your fit of the giggles has quite ruined your chignon."

Harriett's hands flew to the loose knot and wild, fraying curls. She didn't have to peer into the mirror to know how frightful she must look. It was a good thing Tabby was no longer around, or her maid would never forgive her.

"In fairyland, this style is all the rage, you know," Harriett said.

And with that, Cora began to laugh.

Harriett lay in bed that night unable to sleep. She couldn't stop thinking about Chris's handsome face or the fact that she might find him in the kitchen this very moment. She had not seen him at breakfast—he had already been up for hours—nor at luncheon either, which was not at all surprising. But dinner had been another matter completely as the gentlemen always took a break to dine with the ladies.

This evening, however, Harriett and Cora had stopped in at the Biddings on their way back from town. The couple was delighted to see them and couldn't wait to show off their precious Pippin and her litter of new puppies—three to be precise. They clustered around their mother in a large basket located near the fire in the library while Pippin dozed. It was a precious sight indeed. Harriett ached to pick up one of the little darlings and hold it close.

"Now you have seen the reason we have not called at Tanglewood of late. They arrived four days ago. Are they not too sweet for words?" Mrs. Bidding said, obviously thrilled by the newest additions to their family.

Harriett crouched down for a closer look and pointed at a puppy with variegated brown and white fur around its nose. "This one has the look of a foxhound, does it not?"

Mr. Bidding nodded. "You are very observant, Lady Harriett. Before Pippin came to live with us, the neighboring estate housed a foxhound. We couldn't be sure the creature was the father until the litter arrived. One look at that puppy, and we knew the truth of it."

"He's adorable," said Harriett, thinking of Lieutenant

Jamison and his dislike of small dogs. Unable to resist the temptation, she added, "If you could ever bear to part with one of these dear creatures, I'm certain the lieutenant would love to take one home with him."

"What a charming idea," said Mrs. Bidding. "If Mr. Bidding and I should decide to do such a thing, I will be sure to place the credit for the suggestion at your door."

"That is very gracious of you," said Harriett, happy to take credit. She would very much like to see the look on Chris's face when such an offer was made.

Mr. Bidding allowed the ladies to enjoy the puppies for a few moments more before ushering them from the room. "We'll let them sleep and continue our conversation in the drawing room, shall we?"

Once settled, Mrs. Bidding soon discovered that the lieutenant and Jonathan had been preoccupied with matters pertaining to business and had been much absent. As soon has she'd heard the news, she insisted that her guests stay for supper, along with a vigorous game of whist afterwards. The ladies were happy to oblige, and a footman was asked to carry a note to Tanglewood, informing Jonathan of their change in plans.

Later that evening, when the ladies at last returned, the gentlemen were ensconced in the library with the doors closed. Cora and Harriett would have popped their heads in to wish them good night if not for the sound of the bailiff's gruff tones and another voice they did not recognize. Apparently, the men were deep in conversation, and the ladies thought it best not to intrude. Harriett had looked longingly at the doors as she walked past, wishing they would open and reveal a certain lieutenant. One look, a few exchanged words, a smile—that was all she would have needed to direct her thoughts towards sleep.

But the doors hadn't opened, looks and words had not been exchanged, and Harriett had returned to her bed-chamber feeling anxious and out of sorts.

And now she could not sleep.

Was he in the kitchen?

She groaned and rolled to her side. It did not matter if he was. She was a well-bred lady and would not go down-stairs. She would *not*.

He probably wouldn't be there anyway. There was no telling what time he chose to sneak into the kitchen. For all she knew, it could be two in the morning. What were the odds that he would be there at—she snatched a timepiece from her bedside table and held it up to the moonlight—almost half past midnight?

Goodness, had she really been tossing in her bed for two hours? This was beyond ridiculous. Honestly, what had Cora been thinking to plant such a notion in her mind?

Another ten minutes passed before Harriett finally gave up and threw the covers aside. If she did not go down and see with her own eyes that he was not there, she would probably be up all night. That was not at all acceptable, and so she would go down for the sake of her health and well being.

She pulled on her dressing gown, glanced in the mirror to make sure her side braid was still intact, and lit a candle before slipping out the door. As she neared the kitchen, she thought she heard some sort of noise that caused her body to stiffen and her ears to strain, but no more sounds came. Harriett berated her overly active imagination and stepped through the door, expecting to find a dark and empty kitchen on the other side. Instead, she found Jonathan coming out of the butler's pantry with what appeared to be forks.

She let out her breath, feeling both relieved and disheartened. It was only Jonathan. Apparently, Cora had been wrong about her husband not being the culprit after all.

"You look disappointed," he said before disappearing back in the pantry.

"No, of course not," Harriett said quickly. "It's just that I'd hoped . . ." She clamped her mouth shut and felt her cheeks burn. Good grief, had she really almost said that she'd hoped to see Chris? Apparently the late hour *did* have a way of loosening one's tongue. If she had any sense at all, she'd flee back to her bedchamber this instant.

A clatter sounded in the larder, and out came the devil himself, carrying what appeared to be a plate of leftover cake. The moment Harriett spotted him in his rumpled shirt and trousers, her heartbeat surged, much to her annoyance.

He grinned at her. "You had hoped to see *me*, didn't you, Harry? Admit it."

Never.

Harriett set her candle on a nearby shelf and stepped away from its light, hoping the darkness would enshroud her flaming face. "I was actually hoping to find Cora here," she said as Jonathan reemerged from the pantry with a handful of forks. That had sounded convincing, hadn't it?

Not according to the skeptical look Chris directed at her. "Because . . . spending the entire day with her was not enough?"

Jonathan snickered, and Harriett felt the sudden urge to stuff a large slice of cake into Chris's mouth. Why must he always be so vexing? "It's only that I . . . forgot to tell her something . . . important. That's all." Apparently Harriett could now add *a dreadful liar* to her ever increasing list of weaknesses. She was deplorable at it.

"Why not tell Jonathan your important news, whatever it is, and he can convey it to Cora as soon as possible?" Chris suggested in his unhelpful way.

"Heavens no," said Harriett. "She's probably already asleep, and I wouldn't wish for her to be awakened."

"Then you are a better person than I," said Jonathan as he set the forks on the table and took the cake from Chris. With swift movements, he sliced off a large chunk, slid it onto a plate, and picked up two of the forks. On his way out of the kitchen, he paused at Harriett's side. "I have not seen my wife all day and fully intend to awaken her. It's a boorish thing to do, I realize, but I hope to gain her forgiveness by presenting this as a peace offering."

Harriett eyed the slice of cake. "I believe it will take much more than that. You have ignored her these past three days."

"I think you're underestimating the power of this particular lemon cake."

"And I think you are overestimating its power."

He chuckled and lifted the plate as though making a toast to her and then Chris. "I wish you both a good night."

He backed out of the room a moment later, leaving Harriett alone with a man who looked far too mischievous for his own good—or hers, for that matter. If there was ever a moment to excuse herself, now would be it. If only she could get her lips to say the words and her feet to move in the direction of the door.

Chris didn't seem to feel the same unease. He plopped down on a stool and pulled out another, gesturing for her to sit next to him. "If it's any consolation, I have been missing you as well. All this talk of money, crops, drainage, and location has wreaked havoc on my overwhelmed mind. I'm in desperate need of the sort of distraction that only you can provide, Harry. Come, I beg you, and share some cake with me. It truly is delicious."

Feeling somewhat appeased despite his annoying use of

"Harry," Harriett did as he bid, but she could not make her body relax. Her back rigid, she waited for him to slice and serve the cake, but instead, he slid the entire mound between them and snatched one of the forks from the table.

"I'm famished," was all he said before helping himself to a mouthful.

Harriett blinked a few times before rolling her eyes. "I think your nursemaid failed to teach you proper manners."

"She attempted to, but I was not what you'd call an adept pupil." He swallowed another bite and gestured to the cake. "If I were you, I'd cease glaring at me and have a taste before there is none left to be had. I meant it when I said that I was hungry."

Harriett almost laughed. There had to be a third of the cake left. Did he truly intend to finish it off? With a shake of her head, she retrieved a fork and took a bite as well, noting with surprise that it was, indeed, delicious. Heavenly, in fact. Moist and light, with a hint of lemon and vanilla, it melted over her tongue.

"This has to be the most divine cake I have ever tasted," she murmured before stealing another bite.

He wiggled his eyebrows. "And it is all ours."

"I wonder what Mrs. Caddy will say tomorrow when she discovers it gone."

"She'll probably want Jonathan to exile me, or at the very least give me a sound lecture. I suppose it's a good thing I have been making myself useful of late."

Harriett studied him for a moment, noticing the weariness behind his stubble-coated jaw and red-rimmed eyes. It was obvious he had not been sleeping much.

"How, exactly, have you been making yourself useful?" she asked, sincerely curious. Ever since her brother, Colin, had married, discussions about tenant farms, renovations, rents, crops, livestock, repairs, servants, and other issues often arose during dinner at Langtry Park. At first, Harriett had thought such conversations tedious in the extreme, but as she came to understand the way of things better, she learned to enjoy them. Problems became riddles to her, and she had always loved solving riddles.

"If you want to know the truth of it," said Chris, sounding a bit sheepish. "I really haven't been all that useful. Jonathan has been doing his utmost to enlighten me on the latest farming methods and the business behind it all, but he is attempting to impress upon me in a matter of days what has taken him years to learn. It does not help that I have always been a slower study than him."

Harriett's eyes widened at this revelation. Could it be that Chris had an actual failing?

"I find that hard to believe," she said.

He shook his head and chuckled. "Whether or not you believe it, 'tis true. Jonathan can read a book once, grasp its concepts entirely, and remember everything he wants to remember. I, on the other hand, need time and repetition to understand."

Harriett felt an odd desire to reach out and comfort him. Why, she couldn't say. After all that had happened, she should be rejoicing that she had finally discovered a weakness in him.

Chris stretched his neck from side to side and grimaced. "The trouble is that because I am still attempting to grasp basic principles, I am no help at all when serious problems arise. Much of our time lately has consisted of me listening while he thinks out loud or discusses possible resolutions with the land steward and solicitor. Anytime he poses a question to me, I can only shrug. It's irritating in the extreme."

Harriett had never seen Chris in such a state. It was both shocking and . . . sort of wonderful, actually. She rather liked this version of him—not in a gleeful sort of way (at least not too gleeful), but in a *perhaps he's human after all* way.

"The worst bit is that I'm beginning to think his offer to invest in my estate was made out of pity. Why else would he willingly invest in an estate run by a man who knows nothing about business or farming?"

Harriett had no idea what he was talking about. What investment? And what did he mean about not knowing anything about farming? "I don't understand why you would say such things. Are you not well versed in the Norfolk method? During our drive, you implied as much."

His chuckle contained very little humor. "I did not. I only said I'd heard of it, and that is entirely different than understanding it."

Harriett's mouth dropped open. He'd only *heard* of it? She thought back to that dreadful drive when that particular conversation had been the undoing of her. She'd practically fallen to pieces over it, behaving like an emotional ninny-hammer. And all this time, she'd actually known more than him?

"Unbelievable," Harriett muttered under her breath, feeling vexed all of a sudden.

"I beg your pardon?" he asked.

"Oh, er . . . nothing." Determined not to let him get to her yet again, she attempted to gather her wits about her. What were they discussing? Oh, yes, his helplessness.

"If you don't mind my asking," she said, "what problems have arisen?"

He set his fork down and turned to face her, leaning his elbow on the table as he eyed her curiously. "Are you truly interested? Because it's incredibly tedious."

"I would not have asked if I wasn't."

He smiled a little as though he didn't believe her, but continued anyway. "The biggest complication is the matter of the land. Tanglewood has only a small section in the northwest corner that is ideal for planting crops, but it's not large enough for Jonathan's purposes. He could fell some particularly large trees and level some additional ground to make the area a bit larger, but a pond and wetlands to the south and east inhibit additional growth."

Harriett considered his words. "Surely he knew of this problem before now."

Chris nodded. "Of course. He's been in communication for some time with the owner of the property to the west. Last November, they came to an agreement that Jonathan could purchase a portion of his property, but that was before Jonathan's potential business associates backed out of the deal. And now that his finances are back in order and he is ready to proceed, Mr. O'Rourke has suddenly experienced a change of heart."

"Why?" Harriett asked.

"He's arrived at the conclusion that his land will be easier to sell in its entirety. If Jonathan wants that particular parcel, he must buy everything."

"I see," said Harriett. "Am I to assume he cannot afford to do such a thing?"

"He can, but he has no need for the rest of the land. We've also discussed the possibility of farming some of my family's land in Cornwall, but if Jonathan's money is tied up here, that is obviously out of the question."

Harriett nodded in understanding, and Chris shot her a curious look as though he could not fathom why she would be interested in this particular discussion. It raised her hackles a little.

"What, you think a mere woman cannot grasp business concepts?"

He blinked and shook his head, appearing annoyed by her supposition. "I believe anyone can grasp any concept they wish to, though I'll admit to being a trifle surprised when you mentioned the four-course system during our last drive together. But tonight, I'm merely grateful to you. Not many women would care to listen to a weary man's ramblings."

"As I told Cora only this morning, I am not most people," said Harriett, half teasing and half hoping he would agree.

"I am well aware that you are not, Harriett," he said with a slight smile. "You are an Original, to be sure."

Harriett had been called that many times during her first London season, but this was the first time the compliment went deeper, as though it included all of her and not just the shell surrounding her head and heart. It soothed and warmed her in that way only Chris had ever been able to do. But had he truly meant it?

She pulled her gaze from his and turned her mind back to the problem at hand. "What about Mr. Shepherd's property? Can you not farm two separate areas? Does he have some land adjacent to Tanglewood's that he might be able to sell Jonathan?"

Chris shook his head as though they'd already considered that. "That side of Mr. Shepherd's property would be even more difficult to drain than Tanglewood's."

"I see," mused Harriett, still thinking. There had to be a solution. There was *always* a solution if a person looked hard enough. "Would Mr. O'Rourke be willing to lease the land?"

Chris shook his head. "Jonathan has no desire to lease it. What would happen should a buyer be found and that buyer did not want Jonathan farming his land any longer?"

Harriett had to concede that would be a problem. Unfortunately, she had no more suggestions to offer at the moment, which left Jonathan with only two options. "So he must either find a way to convince Mr. O'Rourke to sell only what land is needed or not invest in your property."

Chris nodded. "Perhaps we can find some sort of buried treasure hidden away somewhere and solve all of our problems."

"I have always loved a good treasure hunt," Harriett said.

His answering smile did not quite reach his eyes, which he rubbed and blinked as though they were difficult to keep open.

Harriett looked at what remained of the cake. Apparently, he didn't intend to finish it off after all, so she collected their forks and stood. "Forgive me for saying so, but you look quite done in, Chris. If you do not go up to bed now, you will probably fall asleep here. Only imagine what Mrs. Caddy might say if she discovers you here with the mostly-eaten cake. For your own sake, you ought to retire. I will do my best to tidy things up."

Before she could move away from him, he grabbed her hand and guided her to sit back down, keeping hold of her fingers. "Not so fast, my lady. I meant it when I said that I'm in desperate need of the distraction that only you can provide. Thus far, all I have done is burden you with my troubles."

"I do not feel at all burdened, sir." Indeed, Harriett suddenly felt breathless and somewhat giddy. The effect this man had on her was something of a wonder.

"Sir?" he asked. "I thought we were beyond that."

"I thought so as well, but you only just called me 'my lady.'"

He frowned and blinked as though he hadn't realized he had. "Forgive me, Harry. I fear my exhaustion has muddled my thinking."

This time, she did not let the name slide. She snatched her hand free and frowned at him. "Obviously it has."

He laughed—not a tired attempt at a laugh, but a real one filled with the richness that warmed her straight through. Only this time, it did not bother her at all. In fact, it felt wonderful, almost like a compliment.

"I knew you'd come through for me," he said, leaning close enough to touch shoulders with her. "You have no idea how much I needed to laugh or how good that felt. I could honestly kiss you right now."

Harriett tried her best not to blush or appear astonished by the suggestion—he had obviously made the comment in jest—but when his smile widened into a devilish grin, she knew she'd failed. He leaned in closer, and his gaze wandered briefly to her mouth before returning to her eyes. She could smell vanilla and lemon and a hint of something else— leather perhaps? A delightful pulse whipped down her arm, and she was hard-pressed not to shiver.

"Admit it," he said. "You *have* missed me."

Harriett nearly agreed that she had, but caught herself just in time. Such a declaration might very well lead to a kiss, and she was not ready for that. A loose tongue was one thing, loose morals quite another.

"Not at all," she said, suddenly anxious to leave before she did something she'd undoubtedly regret. In the wink of an eye, she slipped off the stool and rose. "Good night, Chris," she added before fleeing the room as quickly as she could.

His answering chuckle followed her down the hall, up the stairs, and all the way to her bedchamber, where it pestered and prodded and kept her awake the remainder of the night.

CHRISTOPHER AWOKE LATE THE next morning feeling greatly restored. He tucked his hands under his head and stared at the tall ceiling, wondering what the day would bring. More hours shut away in Jonathan's cramped study? *Please no.* Christopher didn't think he could fit any more information into his overcrowded mind. He needed a reprieve from anything to do with business or farming or problem solving. But would Jonathan agree? Probably not. Although Harriett *had* hinted that Cora had been feeling neglected, so maybe Jonathan could be convinced to set business aside for the day and enjoy some time with the ladies.

Dragging himself from the comfortable bed, Christopher dressed quickly and went to the breakfast parlor, where he found a sideboard filled with everything from bacon and poached eggs to toast and marmalade. Apparently, the others had already come and gone, so Christopher began piling his plate high with food, determined to fill his belly before he subjected himself to whatever Jonathan had planned.

The moment he sat down, Watts walked into the room.

"Good morning, Lieutenant Jamison," the butler said. "I

apologize if the food is a trifle cold. We tried our best to keep it warm, but I'm not sure we succeeded. If you'd like, I can ask Mrs. Caddy to prepare something fresh."

"Gads, no," said Christopher, thinking the offer absurd. "It is my fault for sleeping so late, not that it matters in the least. During the war, I learned to eat anything regardless of its temperature. This looks delicious, by the way. Please convey my thanks to Mrs. Caddy." Perhaps a kind word from him would soften her heart regarding the mostly-eaten cake.

"Yes, sir," said Watts. "In the meantime, Lord Jonathan has asked me to inform you that he and Lady Jonathan have driven to town this morning to meet with their solicitor. They will return some time this afternoon."

Christopher almost smiled at his good fortune. That meant he had at least a few hours to do whatever he wanted, and what he wanted most was to enjoy the company of a certain lady. "Is Lady Harriett about?" he asked as casually as he could.

"I saw her leaving the house on my way here. She was dressed in a riding habit, which I can only assume means that she intends to exercise one of the horses."

"Indeed." Christopher looked down at his plate, debating between his hunger and Harriett. If he left now, he might be able to catch her.

"Will there be anything else, sir?" Watts asked.

"No, I thank you."

"Very good." The butler bowed and left Christopher alone with his full plate. He snatched what remained of the toast, shoved a piece of bacon into his mouth, and left the room, finishing off the last of the toast as he walked out into the humid March morning. Clouds and light rains had settled over Askern sometime during the night, bringing with it a slight chill in the air, but Christopher did not mind in the least. The dampness reminded him of the sea, and the scent of vegetation reminded him that he was glad to be away from the sea.

He strode towards the stables, but immediately slowed his steps when he spotted Harriett leaning against a wooden fence and saying something to the chestnut horse standing on the other side—Christopher's horse. Apparently Charlie had taken Wicked out of his stall already—or, more likely, the animal had escaped sometime during the night as he often did. Only yesterday, Charlie had said that tending to Wicked was a job in and of itself.

"You are a sneaky beast, aren't you?" Harriett said to Wicked as Christopher approached quietly from behind. "I've never known a horse who could free himself from his stall as easily as Charlie says that you can. According to him, you are brilliantly wicked." She studied the horse a moment longer. "I think you must be loyal as well. Charlie also said you never stray too far from the lieutenant. Is that true? Has he earned your allegiance then? Is he a good master?"

Wicked responded by sniffing the ground.

Christopher chuckled, and the sound caused Harriett to spin around, looking like a child caught sneaking away from her studies. Christopher knew the look well. He'd worn it often throughout his childhood.

"For all his brilliance, he doesn't speak, you know."

"Of course I know." Harriett's cheeks turned a rosy hue, and Christopher had to stifle another laugh. She looked most fetching in the shade of bluish-gray she wore. She could have blended in with the sky, but she didn't. She stood out, radiant and stunning. How had he ever missed her that first day at the side of the road?

He propped his elbows on the fence beside her and

watched Wicked thoughtfully. "If you must know, I am a remarkable master. Wicked is lucky to have me. Most people would not put up with his tricks."

She nodded. "He is quite beautiful, isn't he? Would he allow me to ride him, do you think?"

"No."

Under the brim of her straw bonnet, her brow furrowed. "Why not?"

"Because you are a woman."

"What does that have to do with anything?"

Oh, how he enjoyed teasing her. "I don't know for certain. Only that he has never taken to a woman before. Perhaps his mother took him to task one too many times as a foal."

"Or perhaps you simply do not want me to ride him."

Christopher hid another smile. "You may attempt to ride him anytime you'd like, Harriett."

Charlie came out of the stables, leading what appeared to be a gentle brown mare. "Daisy's ready ter go, milady," he announced, passing the reins to Harriett. "Will you be wantin' Wicked saddled as well, sir?"

"Yes, thank you."

Charlie nodded and ran off to complete the task while Harriett began to stroke Daisy's neck and talk quietly to the animal.

Christopher found the sight charming. She certainly had a way with animals, judging by how she interacted so naturally with Daisy, Wicked, and even Pippin. She did not force herself upon them. Rather, she allowed them to come to her, and in so doing earned their trust much more quickly. He wouldn't be at all surprised if she'd already won Wicked over as well.

"You won't mind if I join you on your ride, will you?" he asked.

"If I do?"

"Then I shall ride a respectable distance behind you so as not to infringe on your solitude."

She laughed and smoothed her hand down her horse's mane before giving it a final pat. "Truth be told, I'm not fond of solitude and would enjoy your company. In fact, I would love to see the parcel of land Jonathan plans to farm. I must admit that our conversation last night has intrigued me."

Christopher tsked as though disappointed by her answer. "And I'd so hoped to avoid any and all discussions about business today. Are you certain you wish to see it?"

"Yes."

He sighed. "Very well. But only if you promise to be your lively self throughout the tour. Once Jonathan begins talking business, he becomes an absolute bore."

Her eyes twinkled playfully. "Apparently you have more mettle than I gave you credit for. I was once so certain that a tedious conversation would send you fleeing back to London directly, but now you've survived three entire days of tediousness and still you are here."

Christopher watched her closely, wondering if his presence still bothered her. Did she wish him gone, or was their friendship at last progressing? He could never be sure with her. "Don't give me too much credit. It is easy to stay when one has a good enough reason to do so."

The look in her eye challenged him to give an honest answer. "What reason is that?" she asked.

Perhaps he ought to have used the plural form, as his answer was not so simple. There were many reasons he stayed and many reasons he felt the pull to return. But he was not ready to share them all with her, and so he settled on the answer she already knew.

"Why, a potential business opportunity, of course."

"Of course."

For a moment, he thought he spotted a flicker of disappointment in her expression, but she was quick to avert her gaze to the stables, and when she looked back at him, it was gone. "Would you kindly give me a leg up, Lieutenant? Here comes Charlie now."

"Lieutenant?" he asked, his tone making it clear he didn't care for the formality.

She smiled a little. "Would you kindly give me a leg up, *Chris?*"

"I would love to." That name was definitely growing on him. Or rather, *she* was growing on him. Her alluring smile, the way her eyes sparkled with mischief, flashed in annoyance, or fluttered self-consciously. To say he found her interesting was an understatement.

Instead of cupping his hands and giving her an actual leg up, he moved closer and caught her about the waist. She appeared startled at first, staring at him with wide eyes, but then she settled her hands on his shoulders and allowed him to lift her onto the sidesaddle. She felt soft and delicate and smelled faintly of orange blossoms. It took some restraint not to pull her off the horse and into his arms.

"'Ere you are, sir," interrupted Charlie with Wicked in tow. "The beast wouldn't let me saddle 'im 'til I'd fed 'im some oats."

"Yes, that sounds like him. Thinks he's the Prince Regent himself."

"That 'e does, sir," Charlie said, shaking his head and laughing.

Christopher quickly mounted Wicked, and Harriett wasted no time touching her whip to Daisy's right shoulder and setting off. Christopher made a mental note to tell her to leave her whip at home should she ever decide to ride Wicked. Whips made his horse skittish.

They rode to the northwest corner of Tanglewood's property, racing across meadows and ducking through dense wilderness areas, until they at last reached the area of land that Jonathan wished to farm. Christopher pointed out where Tanglewood's property ended and Mr. O'Rourke's began. Then he showed her the muddy wetlands that would prohibit expansion, and finally reined in Wicked near the edge of the pond so that she could see for herself how unfeasible it would be to attempt to drain and fill it.

"It's nearly six meters deep in the middle," Christopher explained.

Harriett nodded and looked to the west, across the expanse of land that Jonathan wanted to farm. "I don't remember seeing a house in that direction. Why have I never heard of Mr. O'Rourke before?"

"Because there is no house and Mr. O'Rourke resides in Northumberland. He purchased the property over a decade ago with the intention of building a house and some tenant farms, but the war brought shortages and increased taxes, making construction too expensive. So he cut his losses and purchased an existing estate in Northumberland instead."

A slight crease appeared between her eyebrows. "If he intended to build tenant farms, he must own a great deal of property. What are the odds he'll be able to sell it to someone other than Jonathan in the near future? Perhaps a new owner would be more willing to part with only what Jonathan needs."

Christopher could only shrug and venture a guess. "Jonathan mentioned that Mr. O'Rourke has been trying to sell the land since he purchased the estate in Northumberland, and from what his solicitor can find, Jonathan has been the only interested buyer during that time. He's hoping Mr. O'Rourke is desperate enough to accept a low payment for the land."

The crease remained between Harriett's eyebrows. "If Jonathan does purchase the whole of it, can he not partition the land himself and sell what he does not want to keep?"

"If it comes to that, I'm certain he will try to sell the rest. But finding a buyer will not be an easy feat, at least not in the near future. That is the reason he needs to get it for a steal. He will likely be saddled with it for some time."

She drew her lower lip into her mouth as her horse danced beneath her. She seemed to have a firm grasp on business dealings, and Christopher had the lowering thought that she could probably manage his family's estate better than he.

Wicked began to grow antsy as well, or perhaps the animal merely sensed Christopher's mood. Did Harriett plan to stay until she figured out some sort of resolution? She seemed quite determined.

At last she gave voice to her thoughts. "If Mr. O'Rourke is anxious to sell, and Jonathan is the only buyer who has ever come along, why does Jonathan not tell Mr. O'Rourke that he no longer wishes to purchase *any* land—be it a parcel or the entire property?"

Christopher frowned at the question. Was the answer not obvious? "Because he *does* wish to purchase it."

"Of course, but does Mr. O'Rourke know how much he wishes it? Who is more desperate? Could Jonathan exercise a little more patience and hold off another year if needs be? Perhaps if Mr. O'Rourke comes to believe that Jonathan is not desperate, he would be willing to take a partial sum for a corner of his land rather than no sum for all of it."

Christopher gave the matter some thought, and the more he thought about it, the more he wanted to think about it. Harriett had planted a very interesting seed that served to engage his mind like no other discussion on business had in the past few days. Mr. O'Rourke had suddenly become an enemy vessel and Christopher the lieutenant who could one day overtake him by means of strategy. It was now a game of wits—a battle of the minds—and Christopher had always played those games well.

Perhaps now he wouldn't be so useless.

A slow smile stretched across his face as he looked at Harriett with new, more appreciative eyes. But he still couldn't resist teasing her. "Why, Harry, I do believe you are even more brilliant than Wicked."

She leveled him a glare that chastised and challenged him. "Brilliant enough to be allowed to ride him?"

Christopher chuckled. "I told you, he does not like women."

"And I told you that he will come to like me."

Christopher didn't doubt it. The two probably had a great deal in common, not that he'd ever tell Harriett as much. She would never forgive him for thinking such things. "Are you wishing to ride him at this moment? Because if that is the case, I will need to switch saddles."

"No, you'll just need to remove yours. I do not need a saddle. Bareback will suit me just fine."

He hesitated, wondering if she really could ride bareback well or if it was her pride speaking. Although Christopher was willing to let her on Wicked, he did not want to see her hurt. "I must warn you that two of my sisters, both excellent riders, have attempted to seat Wicked, only to be unseated moments later. I may jest about him not liking women, but it may well be the truth."

Unperturbed, Harriett slid from her perch and tied Daisy to a nearby tree branch. She brushed her gloves together and approached Wicked, cautiously smoothing her hand down his nose and along his jaw. "You'll allow me to ride you, won't you, Wicked? I don't believe you're wicked at all, merely a tease like your master."

Christopher swung down, knowing he would not be able to talk her out of it. He made short work of loosening the girth, removing the saddle, and tossing it over a low hanging tree branch before taking hold of the halter and staring the animal in the eye. "Treat her right, beast, or there will be no oats for you tonight."

Harriett cocked her head at him. "My, aren't you protective? Have a care, Chris, or I might start to think of you as a gentleman."

He took her by the shoulders, needing to see the confidence in her eyes. "Are you certain you can ride him bareback? I'd hate for you to take a fall."

"Are you concerned for my welfare, Chris?" The delighted sparkle in her eyes showed that she knew he was. The minx.

Uncomfortable with sentimentality, Christopher responded the way he usually did—with flippancy. "I'm worried about my own. Should you break an arm or a leg, it is I who will have to come to your rescue. Not only that, but I will likely be blamed for ruining yet another one of your garments."

She took his jesting in stride, though her eyes contained a hint of disappointment. "In the unlikely event that I do take a fall, I promise to hold myself entirely to blame."

He nodded, knowing her mind was set on riding the animal. With careful movements, he took her by the waist and lifted her, catching another whiff of orange blossoms in the process. He kept a hand on her back as she situated herself, hoping the finicky horse would allow her to remain. Only after she'd collected the reins did he release her and step away.

"See?" Harriett said as Wicked took a few steps backwards but did nothing more. "Your worry was for naught."

Her whip caught Christopher's eye as she transferred it to her right hand, and he quickly stepped forward to intervene. "Harriett, do not use your—"

Too late. She tapped Wicked's shoulder, and the horse immediately reared. Christopher rushed forward to catch her, but she'd already slid to the ground, landing on her feet near the edge of the pond. Her arms waved in a large, circular motion before she lost her balance, squealed, and fell backwards into a shallow, marshy area.

Much to Christopher's surprise, she did not immediately scramble to get out. Instead, she sat there, blinking as though in shock.

"You unseated me, you scoundrel!" She finally glared at the horse. "Apparently, you are very wicked indeed."

Christopher smiled, happy to see that she seemed unharmed. He inched forward a little, trying to get close enough to offer a hand without falling in himself. "I did try to tell you that he does not like women—or perhaps it was your whip. He's never liked those much either. Try not to take it personally."

He probably should have kept that last part to himself because she turned her glare on him, obviously not appeased by his words. "You might have told me that before setting me on top of him."

"Yes, that would have been best, but I didn't think to say anything until it was too late. Now take my hand before your habit soaks up every last drop of water." Crouching low, he wiggled his fingers, encouraging her to accept his help.

She lifted a muddy glove and placed it in his. As he'd suspected, it felt frigid and slippery, and he made quick work of getting her out of the pond. She was drenched from her waist down, and the majority of her blue-gray dress was now a charcoal gray. He wanted to wrap his arms around her to keep her warm.

She pulled her hand from his and hugged her arms to her shivering body. "You should be glad to know that other than a ruined habit, I am unharmed and you will not be required to carry me back to Tanglewood."

As much as he would have enjoyed holding her, he quickly pulled off his coat and draped it around her shoulders. "'Tis a relief, though I pity Daisy the task. Your skirts must weigh a great deal more than they did before."

Her eyes widened in disbelief. "Is that all you have to say, sir?"

"What more is there to say? You did promise that should you take a fall, you would hold yourself entirely to blame."

She scowled. "To think that I was actually beginning to think well of you."

That was news to him. Happy news. "Not to worry. I'm certain it's only the cold. As soon as we get you home, it will pass and you will think well of me once more. Now let me help you onto Daisy. You must be chilled to the bone."

He tried to put an arm around her to guide her towards her horse, but she shrugged off both his arm and his coat, handing it back to him.

"I'm no longer in need of your assistance, Lieutenant. Good day to you."

She lifted her water-laden skirts, trudged to collect Daisy, and led her to a fallen log, which she used as a boost. After a struggle, some awkward movements, and a few unladylike expressions, she at last mounted and cantered away.

Christopher let her go, knowing from many years of experience with his sisters that if he tried to say anything more, he would only worsen matters. Other gentlemen might know how to soften Harriett's heart, but Christopher didn't. He knew how to tease and prod and make light of situations, but when that fell short, so did he.

10

THE MOMENT WATTS SPIED Harriett in her disheveled state, he sent for Tabby, who fretted and fussed all the way up to Harriett's bedchamber. More servants came bearing warm water for a hot bath, and Sally, the housekeeper, soon appeared with a tray filled with the most delicious tea and an assortment of sweet rolls.

The servants' kindness was a balm to Harriett's bruised heart, and she luxuriated in the blessed feeling of being looked after. When at last she left her room, she felt cleaner, warmer, and refreshed. But that did not mean she was anxious to speak with the lieutenant again. She took her time walking down the long hallway, her troubled thoughts drifting in his direction. Why did he always seem to find her humiliation a source of amusement? Yes, he had been good enough to pull her from the pond and place his coat around her shoulders, but that was the extent of his kindness. He had not bothered to inquire about her welfare or even apologize for his failure to mention that his horse did not care for whips.

His actions, or lack thereof, had injured her. During the chilling ride back to the manor, she had come to the unhappy realization that she craved more from Lieutenant Jamison than flippancy and invigorating conversation. She wanted him to care about her and show her some concern— *genuine* concern. But was he capable of such sentiments?

Harriett had no answer to that. She only knew that she wanted him to be capable of it.

When she reached the stairs, she slid her fingers across the smooth and satiny banister as she descended slowly. Voices reached her ears, originating from the drawing room, and she paused to listen. Had Cora and Jonathan returned?

"No bedchambers available?" came an unfamiliar feminine voice, followed by light laughter. "Don't be ridiculous, Christopher. In a house as large as this, of course there are rooms to spare. Why wouldn't there be? Or is there a house party in progress that you have neglected to mention?"

A heavy sigh sounded. "No, Mother," came Chris's voice. The mere sound of it set Harriett's heart to pounding, but she was quick to push it aside as another thought took over. His mother was here?

Intrigued, Harriett quietly descended a few more stairs and leaned over the banister to better hear the conversation.

"One would think you did not want us here," came a deeper voice. His father's, perhaps? How very interesting.

"Of course he wants us here," his mother insisted. "He wouldn't dare to think otherwise, would you, darling?"

"No, Mother," Chris said again. "I only meant to say that since you did not see fit to send word that you were coming, no rooms have been made ready."

"But your father did send a note ahead, did you not, my love?"

"Er . . ."

Harriett had to stifle a giggle. She really should not eavesdrop, but this conversation was proving most diverting.

Christopher's mother didn't seem at all put out by her husband's lapse. "No matter. We are here now, and Jonathan is an old and dear friend. I'm certain he will see to the arrangements as soon as he returns. But if you truly think we are imposing, your father and I can easily settle in at the inn in town."

"Of course you are not imposing," said Chris, the disgruntled tone of his voice contradicting his words.

His mother seemed to pay it no mind. "Yes, I'm quite certain you are right. Now sit down, dearest, and tell me all about this lovely lady who has set her cap at you. Where is she, by the by? I own, I am most anxious to make her acquaintance."

Harriett wasn't quite sure what to make of that. She frowned. A young lady had set her cap at Chris? Surely not. As far as Harriett knew, the only unmarried lady the lieutenant knew in Askern was herself, and his mother couldn't possibly think that—

The front door opened, and in walked Watts. He stood aside to allow Cora and Jonathan entrance as well.

"I put them in the drawing room and directed Sally to ready two rooms as quickly as possible," Watts explained.

"Thank you," answered Cora. She was the first to spy Harriett on the stairs, and her brow furrowed in confusion.

Harriett immediately straightened, realizing how odd she must look leaning over the banister.

"Hello, Harriett," said Jonathan, his mouth twitching. "Are you quite comfortable?"

"Quite," she responded as she quickly walked down the remainder of the stairs, trying her best not to blush.

Jonathan snickered and Watts cleared his throat. "Forgive me, Lady Harriett, for not being here to introduce you to our recently arrived guests. The rest of the staff is occupied at the moment, and when I spied Lord and Lady Jonathan's carriage approaching, I went out to meet them."

Harriett waved his concerns aside. "No apologies necessary, Watts. I have only just come down."

Cora stripped off her gloves and laid them on a table. "You probably know this already, but Mr. and Mrs. Jamison have arrived from London and are awaiting us in the drawing room. Would you care to join us?"

"I would love to," Harriett answered honestly. After what she'd heard, she'd very much like to meet Chris's parents and discover more about this mystery woman who'd supposedly set her cap at their son.

As they walked into the room, the lieutenant stood immediately, appearing nervous. The glance he directed at Harriett could only be described as wary. Was he worried about her reaction after this morning's debacle, or did his wariness have more to do with what she may or may not have overheard?

Only time would tell.

Harriett turned her attention to his parents, noting that Chris shared his mother's blonde locks and his father's height and regal bearing, though neither parent had his stormy gray eyes. His father's were a nondescript green and his mother's a slightly darker version, like the color of moss. The pair made a handsome couple—Mr. Jamison, with his dark, windswept hair, and Mrs. Jamison, with her lovely high cheekbones, curls about her face, and bright smile. They didn't seem at all stuffy, which made Harriett like them even more.

Jonathan greeted Mrs. Jamison with a kiss to her hand. "How good it is to see you again, Mrs. Jamison. It has been too long."

"Far too long," she answered.

"I must say, you have a fine estate here, Jonathan," Mr. Jamison inserted.

"It is good of you to say as much, sir," Jonathan said. "I hope you don't mind, but I took the liberty of directing my staff to bring in your luggage. Sally has been overseeing your rooms and will alert us the moment they are ready for you. In the meantime, may I introduce my wife, Lady Jonathan Ludlow, and our dear friend, Lady Harriett Cavendish? She will be with us for the remainder of the month, at which point she is to meet her mother in London."

Mrs. Jamison dropped into a respectful curtsy, and when she rose, her gaze lingered on Harriett before returning to her host. "Pray forgive us for descending on you so unexpectedly, Jonathan. When Christopher wrote to us about the lovely time he has been having here at Tanglewood, we simply had to come and see you again. We are honored to make your acquaintance, Lady Jonathan, and Lady Harriett, it is a pleasure to meet you as well. You are every bit as breathtaking as Christopher described in his letter."

Breathtaking? Harriett directed an inquiring glance at Chris, only to see him grimace and touch his fingers to his brow as though he felt a headache coming on.

She smiled as she looked back to his mother. "How kind you are, Mrs. Jamison, and how happy I am to make your acquaintance as well. But are you certain you did not mistake 'breathtaking' for . . . lively or interesting?"

"Oh yes, quite certain." Much to Harriett's surprise, Mrs. Jamison reached out to clasp her hands as though they were already the dearest of friends. "Forgive me, my lady, but I have heard enough about you that I feel as though we are already acquainted. Will you not come and sit with me a moment? I would love to speak with you."

Chris materialized at Harriett's side and took his mother's hands in his own. "Mother, you have had a long and tiring journey. Wouldn't you prefer to take tea in your bedchamber and rest a little before dinner? There will be plenty of time for a cozy chat later on."

Mrs. Jamison patted her son on the arm, directing her remarks to Harriett. "Such a dear boy. He is always so concerned for my well being. At one point I was certain he was destined for the church."

Harriett nearly snickered at that but managed to swallow it down. "Perhaps he still is," she said. "He's quite adept at sermons and reading from the Bible."

His mother appeared surprised by this news. "Is that true?"

"Lady Harriett is only teasing me, Mother." He shot her a stern look, daring her to refute him.

She smiled. "I do enjoy teasing him on occasion. But you are indeed lucky to have such a . . . *thoughtful* son."

Watts entered the room and whispered a few words in Jonathan's ear. A moment later, Jonathan announced that the rooms had been made ready and Mr. and Mrs. Jamison were free to retire whenever they wished.

"I must admit that some rest would do me a great deal of good," said Mr. Jamison. "The inn we stayed at last night left much to be desired in the way of comfort. Shall we go up, my dear?"

His wife hesitated only a moment before nodding. "I shall see you later," she told Harriett, giving her hand a gentle pat.

"Jonathan and I would be honored to show you to your rooms," said Cora, sneaking a curious look at Harriett, no doubt wondering about the odd exchange.

Harriett had no answer for her. She could only smile

and give a slight shrug, thinking she would very much like to have a cozy chat with Chris at the moment.

Once the foursome had exited the room, Watts positioned himself just outside the open doors, close enough to act as a chaperone and far enough away to allow them a private word. Harriett had to admit that she was developing a great fondness for the man's kindness and tact. Not for the first time, she thought that Chris could learn a great deal from the butler.

Harriett sank down onto a cream brocade chair and turned her attention to Chris, who appeared even more wary than before judging by the way he could neither stand still nor meet her gaze. She clasped her hands in her lap, waiting for him to begin what she hoped would be an enlightening conversation.

After a few moments, he lowered his handsome frame to the sofa nearest to where she sat and pasted a smile on his rugged face. "You do not seem to have suffered any lasting damage from this morning's adventures. In fact, you look quite . . . lovely."

The compliment lost a great deal in its delivery, and Harriett shook her head slightly before leveling him with a no-nonsense stare. "Only lovely?" she asked. "Not . . . *breathtaking*?"

"I, er . . ."

"Sir, please tell me that I am not the unnamed woman who has purportedly set her cap at you."

His eyes widened for a moment before he pressed his lips together and dropped his gaze to the floor. "I did not write those exact words."

"Only implied them?" she guessed.

He shifted uncomfortably, still avoiding her gaze. "I may have said something to the effect of . . ."

When he did not continue, Harriett leaned forward. "The effect of what, *Lieutenant?*"

He glanced at her briefly before clearing his throat. "I may have implied that you were . . . pursuing me." The last two words came out in a rush as though he did not want them to be understood. But Harriett had understood them perfectly.

Her eyes widened, and she sat back slowly, staring at him. Was he in earnest? Had he truly told his parents that *she* was pursuing *him?* She had no response to that. She was . . . speechless.

"It was not a lie," he said. "At the time I penned that letter, you *were* pursuing me."

"I beg your pardon." A great many words were flowing into her head now, none of them very ladylike.

"Yes, the way one might pursue an enemy."

She glared at him. "From your mother's reaction to me just now, you obviously did not convey your meaning with any sort of clarity, sir."

"No," he admitted, squeezing the bridge of his nose with his fingers. "I did not."

"Would you care to explain why?"

"Not really, no." He let out a haggard breath and dropped his head against the back of the sofa, lifting his gaze to the ceiling. After a time, he dragged his body forward once more and rested his elbows on his knees. For the first time since she had known him, she saw what appeared to be humility creasing the corners of his eyes.

He drew in a deep breath and began telling her about his family's straitened circumstances, about his youthful avoidance of all things responsible, and about his reasons for going to war. He told her about what he'd learned, what he'd gained, and what responsibilities awaited him upon his return. Harriett learned of his promise to marry, the reason he'd come to Askern to visit an old friend, and finally, the plan he and Jonathan had hatched to keep his mother at bay.

The conversation proved most enlightening and not in a good way. His parents had taken their son at his word, and were now at Tanglewood, intent on meeting the lady who had been "pursuing" their son.

In the end, Harriett didn't know what to feel. Pity? Annoyance? Frustration? Anger? While she understood why he had done what he had, he had placed her in an uncomfortable and precarious position. That alone should have angered her. But she did not feel angry, exactly, not when he appeared so . . . worried. The man who sat before her was no longer the arrogant and invincible Lieutenant Jamison who had first appeared on Tanglewood's doorstep. He was merely a man.

"I know that I have no right to ask this of you," he said, "but if you can bring yourself to . . . feign an interest in me, at least until Jonathan and I have concluded our business, I'll . . ."

When he did not continue, Harriett lifted an eyebrow. "You will what, Lieutenant?"

His brow furrowed, and a genuine sadness crossed his features. "I wish you would call me Chris."

"Why? Because it will make this"—she gestured from her to him—"pretense between us more believable?"

"No." He leaned forward and peered at her with an intensity she had never before seen in him. "Right now it is just you and me, Harriett. No pretense whatsoever."

Harriett wasn't quite sure what to make of his words— or anything, really. She only knew that his parents seemed like good people and it would be cruel to deceive them. "Let us say that I agree to participate in this little sham of yours.

What will happen in a week or two when you have concluded your business here? What will you tell your parents then?"

He gave the matter some thought before shrugging. "That you came to your senses and realized I could never be worthy of you."

Harriett nodded slowly, not liking that scenario at all. "So I will become a cold-hearted flirt capable of crushing your heart and their dreams?"

"Would you prefer for me to conclude that *you* are not worthy of *me*?" A slight smile tugged at his lips with the suggestion.

Her gaze narrowed. "No. I would prefer that you explain to them right now why you have misled them."

His smile faded, and he sighed, raking his fingers through his hair and causing more of it to fall across his forehead. When his eyes met hers again, they conveyed a deep emotion that she couldn't decipher. "You are right. I should explain, and I will . . . eventually. But can we not wait another week? The fact of the matter is that I have not seen my mother this happy in ages. It's as though she has been freed from a heavy burden, and my father as well. I am loath to take that away from them, at least for the time being."

Harriett felt a tug on her heart and considered his appeal to her emotions vastly unfair. Why should this be her burden to carry? She didn't wish to bring his parents pain anymore than he did, but how could deceiving them be a good idea when the truth would surface eventually?

"Will it not worsen matters to wait?" she asked.

"I don't believe so," he said, his eyes pleading with hers. "Ten days, Harriett, and I swear to you I will tell them the truth. In the meantime, I beg you to let them bask in their happiness while I help Jonathan acquire his land. As soon as

I have accomplished that, I will behave in a boorish, unforgivable manner, and you can administer a stinging slap to my face and proclaim that you never wish to see me again. Would that be an agreeable ending to our ruse?"

Harriett lifted an eyebrow. "By 'boorish,' do you mean that you will splatter me with mud, laugh when a bird ruins my pelisse, and allow me to be thrown from your horse? If so, I ought to administer a stinging slap to you now."

"Touché." He smiled. "Perhaps it would be better to promise that I will do my best to *not* behave boorishly from now until then."

Harriett pressed her lips together, wondering how they had reached the point where she was actually considering going along with his ridiculous scheme. Would they really be doing both his parents and Jonathan a service by feigning a romantic interest in each other? It seemed ludicrous, yet . . .

Harriett closed her eyes and shook her head, not knowing what to say.

Christopher slid to the edge of the sofa and took hold of one of her hands. His touch sent delightful sensations up her arm and into her chest, where they knocked on the door of her heart. She studied his handsome face, wondering if she dared to let him in.

"Please, Harriett," he said softly. "I will do anything."

Attempting to ignore her thumping heart, she swallowed. "Anything?"

"Anything."

As she continued to study him, it occurred to her that she finally had Lieutenant Jamison where she'd wanted him all along—at her mercy—and that was a very good feeling. The fact of the matter was that ten days was not so very long, was it? And at the end of it all, if the lieutenant was willing to give Harriett a valid reason for disliking him, would it really be so bad? Would the Jamisons be more saddened to learn the truth at a later date than they would now?

She didn't know the answer to that, but she knew that saying no to Chris when he looked at her in such a way was nigh unto impossible.

"Very well," she finally agreed, tugging her hand free. "But If I am to play this part, I'll require something in return."

"Anything," came his answer.

She gave him a look that challenged him to deny her. "From now until the time you return to your boorish ways, I would like for you to make a complete cake of yourself over me."

11

As the group gathered in the drawing room following dinner, Christopher learned fairly quickly exactly how much of a cake Harriett meant for him to make of himself. She approached him with a beautiful smile, complimented him on how well he looked, and tucked a note into his hand before joining his mother on the sofa.

He fingered the note as his eyes lingered on her. The elegant slope of her neck and shoulders, the curves that attracted his notice every time he saw her, and her natural grace and elegance. Add to that her sparkling eyes, her vibrant ebony hair that caught the highlights from her golden gown, and her kissable lips, and Christopher could not deny that she was indeed breathtaking.

His thoughts returned to the previous night, when he'd nearly kissed her after they'd finished their cake. Looking back, he almost wished he would have if only to see what her response would have been. Would she have returned his kiss, or would he have angered her beyond redemption? He couldn't say, only that his fear of the latter had caused him to shy away.

Christopher still had no idea how he had convinced her to play the part of an infatuated lady, but she'd risen to the occasion with gusto. All throughout dinner she had flashed him smiles, secret looks, and exchanged words with his mother, giggling and laughing all the while like a giddy debutante. If it were anyone else, such antics would annoy him in the extreme, but Harriett transfixed him. At some point during dinner, something shifted inside him, and he found himself wanting her overtures to be real instead of feigned.

He bit his lip as he glanced down at the note. He probably should tuck it inside his jacket for later perusal, but his curiosity could not be quieted. He casually turned away from the others and quickly broke the seal, finding a slip of Foolscap tucked inside the note.

> *Chris,*
> *How very romantic of you to write me a sonnet. Do say you will read it aloud to me this evening. I'm certain your parents will be most impressed by your clever and charming way with words. I'm certain I will be as well.*
> *Yours,*
> *Harriett*

He had to press his lips together as he scanned the slip of paper. Surely she did not mean for him to actually read this aloud. Only a dandified buffoon would write something so absurd, let alone recite it in public.

He glanced up and caught her grinning at him. An unspoken challenge sparkled in her eyes, daring him to make an utter cake of himself. *A promise is a promise,* she seemed to say.

"What is that you are reading?" asked his mother.

He quickly folded the note and stuffed it into his pocket. "Nothing."

Harriett leaned towards his mother with a sly look. "I believe he is spinning a Banbury tale, Mrs. Jamison. Look, I do believe he's blushing."

Christopher scowled. "I assure you, my lady, I am *not* blushing."

"I beg your pardon," she said. "Perhaps I ought to have said that you appear flushed. Is that more masculine?"

"I think you are right, Harriett," added Cora. "He does look a trifle pink."

Christopher eyed Cora with suspicion, wondering if she had aided in the writing of the sonnet. It did not take much imagination to picture both ladies giggling over tea as they revised the words to "The World is Too Much with Us" by Wordsworth. How charitable of them to give him credit for their ghastly creation.

"Is it a love note, do you think?" Cora speculated.

"I hope not, or I shall be quite jealous," said Harriett.

With all eyes on him, Christopher hesitated, wondering how to extricate himself from this situation. Like it or not, the sonnet would have to be read—the ladies would see to that—but Christopher refused to be the one to read it. Making a cake of himself was one thing. A fool quite another.

Christopher withdrew the note from his pocket, fingered it a moment, and sighed, holding it out to Harriett. "This is for you, my lady. Do with it what you will, but tread carefully. It may or may not contain a piece of my heart." He had to force himself to say that last part.

Cora coughed to cover up a giggle while his mother smiled proudly. Jonathan and his father looked on with interest, and Christopher could only pray that Harriett would not wish to read it aloud either.

She accepted the note with a gracious, "You intrigue me, sir," and went on to make a pretense of reading the poem. Christopher had to give her credit for appearing properly delighted and touched by its contents.

Once she'd finished, her hand covered her heart as she peered at him. "What a beautiful sonnet, Lieutenant. I shall always treasure it."

"Do say that you will read us a line or two from it, my dear," begged his mother. "I had no idea my son had a talent for poetry."

"Only a line or two would not do it justice, Mrs. Jamison. You must read it in its entirety if you wish to acquaint yourself with his talent." Harriett directed a look of adoration his way before handing over the slip of paper.

"I should very much like to hear the poem as well," inserted Jonathan, making Christopher want to snatch it back and toss it into the fire. Only with great effort was he able to take a seat and look properly self-conscious.

His mother held the note out in front of her and squinted at it. "I can see you took your time with this, Christopher. Your letters are much improved."

Harriett's lips twitched, and Christopher barely refrained from rolling his eyes. He wished his mother would get on with it and be done.

After more shifting and squinting, she began.

"Lady H— is much with me; late and soon,
With hope unfeigned, I lay waste my powers;
Nothing in her is remotely dour,
I have given my heart, a stirring boon!
Her ebony hair bares her beauty to the moon;

Her sky blue eyes hold me captive all hours,
Her fair skin resembles pale-peach flowers;
For her, for everything, I am most in tune;
She moves me so. Oh yes! I'd rather be
A dandy bedecked in fashions outworn;
Then lose her. And so I sit on this bench,
Catching sights of her that make me less forlorn;
She speaks to another and my heart does wrench;
But one smile my way, and I am reborn."

His mother had tears in her eyes when she finished reading. Actual tears! Had she really thought it beautiful? It wasn't even a true sonnet. It didn't take a mathematician to notice that many of the lines contained more than ten syllables.

Harriett was certainly not crying. She and Cora appeared vastly entertained while Jonathan would undoubtedly succumb to a fit of laughter any moment. And Christopher's father—well, his father looked very much surprised, and not in a good way.

"My dear boy, that was extraordinary," spoke his mother. "I had no idea you could be such a romantic."

Good gads. Christopher would never hear the end of this. He could already see it in Jonathan's gleeful expression. What else did Harriett have in store for him? Ten days would feel like an eternity if he would be required to make a spectacle of himself every evening. But how to convince her to lower her expectations so he wouldn't be completely emasculated by the end of the week?

Christopher walked over to Harriett, bowing low over her hand. "Lady Harriett, it is a beautiful evening. Will you do me the honor of taking a stroll with me in the gardens?"

"What a wonderful idea. I would love to." She rose and

accepted his arm, looking every inch the kitten who had just outwitted a dog. She turned to the others. "Do say you will join us."

"Of course we will," said his mother, quickly rising and gesturing to her husband. Jonathan and Cora linked arms as well, and they all adjourned to the great hall, where a few maids were sent to collect the ladies' coats and gloves.

As Christopher helped Harriett into a deep burgundy pelisse, he lowered his voice so only she could hear. "How many pelisses do you own, exactly?"

She glanced over her shoulder and smiled. "If I continue to keep company with you, not nearly enough."

"Ah, but I have promised to be on my best behavior from this point forward, haven't I?"

"You also promised to make a cake of yourself over me, and so far the only thing you have done of your own accord was to accompany me into dinner and see that I was comfortably situated."

Christopher frowned as he pulled on his gloves, wondering what more she had expected of him. Had she wanted him to raise his glass and call out a toast in her honor? Stare longingly into her eyes over dinner? Rhapsodize about her many virtues and attributes?

Apparently so, judging by the sonnet she had written.

They followed the others outside, and he breathed in the crisp, evening air. The sun hovered over the tops of the trees, threatening to depart within the hour. Christopher should have been in London by now, attending dinner parties, afternoon teas, balls, and inviting eligible young ladies for a drive through the park. Instead, he was here, strolling through Tanglewood's gardens with the most complex and alluring woman he had ever known—a woman who was only pretending to be interested in him.

Christopher had implied that Jonathan still needed him, but the truth of the matter was that until the issue with the land was settled, not much more could be done. Christopher could leave tomorrow if he chose and return at the conclusion of the London season, just as he'd initially planned to do. He could begin the hunt for his future wife, allow Jonathan the time he needed to settle matters with Mr. O'Rourke, and come again once everything had settled down.

But he remained. Why? Did he truly think he could help Jonathan sort things out with Mr. O'Rourke? Did he really want to see his mother enjoy her happiness a while longer? Perhaps those played a small part in his decision, but if Christopher was being truly honest with himself, the real reason he wished to stay was holding onto his arm, glancing up at him with a mischievous gaze, and undoubtedly plotting more ways to unman him.

Christopher really needed to put a stop to that.

"Tell me, Harriett." He slowed his steps so that they could speak without being overheard by the others. "Are you fond of men who fall all over themselves for you? If I had written a sonnet in earnest, declaring my rapture for your hair and eyes and complexion, would you be swept off your feet by such tactics, or would you begin avoiding me like the plague?"

Harriett smiled a little and shrugged. "In all honesty, the latter."

"Then why would you place me in such a role? And why would you suggest to Mrs. Bidding that I would consider it a great honor to be gifted with one of Pippin's puppies? Yes, Cora let that little fact slip earlier today, but I cannot understand it. Do you wish for me to drive you away by behaving like a buffoon instead of a boor? Is that it?"

"Heavens no," said Harriett, slowing her steps until they had ceased walking altogether. When she turned and looked at him again, there was a hint of sorrow in her expression. "I am sorry for tonight. Truly. I suppose that after all that has happened between us, I wanted to, I don't know . . . have a little comeuppance. I thought it humorous and fun, but if I have offended you with my antics, then I was in the wrong. I'm sincerely sorry. You are not a buffoon, Lieutenant, and I would never wish you to be."

Surprised by her words and her earnestness, Christopher was at a loss how to respond. He hadn't expected such a sincere apology, especially not from Harriett. He'd expected a witty rejoinder.

Yet here she stood, genuinely remorseful for something that had been . . . well, inconsequential really. Although he hadn't appreciated being made to look the fool, Christopher couldn't deny that he probably would have done the same had the situation been reversed.

How many times had she asked for an apology from him, only to receive flippancy in return? How many times had he put her or someone else in an awkward situation so that he could laugh at their expense? All's fair in love and war had been a motto he'd often adhered to, but now, with Harriett looking so worried that she had offended him, he realized that all was not fair, not really.

For all of his posturing and Bible readings, apologies had never come easily for him, nor sincerity either. Christopher had always preferred to keep conversations superficial and had even prided himself on his ability to remain buoyant in any situation. But now, looking into Harriett's mesmerizing eyes, he realized that sincerity was not a weakness. It was something to be commended.

Feeling humbled and undeserving of her apology, he

tucked her arm through his, pulling her close as they resumed their walk. "You have nothing to apologize for, Harriett. The sonnet was a clever move on your part, and you could not find a more deserving recipient than me. And besides, you made my mother very proud and entertained the others most beautifully."

"I was rather entertained myself," she admitted.

"So I noticed."

They continued on in silence, giving Christopher time to reflect upon the woman at his side—a woman who was rapidly finding a place within his heart. The words of her sonnet had not done her justice. They had focused only on her superficial qualities, which were indeed remarkable, but had mentioned nothing about who she truly was.

Why had she left that part out?

Christopher glanced at her, wishing he could see past her beautiful face and into her thoughts. After a moment or two, he felt compelled to say, "I wish you had allowed me a little say in the contents of the sonnet. It praised only your beauty and mentioned nothing about your wit, intelligence, and uncanny ability to put me in my place. Is there a reason you did not list those traits as well?"

His words seemed to please her, for she smiled. "You will have to ask Mr. Thomas Chant that question, not I. It was he who composed that sonnet, right before he offered for me last season."

Christopher was relieved to hear her say as much, although he had to wonder at her reasons for holding onto the poem. "You must treasure it a great deal to have kept it all this time."

"Indeed I do," she answered lightheartedly. "Anytime I am feeling low, I pull out that poem and cannot help but laugh. Perhaps it is cruel of me to find so much humor with

Mr. Chant's efforts, but I cannot bring myself to part with it just yet. It has become too dear to my heart."

"Do you regret not accepting his suit? You could have an entire drawer filled with sonnets at your disposal."

She shook her head prettily. "One is all I need. But I must confess that it has become even dearer to me now. I will never forget the look on your face when your mother read it aloud." She smiled, and Christopher couldn't help but respond in kind.

He slowed his steps and paused to cover her hand with his own. "Promise me that you will not make me the author of any more poems."

She blinked innocently at him. "Considering I am pursuing you as an enemy would her prey, I'm afraid I cannot."

"I thought we agreed that you would pursue me for other, more romantic, reasons."

"Yes, well, that is something I wish to discuss with you, Chris. I am a lady, you understand, and as such it is not seemly for me to pursue a man for any reason. So from this point forward, I believe it should be *you* who pursues me and not the other way around. You can consider it practice for the upcoming season. You must learn to woo a woman, after all, if you want to have any hope of capturing her heart."

Her tone was playful and mischievous, but as Christopher thought over her words, he wondered if he could ever hope to capture a woman's heart—a woman very much like Lady Harriett Cavendish.

"Is there any hope for me, do you think?" He kept his tone flippant, but he very much cared about her answer.

She freed her hand from his arm and stepped in front of him as though studying him. She dusted off his shoulders, fiddled with his cravat, and straightened his lapels. After she'd finished, she concluded, "I believe so. You are handsome, intelligent, amusing, and even kind when you wish to be. You simply need to work on your . . . comportment a bit more."

He raised an eyebrow. "How so?"

She touched the tip of her finger to her lower lip and thought a moment. "Well, when a lady enters the room, for example, you should stand immediately and focus your attention solely on her."

"Do I not already do that?"

She made a face as though sometimes he did and sometimes he didn't. "By *focus*, I mean that instead of teasing or torturing her, you should offer a compliment and speak to her as though she were the only woman in the room. Not for too long, of course, but for a few moments at least. If you make a woman feel as though she is the center of your world, she will not come away from the experience unaffected."

At that moment, Christopher felt as though he was the center of Harriett's world, and he was most certainly affected. "Is that all I need to do?"

She laughed a little, shaking her head. "I'm afraid that is only the beginning, Lieutenant."

"Chris," he corrected.

"*Chris*," she repeated. "You must also learn how to make heartfelt apologies, show genuine concern when a woman experiences a misfortune, and treat a lady as though she is . . . well, a lady. Laughter and facetiousness are all well and good, but when a woman is suffering from discomfort or humiliation, laughing at her will only worsen the situation."

It all seemed like a great deal to think about, and Christopher didn't know if he was capable of too much sincerity. But he could also see the wisdom in her words and how his teasing could be hurtful at times. Perhaps that was something he could improve upon.

He nodded, taking hold of her gloved hand and placing it between his own. The scent of orange blossoms invaded his senses, making him want to touch her cheek, curl his fingers around her lovely neck, and draw her to him. Would she let him?

"And if I desire to kiss a woman?" he asked, his body mere inches away from hers. "How would you suggest I go about that?"

Her reaction surprised him. Rather than scowl and reprimand him for voicing such an improper thought, a slight blush tinged her cheeks. She shrugged and looked away. "I cannot say. The only man who has ever attempted to kiss me received a hard slap to his cheek."

Christopher laughed, wanting to kiss her more than ever. What would it feel like to hold her close and sample those lips? Would she slap him as well, or would she melt against him the way he hoped she would? Someday, he vowed he would have the courage to find out, and he very much looked forward to that day.

"Can I ask what you might consider an odd question?" he said, thinking back to the note that had accompanied the sonnet.

"Yes, though I will not promise to answer it."

"I couldn't help but notice that you spell Harriett with two Ts rather than the usual one. Is there a reason for that, or did your parents not know how to spell?"

She laughed lightly. "You really are quite the observer, aren't you? Most people don't notice the spelling and very few invitations that come in my name are written correctly. The truth of the matter is that the name Harriett was not my mother's first choice for me—she thought it too ordinary—but my father had always adored it, and since she adored him, I was christened Harriett. My mother insisted on the second T because she did not want me to be ordinary. She wanted me to be uniquely me, whoever that turned out to be, and the extra T was her way of reminding me, or perhaps prodding me, in that direction."

"Your mother was a wise woman," Christopher found himself saying, believing it to be true. Harriett was the most unordinary woman he had ever known. Her uniqueness extended beyond her beauty and into her soul, just as her mother had hoped it would. At one point, he might have considered the name Harriett nondescript, but not anymore. Now, he thought it perfect.

Before he yielded to the ever-increasing urge to kiss her, he took her hand and tucked it through his, guiding her towards the statue at the center of the garden where the others were clustered.

Not long after, Cora proposed a game of shuttlecock, as she had discovered a pair of battledores—or rackets—in one of the outbuildings the other day. It was a game usually played by women and children, but Jonathan and Christopher had always been fond of a lark and agreed it would be fun. So a footman was sent to retrieve the items while Christopher's parents settled down on a nearby bench, content to observe.

The game began as soon as the footman returned, with two persons playing at a time. When one of them failed to return the shuttlecock, he or she had to give up the baddledore to another player before play could continue. Christopher had always been good at the game in his youth and very seldom missed the shuttlecock. As the last of the light faded from the sky, he was officially declared champion.

His parents cheered from the bench, and Harriett shook her head as though she was not at all surprised. "Have you ever not come away the champion, Chris?" she asked wryly.

"Yes," he said, thinking of several skirmishes he'd lost during the war and the tricky and diverting game he now played with Harriett. When it came to shuttlecock or other meaningless games, Christopher didn't care a groat whether he won or lost, but when it came to more important things, he very much did care.

And Harriett, he was coming to realize, was most definitely one of those things.

As the hour approached midnight, Christopher found Jonathan seated at his desk in his study, composing some sort of letter.

Christopher dropped down in a chair opposite the desk, propping his boots on a nearby ottoman, and leaned back to tuck his hands behind his head. After such a precarious start to his day, he would have never guessed it would conclude on such a happy note.

The quill scratched across the Foolscap for another line or two before Jonathan stopped writing and glanced up. "There is no need for you to stay up late again, Christopher. I am sorry that things have not gone as planned. I feel like a widgeon for asking you to remain in Askern when so little has come of it. Even worse, I convinced you to imply something to your parents that is not true, and now they are here with the hope that you and Harriett will one day make a match of it. Honestly, I did not mean for any of this to happen. You would've been better off returning to London as you'd originally planned."

Christopher paid the apology no mind and nodded towards the desk instead. "Are you making Mr. O'Rourke an offer for his land?"

"Yes, but I'm certain this is only the beginning. The offer comes nowhere near to what the property is worth, and he will undoubtedly think it laughable. But I cannot bring myself to pay its worth when most of it holds no value for me. I'm hoping that we can eventually reach a compromise that will not put me in the poorhouse."

Christopher nodded and closed his eyes, feeling fatigued. The day had finally caught up with him, not that he was ready to give up on it just yet.

"Something Harriett said this morning got me thinking," he said, not ready to reveal exactly what she'd said just yet. If this turned out to be a bad idea, he planned to take full credit.

"You? Thinking?" teased Jonathan. "Should I be concerned?"

"Perhaps," said Christopher dryly, prying his eyes open. "I realize I know very little about estate management or negotiating, but it seems a poor investment to buy up so much land when you don't need it. I can't help but wonder if you are giving up too soon on changing Mr. O'Rourke's mind. He was willing to sell at some point, after all. Perhaps with the right approach, we can bring him around again."

Jonathan shook his head. "That was before he sought his solicitor's advice, which I cannot fault him for. It is what I would have done in his situation and the wisest move for him to make."

"Yes," said Christopher. "But it is not the wisest move for you to make, is it? And you must do what is best for *you*, Jonathan, not what is best for him."

Jonathan sighed, sounding depleted. "He is unwilling to sell only a parcel, so I fail to see what more can be done."

Christopher dropped his boots to the ground and leaned forward, resting his elbows on his knees. He nodded at the letter. "Once you send that to him, you will be showing your hand, and he will know that you are willing to buy all of the land if you can agree on the price. But if you explain to him that you are unwilling to buy land you do not want or need, I wonder if he will not reconsider."

Jonathan steepled his fingers under his chin, the way he always did when deep in thought. At last he said, "And if he does not fall for my bluff? What then? I would need to approach him again about buying the entire lot, and at that point he will know exactly how much I desire the land and will not be as willing to negotiate."

"It is a gamble," agreed Christopher, "but one worth taking, I believe. If you think about it, Mr. O'Rourke has already shown that he is willing to part with a portion of his land, and given the choice between selling some or none, I'm willing to wager there is a high probability that he will choose some."

Jonathan fingered the letter as though undecided about which course to take. "You make a good argument."

Encouraged, Christopher pressed on. "During the war, I became very good at anticipating the moves of my enemies. It's what kept my crew safe and contributed greatly to our success. I tell you this not to brag, but to prove that I have good instincts. And my instincts are telling me that Mr. O'Rourke will come around eventually. It may take a month or two or even a year, but he *will* come around. He would not have been so quick to take you up on your offer before if he wasn't inclined to sell."

Jonathan nodded slowly, and after a few moments, he picked up the paper, wadded it into a ball, and tossed it at the fire. It curved to the left, struck the mantle, and rolled to a stop on the rug.

Christopher grinned at his friend. "That is why I bested you at shuttlecock. You always were a bad shot."

"And you're a bad poet."

"As opposed to you?"

Jonathan chuckled. "Touché."

Christopher stretched his arms over his head before stifling a yawn. "I'll have you know that I did not pen one word of that sonnet, not that it matters. You will hold it over my head forevermore regardless."

"Of course I will. You have to admit that Harriett has proven to be a worthy opponent, wouldn't you say? Or has she become more to you than that?"

From the knowing look in Jonathan's eyes, he had already surmised that she had. Christopher had never been able to fool his friend, but that did not mean he was ready to admit to anything just yet.

"Yes. She's become a wretch."

Jonathan snickered. "I should've known you'd say as much. You can never be serious for too long, can you?"

"No." Christopher let out a heavy breath and heaved his body up, stifling another yawn. "Now that we have settled the matter with Mr. O'Rourke, I'm off to bed. Good night, my friend."

He was nearly to the door when Jonathan's voice halted him. "Christopher, a word of advice before you leave, from one friend to another."

His hand on the knob, Christopher looked over his shoulder.

The sound of Jonathan's fingers thrumming against his desk filled the silence. After a moment, it ceased, and Jonathan said, "You and Harriett will soon go to London. From what Cora has told me, she was highly sought after last season, and I think it safe to say that she will be a favorite this season as well. I only tell you this because . . . well, if she *has* become something more to you than a diversion, you would be wise to make the most of your time here."

"Are you doubting my ability to compete with other men?"

Jonathan shook his head slowly. "I'm only saying that if you cannot manage to turn her up sweet when you are the only unmarried man in the vicinity, the likelihood of doing so in London will be slim."

"*Que sera sera*," Christopher said lightly, waving a dismissive hand as he exited the room. But as he walked back to his bedchamber, he knew he hadn't fooled Jonathan. "What will be, will be" was a pretty phrase, and one he had tossed out a time or two over the years, but Christopher had never truly meant the words. That sort of attitude bordered on apathy, and he was anything but apathetic. Yes, there had been times in his life when he'd had to accept undesirable outcomes, but not before he had done everything in his power to alter them. Life was meant to be lived, not observed, and Christopher had always adhered to the notion that if he had the will, there had to be a way.

Unfortunately, when it came to Harriett, it was "the way" that eluded him.

THE ARRIVAL OF MR. and Mrs. Jamison marked a change at Tanglewood Manor. The house seemed less quiet, Christopher and Jonathan no longer made themselves scarce, and the days began to fill with outings and diversions, rushing past Harriett like the earth beneath a galloping horse.

The most intriguing change of all was Christopher. He was the first to stand when Harriett entered a room, the first to walk to her side, the first to extend a compliment of some sort, and the first to offer his arm when dinner or luncheon was announced. During their outings, he was attentive, but not too attentive, kind, but still a tease, and . . . well, charming. In essence, he became the perfect gentleman.

It confused Harriett somewhat. Was he attempting to heed her advice? Was it real? Or was he merely playing the part of a doting suitor for his parents' benefit?

When the weather was fair, they picnicked, played lawn bowls or shuttlecock, and tried their hand at shooting. When the weather turned foul, they organized various card games, played spillikins, and entertained themselves with a lively game of charades.

One afternoon, Chris and Jonathan accompanied the

ladies on a shopping excursion to town. Cora had insisted that Harriett replenish her depleted wardrobe with at least a few things, such as a new bonnet, and Harriett finally consented.

Inside the millinery shop, she fingered a straw bonnet, wondering if she could also wear it in London as well or if it was too countrified. If only she had a better eye for such things.

"I like it," Chris said, stepping up next to her. "It is well made, a good balance of town and country, and best of all, the colors suit you well."

She looked at him askance. "I had no idea you were such a fashion aficionado."

He shrugged and casually leaned against the counter, folding his arms. "I have five sisters and was often required to accompany them on shopping excursions. I learned a great deal over the years, more than I ever hoped to know, if you want to know the truth."

Harriett ran her fingers down the gold and burgundy ribbons, still undecided. "My modiste *has* told me that gold and this particular shade of burgundy becomes me." Why had she said such a thing? It sounded so childish, as though she didn't know her own mind, which admittedly, she didn't. But he did not need to know that.

"That bonnet will more than become you," he said.

The compliment surprised her, and Harriett searched his smiling eyes for a sign of sincerity. For all his recent charming ways, she could never be sure of what he truly thought. It all felt too surreal.

"Do you mean it?" she asked, hoping for assurance that he did.

Unfortunately, he did not comply. "Harriett, if you do not care for this bonnet, it is of no consequence to me. Most bonnets would become you, I imagine, and there are a great many to choose from."

"It's not that I don't care for it," she hedged, feeling silly for having such a ridiculous flaw. She was a lady, after all, and should be well versed in matters pertaining to fashion.

"Then what?" he asked, probably wondering why she was making such a fuss over something as insignificant as a bonnet.

She sighed, suddenly exasperated with herself *and* him. If he had not been the cause of so many ruined garments, she would not be in need of a new bonnet now. Why had Cora suggested that the men accompany them anyway?

"Harriett, do you like this bonnet or not?" Chris asked.

She may as well tell him the truth. Perhaps he would even surprise her by not teasing her about it incessantly. "I do not know because I have very little fashion sense, if you must know. That is why I never go shopping alone."

His eyes widened slightly before his maddening mouth quirked into a smile. "Surely, you jest."

"No, I do not," she said curtly. "The only reason I paused to consider this particular bonnet is because I have learned that those colors look better on me than others. But is the poke too large, are those flowers gaudy or countrified, or is the whole creation too simple? These are things I do not know. Fashion changes so rapidly, and I have never been able to maintain its pace."

Harriett frowned at the bonnet, wondering why she had agreed to this excursion. She would be meeting her mother and sister in London soon enough and could get by with what she had until then. And where was Cora when she needed her?

Harriett glanced around the shop, spotting her friend examining some ribbons across the way. But before Harriett could go to her, Chris caught her arm, bringing her attention back to him. With a look she could only describe as tolerance, he removed the bonnet she wore and replaced it with the one on display. He made quick work of tying the ribbons before taking hold of her shoulders and looking her over.

"As I said, most bonnets would look well on you, but this particular one suits you perfectly. It deepens the color of your eyes, adds vibrancy to your skin, and lends an air of intrigue. You look beautiful, Harriett, and if you do not purchase it at once, I will do it for you."

The earnestness in his expression caused her heart to thump loudly in her ears, drowning out all other sounds. She feared she was growing to like this version of Chris altogether too much. With every passing day, her heart and mind swayed more and more in his direction. But did she dare hope that his heart swayed back? The fact of the matter was that a woman should trust the man she gave her heart to, and she did not trust Chris—not completely, at any rate, and especially not with her heart. She merely *wanted* to trust him.

"He's right you know." Cora entered the conversation, her eyes twinkling. "That bonnet is beautiful on you."

"I cannot say the bonnet moves me as much as it does Christopher," added Jonathan, his lips twitching, "but I concur that it looks well on you."

Chris's hands fell away from her shoulders, and his usual flippancy returned. "What do you mean it does not move you? Are you so unfeeling, Jonathan? I vow, I could write a sonnet about the loveliness of this particular bonnet."

"Please do not," said Jonathan with a chuckle. "We have heard more than enough of your sonnets to last a lifetime."

"Agreed," Chris said, turning back to Harriett. "You have now had three people praise this bonnet's merits. What more can we say to convince you?"

"Nothing," she said, ready to be done with this conversation. "I am quite convinced."

"Did you hear that, Jonathan?" he touted. "I told you I had a knack for strategizing."

"You also have a knack for boasting."

Chris chuckled. "Perhaps."

Harriett managed a smile, but her heart was not in it. Whatever spell Christopher had cast over her earlier had melted away with his teasing. She had been so certain of his sincerity, and had nearly fallen for his pretty words, but now it seemed as though he had only been playing a part in their ridiculous charade. How silly of her to be so affected.

Harriett pulled the ribbons loose and removed the bonnet before handing it over to the woman behind the counter. As she wrapped it up, Harriett thought about the power of words and how a few simple phrases had made her believe in the bonnet's beauty one moment and disbelieve it the next.

It was at times such as these that she wondered if she would ever be able to believe in Chris.

Near the end of their ten-day agreement, Jonathan and Cora planned a riding excursion to some old ruins one morning. Harriett looked forward to an invigorating ride, hoping it would help to clear her head. After dressing in her warmest, deep blue riding habit—one that Tabby had managed to resurrect from Harriett's spill into the pond—she pulled on her gloves, retrieved her whip, and left her room behind.

She emerged into the brisk morning air to see that six horses had been saddled and tied to a fence. Chris was already there, holding onto Wicked's halter, but it wasn't until Harriett looked over the horses that she realized he had outfitted the chestnut horse with a side saddle. She blinked, searching his expression. Had he done that for her, or had a groom placed that saddle on Wicked by accident? Her heart fluttered a little faster as she strode across the path to meet him.

"Is this for me?" she asked, gesturing to the saddle.

Chris responded by taking the whip from her hands and tossing it aside. "We had a talk, Wicked and I, and I informed him that if I can be on my best behavior, so can he—assuming you are willing to grant him a second chance, that is."

Harriett looked over the horse, admiring the rich color of his coat and his sleek lines. He appeared so *un*wicked at the moment, yet still beautiful and powerful.

Powerful enough to toss you off again, came an inner voice of reason. Harriett could still feel the bruise on her leg from where she had landed on a rock in the pond and remembered the unnerving feeling of falling from the horse's back. But she refused to let that dissuade her.

"And if he is not on his best behavior?" she asked.

"There is no telling with him, of course. But to be on the safe side, we will stay away from ponds and prickly bushes. And birds, if at all possible," he added with a grin.

"You certainly know how to allay a woman's fears, don't you?"

He looked ready to say something, but the arrival of his parents silenced him. His mother pointed at Wicked as she crossed the yard. "Christopher, you are not going to let Harriett ride that demon, are you?"

"Harriett has been wishing to do that very thing, and I have decided that for this morning only, her wish is my command."

"Only this morning?" Harriett quipped, attempting to push aside her fears.

"Yes," he said. "If not, you would undoubtedly abuse your wishing privileges most abominably."

"You are probably right," she conceded.

His mother looked from one to the other as though they'd gone daft. "Harriett, I cannot, in good conscience, allow you to ride this beast. Christopher, you must remove that saddle at once."

"Please do not ask that of him, Mrs. Jamison," said Harriett. "Wicked was unkind enough to unseat me the last time I attempted to ride him, and my father taught me that a horse cannot respect a cowardly rider. So you see, I must ride him again so that I might earn his trust as your son has done."

Mrs. Jamison's eyes widened, and her mouth dropped open. "He has unseated you before? Christopher, how can you even think to let Harriett ride a horse who has already shown his wicked nature?"

"I'm afraid I have to agree with your mother on this," added Mr. Jamison. "I will not see Harriett come to any harm on my watch."

Touched by their concern, Harriett laid a hand on Mr. Jamison's arm and attempted to lighten the tone. "You needn't worry, sir. Chris had a stern talk with Wicked and has assured me that nothing will go amiss this morning."

"A stern talk?" Mr. Jamison spluttered. "What nonsense is this?"

Harriett laughed. "Forgive me, Mr. Jamison, I was only jesting. Perhaps it would help if I told you that the first time I attempted to ride Wicked, I had my whip with me and quickly learned that whips make him skittish. As you can see, your son has been good enough to set my whip aside so that

I will not upset Wicked this time around. So you see, there is nothing to fear." She glanced at Chris. "Isn't that right, sir? Wicked is not adverse to anything else, is he?"

"No—at least none that I am aware of."

"Then I am quite determined." Harriett spoke with a confidence she did not entirely feel, but she would never forget the lesson her father had once taught her. If Chris was willing to allow her another opportunity, she would be a fool to let this particular wish go ungranted.

"I still cannot approve of this," Mrs. Jamison said, appearing only mildly appeased.

"Then you may hold me entirely to blame should Wicked behave wickedly." Christopher moved to Harriett's side and took her by the waist. "Ready?"

At her nod, he lifted her easily into the saddle and waited for her to situate her legs and adjust her skirts before taking a step back.

"Not to worry, Mother," he said. "I have seen Harriett ride and believe her to be an excellent horsewoman. I have complete confidence in her abilities."

Did he mean that? Harriett wasn't entirely certain, but his words warmed her heart. Some might think it uncaring of him to allow her to ride such a temperamental animal, but Harriett didn't see it that way. She viewed it as a compliment. Christopher's gesture showed that he not only believed in her but valued her opinion, and what woman wouldn't appreciate that?

She could only hope she would not disappoint him. Or Wicked. She'd rather not take another spill if she could help it.

"How am I to direct him without the whip?" she asked, not liking the sensation of not being in control.

"Simple. If you would like him to go left, tug the reins to the left. If you'd like him to go right, tug right. If you want him to stop, say halt. Pull back on the reins slightly to slow him down, and click your tongue if you'd like him to move or increase his speed."

"Sounds easy enough," Harriett said, relieved that Wicked had not seen fit to drop her in the dirt just yet. "Might I take him for a quick jaunt about the yard while we wait for Jonathan and Cora?"

"Of course." Christopher stepped aside, gesturing for her to go ahead.

With the reins firmly in her grip, Harriett clicked her tongue. All eyes watched her as she guided the horse around in a large circle. He side-stepped a few times and tossed his head in a defiant manner, but as they neared Chris once more, he seemed to settle. By the time Cora and Jonathan joined them, Harriett was ready to ride.

She leaned forward to give the horse a thankful rub. "Mr. and Mrs. Jamison, I hope that Wicked and I have put your fears to rest."

Mrs. Jamison chose not to answer right away. Instead, she mounted her own steed, with assistance from her husband, before turning back to Harriett. "I will not rest easy until our ride is complete and you are off that wretched horse."

"He does not take kindly to name calling, Mother," said Chris.

"And I do not take kindly to being ignored," she returned.

Chris barked out a laugh, causing his mother to smile a little. Harriett interpreted her expression as a fondness for an incorrigible son and had to smile a little as well. As much as she wanted Chris to change in other ways, she would never wish away this aspect of his character. It made him far too endearing.

As soon as all riders had mounted, the party followed Jonathan and Cora around the house and across a meadow. It didn't take much coaxing to spur Wicked into a gallop, and Harriett reveled in the feel of his smooth and steady pace. With the wind whipping at her face and the sun high overhead, she felt perfectly happy.

As they slowed on the far side and moved into a dense thicket of budding trees and dormant underbrush, Chris fell in beside her. "It appears as though Wicked has taken to you. Should I be envious?"

"Very." Harried leaned forward and gave the horse another pat. "He's a beautiful animal. I cannot say I've ever experienced such a smooth ride. It felt as though I was soaring across the meadow. What would you say if I offered to buy him from you?"

Chris chuckled. "I would turn you down with my sincerest apologies."

"You? Apologize sincerely? No, I don't believe it."

Placing his hand over his heart, Chris feigned offense. "You injure me, my lady. Pray tell me, when have I not been sincere?"

"When *have* you?" she countered, curious as to how he might answer. "Take Wicked, for example. Did you let me ride him this morning to show your parents how besotted you are over me, or did you do it to be kind—because you knew I have wanted to ride him?"

He didn't answer right away, nor did he look her in the eye. After a moment, he said, "I'm not sure I follow. Wouldn't both reasons prove me sincere? After all, I'm either attempting to please my parents or you—possibly even both—am I not?"

"I suppose," she murmured, not at all happy with the way he skirted around her question. He could be so maddening at times.

"Now that I think on it," he added. "I can see that your question has nothing to do with my sincerity and everything to do with my allegiance. You're wondering who I saddled Wicked for—you or them—are you not?"

"No," she said quickly. "You have mistaken my meaning entirely. It does not matter who you did it for. What matters is the *reason* you did it."

"I still do not follow. I did it as a kindness to both you and my parents. What other reason is there?"

Harriett clenched her jaw to keep from uttering her unkind thoughts aloud. How could he be so endearing one moment and so vexing the next?

She ducked under a low tree branch and grumbled, "I do not know why you are so set on pleasing your parents when you only mean to displease them in a few days' time."

"I'm hoping that all the pleasing will counteract the displeasing."

"I wouldn't count on it. Your mother has grown quite fond of me, you know. I rather think she prefers me over you."

He slowed his horse to let her go ahead of him through a narrow section. "I don't doubt it. You are a great deal easier to like."

Harriett glanced over her shoulder, wondering if he truly believed that. "I was only jesting, Chris. A mother could never love another's child more than her own."

"She could if that other person is you."

The way he said it—without pretense or sarcasm—caused Harriett's heart to drop to her toes. Did he mean it or had he said it to flatter her? As he came up beside her once more, she snuck a glance at him, spying the familiar glint of humor in his eyes. It annoyed her. Could the dratted man ever stay serious for longer than a moment?

They reached a rapidly flowing stream, which Wicked plowed across without hesitation. Droplets of water splashed across Harriett's skirts as they did so, but she scarcely noticed. Her thoughts were too preoccupied with trying to understand the man behind her. If only she could be allowed access to his mind, even for a short while. She would dearly love to see his true thoughts and feelings. At times, he seemed to care about her, but to what extent? Did he wish for something more than friendship, as she was coming to hope for, or was he content to say goodbye after he'd completed his business with Jonathan?

"Come now, you stubborn mule. It's only water," muttered Chris from behind.

Harriett pulled Wicked to a halt and looked back to see Chris and his horse on the other side of the stream.

"He won't cross," said Chris, attempting to urge his horse onward. But the animal backed up instead, tossing his head and appearing ready to bolt.

With a muttered curse, he swung down, grabbed the horse by the halter, and attempted to lead it across, but the horse would not take even a step into the water.

Chris shook his head at Harriett. "Apparently he doesn't care if he sees the ruins or not," he told her, then raised his voice to call out to the others, "Father! Jonathan!"

It didn't take long for the entire group to congregate near the stream. As soon as Jonathan realized Chris's predicament, he scowled. "I should have sold that beast last year. He's the most finicky creature I've ever owned. Perhaps we should return to Tanglewood and postpone the ruins outing until tomorrow. I'm certain the Biddings will allow us to borrow one of their less-particular horses."

Chris waved the suggestion aside. "Don't be ridiculous. There's no telling what the weather will be like tomorrow, and we are already well underway. I've seen enough ruins to last me a lifetime, so please continue without me. I'll take this stubborn mule back to the stables and await your return at the manor."

"And leave you to your own devices?" Jonathan said dryly. "I'm not sure that is the best idea. I'm likely to find a snake in my bed later tonight."

Harriett sighed, knowing she could not allow Chris to remain behind on his own. She was riding his horse, after all. It should have been her who was stuck on the other side of the stream—not him. "I shall stay with Chris," she said.

"I can stay as well," Cora offered.

"And I," added Mrs. Jamison.

"What would be the point in that?" Harriett asked. "Mr. and Mrs. Jamison, I know how excited you are to see the ruins, and Cora and Jonathan know the way, so pray carry on without us. It is but a short ride back to the house, and we'll see to it that luncheon is ready upon your return."

Mrs. Jamison looked hesitant. "I don't know. I would very much like to view the ruins, but I shouldn't leave you and Christopher alone without a proper chaperone."

"Truly, there is no need to worry, Mrs. Jamison. This is the country, after all, and Chris will behave as the perfect gentleman during our ride back, won't you?"

"As perfect as I am able," came his reply. He was still trying to pull the horse into the water with no luck. His boots were wet and his trousers were damp as well.

"I see no harm in leaving them alone," inserted Mr. Jamison with impatience. "They're practically betrothed, after all."

Harriett's eyes widened slightly, and she glanced at Chris for help, but he was too preoccupied with the horse and didn't seem to hear his father. From the glare Mrs.

Jamison sent her husband and the amused looks on Jonathan and Cora's faces, everyone else had heard plain as day.

Mrs. Jamison attempted to ignore her husband's indelicate remark. "Perhaps you are right, Harriett. It is but a short ride back to the manor. Once you explain, I'm certain the servants will understand why you have returned alone."

"My servants know better than to gossip, Mrs. Jamison," said Jonathan. "Now let us be off, shall we? I'm beginning to get hungry already."

"It is a good thing I asked Mrs. Caddy to pack us some sweet rolls then," said Cora.

Jonathan's gaze softened as he smiled at her. "You know that I adore you, don't you?"

"Yes, you make that very clear." She smiled, looking for all the world like the happiest of women.

Harriett tried her best not to envy her friend too much. Jonathan had never been one to hide his feelings regarding his wife. The way he looked at her, the way he spoke to her, the way he always gravitated towards her with no one prodding him or reminding him to do so. What would it feel like to be loved in that way?

"Be off with you," said Chris with a dismissive wave of his arm.

Cora nodded. "Enjoy your ride back to Tanglewood. We shall see you shortly."

As Harriett watched them canter away, a feeling of unease settled in her stomach. What had she been thinking to offer to stay with Chris? That was the problem. She hadn't been thinking, only feeling. She wanted to be near him, converse with him, and spend more time with him, all the while knowing it would probably not end well for her. Perhaps this was how a bear felt when drawn to a hive surrounded by swarming bees. Harriett wanted to draw near, but would she find honey within, or would she merely receive a series of painful stings for her efforts?

Her foolish, foolish heart.

Harriett guided Wicked back across the stream while Chris remounted, and they began to pick their way through the trees and brush once more.

"You did not need to stay behind with me, but it was good of you to do so," said Chris.

"How could I not?" she said dryly. "I am pursuing you, after all, and what woman wouldn't leap at the opportunity to be alone with the man she adores?"

"*Do* you adore me, Harriett?" he asked, his tone half teasing and half something else.

"Do you adore *me*?" she countered.

He chuckled. "Jonathan and Cora must be having an effect on us. We're beginning to sound like them."

Would that be so terrible? Harriett thought, feeling frustrated with both him and the situation. How much longer would this continue? "Your parents think we are nearly betrothed, Chris. I feel terrible deceiving them as we have done. We need to tell them the truth."

"What truth is that, Harriett?" he asked.

"That you have no intention of proposing."

"And if I did propose?" he teased, his eyes sparkling with humor. "What would you say?"

Harriett was not in the mood to joke about something like this. "You must stop your teasing, Chris. This is not a laughing matter. When the truth comes out, your parents will not be at all amused, I promise you that."

That seemed to have a sobering effect on him. "No, I daresay they will not. They will probably want to turn me over their knees and take a whip to my backside."

"Will you tell them the truth then?" Harriett implored.

"I've noticed you and Jonathan have not been as preoccupied with matters of business as of late. Are you even needed here any longer?"

Christopher hesitated as though deliberating how to answer. At last, he said, "I convinced Jonathan to do as you suggested and cry off from the deal. He wrote to Mr. O'Rourke and explained as much, and now he is waiting to see if there will be a reply. If you can bring yourself to carry on for a bit longer, I would like to stay on another day or two to see if that reply comes."

Harriett's eyes widened at this revelation. He had acted on the suggestion she had made? Her heart warmed at the thought, but then a nagging doubt entered her mind. How had it all come about? Had Chris presented the idea as his own, or had he included her name in the conversation? The world of business was a man's world, and most men had far too much pride to tolerate or appreciate a woman's involvement in their affairs. Chris didn't seem to share that way of thinking, which she was grateful for, but did Jonathan know that? Would she receive thanks if everything came out all right or be held to blame if they did not?

"I hope he hears something favorable soon," said Harriett.

"As do I."

Why? she wanted to ask. *So Jonathan will not have to fret much longer, or because you're ready to be on your way to London?*

Perhaps it was both.

"Look at that." Chris pointed at something up ahead and urged his horse to the left, dodging around a few bushes and ducking under some branches. Curious, Harriett followed, slowing Wicked to a crawl to avoid snagging her bonnet or skirt. When at last she caught up to Chris, she found him stopped near a large oak tree where the wilderness met the meadow. On the other side of the clearing, Tanglewood loomed before them, looking grand and majestic.

Chris swung down from his horse and peered up into the center of the tree.

Harriett craned her neck to see what had captured his attention. What was so intriguing about this tree? Had he seen an animal on one of its branches? Perhaps a rare bird of some sort? Was he luring her near with the hope she'd be the recipient of more droppings?

"I've never seen a tree that has begged to be climbed more than this one. From that branch there"—he pointed up—"I'll wager a person would have a spectacular view of Tanglewood and the surrounding countryside. Shall we investigate?" He made short work of tying his horse to a low branch before approaching Harriett.

She blinked at him in surprise. "You are not suggesting that we climb this tree, are you? Because a lady does not climb trees, Lieutenant, and a gentleman would never ask her to do such a thing."

He reached for her waist and lifted her down from the horse, setting her gently on her feet. "Of course not. I only suggested that we investigate. We have some time to spare, after all. Why not take a short break under the canopy of this beautiful and interesting tree?"

"How does one 'investigate' a tree, precisely?" she asked, all too aware of his hands still at her waist and the jittery feelings his touch evoked.

He smiled. "Have you not learned to trust me yet, Harriett?"

She hesitated, not knowing how to answer. Did she trust him to keep her safe from physical harm? Yes. She would not have ridden Wicked this morning if she hadn't. But when it came to matters of the heart, she could honestly say that no, she most certainly did not.

Her silence seemed to bother him. His eyes crinkled at the edges and his mouth turned down in a slight frown. "You don't trust me," he said quietly.

"It isn't that," she said. "I simply don't feel as though I know who you truly are. I've glimpsed a peek here and there, perhaps, but you seem to hide the real you behind flippancy and sarcasm, and I cannot help but wish that . . ." She pressed her lips together and looked away from his eyes, attempting to hide the blush she felt warming her cheeks. She'd almost told him that she wished she knew how he truly felt about her. Goodness, how could she even think such a brazen thought, let alone give voice to it?

She definitely should *not* have offered to stay behind with him.

His fingers grazed her chin, and he gently lifted her face to his. "Tell me, Harriett, have you forgiven me of all my earlier offenses?"

Peering into his eyes, she realized how much had changed since those first days when she had viewed him only as a shell of a man with a handsome face. In so many ways, she knew him a great deal better now. She knew he had imperfections and vulnerabilities just like everyone else. She knew him to be a caring son, a loyal friend, and a good person. She also knew him to be an incorrigible, mostly harmless, tease. What she didn't know was where his feelings and intentions sat with regard to her.

"Yes," she finally whispered.

"Then you do know me," he replied. "We've had our fun, you and I, but surely you know that I would never purposefully do anything to harm you, don't you?"

"Yes," she answered, even though she didn't quite believe it. With a few words or actions, he could shatter her heart into bits and pieces the way one could shatter a window with a well-aimed rock. He wouldn't do it intentionally, of course, but he could still do it. All he would have to do was return to London and begin his search for another woman who wasn't her.

He took a step closer, bringing their bodies within inches of one another. Her breath became short and ragged, and her heart sounded like the pounding of hooves during a horserace. Ever so slowly, he moved forward until his mouth grazed hers in the lightest of touches. A myriad of sensations unlike any she had ever felt ran through her entire being, engulfing her in something beautiful and exquisite. As the pressure of his kiss increased, she gave in to her emotions, returning the touch with a fervor that surprised even her. This felt nothing like the clumsy kiss Mr. Fisher plastered on her near the end of her first season. That one had been distasteful in the extreme. This one made her reel with its power. She now understood why a woman would want to kiss a man. Chris made the experience magical, transporting her to a place that felt nothing less than sublime.

When at last he drew back, she spotted something warm and affected in his expression, something she wanted to see more than anything else. But in the span of a blink, it vanished, leaving her wondering if she had seen it at all.

His usual sparkle of amusement returned. "What, no stinging slap?" he asked, his voice teasing.

His words swept the magic away, leaving Harriett to wonder at his reasons for kissing her in the first place. For a brief, wonderful moment, she had allowed herself to hope that the kiss had meant that he was coming to care for her as she did him. But perhaps he'd only done it to prove that he could succeed in doing what no other man had—receive a kiss from her without an accompanying slap.

He continued to hold her by the shoulders, and Harriett let him because she craved his touch. She willed him to say something tender, something kind, something meaningful— but he merely fingered several locks of hair that had come free from her pins.

"Tabby is going to wonder what you've been up to. What will you tell her?"

Harriett forced her body to move away from him. She ought to have known not to expect anything tender from him. As she tucked her hair back into her bonnet and re-tied her bonnet strings, which had also loosened, she answered with a flippant remark of her own. "I shall tell her the truth, of course. That you have manhandled me most abominably."

"You didn't seem to think it too abominable at the time."

She feigned an indifference she did not feel and shrugged. "You were kind enough to allow me to ride Wicked this morning. Such a thoughtful gesture is not deserving of a slap no matter how much I may or may not wish to administer it."

Harriet's gaze sought out Wicked, who happened to be grazing next to a large, fallen log. It felt like an answer to an unasked prayer. Without another word, she strode to the animal's side, stepped on the log, pushed the toe of her boot into the stirrup iron, and lifted herself into the saddle. She took a moment to adjust her leg around the pommel and arrange her skirts before returning her attention to the lieutenant. "Shall we race back to the stables?"

His smile didn't quite reach his eyes. "Do you think that fair—with you on Wicked and me on this stubborn mule?"

"I think it more than fair." Without waiting for him to

mount, she clicked her tongue and sent Wicked on his way. The pounding of hooves sounded beneath her as she flew across the meadow, wishing she could outrun a great many things. But for now she would settle on the lieutenant.

HARRIETT AWOKE EARLIER THAN usual, or perhaps she'd never really fallen asleep—at least not a deep, restful sleep. Rather, she had suffered through one fitful doze after another all night long, with images of Chris kissing her plaguing her thoughts and dreams. Why had he kissed her? The question plagued her mind over and over again, making her yearn for one answer while fearing another. By morning, she knew that he had claimed a large portion of her heart, and nothing she could do from this point forward would protect it from being smashed to bits if that's what he chose to do with it.

Harriett attempted to roll over and go back to sleep, but her mind would not quiet, so she tossed her covers aside and went to the window, peering across the landscape with a frown. If she ever developed lines of consternation around her mouth and eyes, they would be Lieutenant Jamison's doing.

The morning was a beautiful one, with only a few clouds marring the sky. The meadows glistened with dew, and the little buds on the trees promised to soon reveal an array of textures, colors, and shapes that would contrast nicely with the darker evergreens. Not for the first time, she contemplated how lovely it would look in another few weeks, when she was no longer here to see it.

It was difficult to believe that Tanglewood had once belonged to her family. How strange life could be at times. Her brother had sold the property because their family had no need of an estate located so far from home, yet as Harriett looked out over the grounds, she couldn't help but feel a pang of regret even though she knew it had all been for the best. If her brother had not sold Tanglewood, Mr. Ludlow would not have come to Askern and Cora would have never met him. Harriett's loss had been Cora's gain, and she could never really regret that.

In truth, the pang had little to do with Tanglewood and everything to do with her decision to visit her friend before continuing on to London. Perhaps Harriett should have missed Jonathan and Cora's wedding and stayed in Danbury instead. Though she may have crossed paths with Chris a time or two in London, it would not have amounted to much, and her world would not feel as precarious as it did at the moment.

At the far end of the meadow, a large tree caught her eye—the same tree she and Chris had stood beneath only yesterday. The mere memory of his kiss sent a blush to her cheeks and a fire to her belly. As she placed her palm over her stomach, she had to admit that the tree was quite magnificent, with its massive trunk and large, gnarled and twisted branches. One particular branch swept low to the ground, as though it had grown that way on purpose, beckoning all who came near to climb aboard.

Harriett had not climbed a tree in ages. As a child, she had scurried up branches and imagined a secret and magical world separate from her own—a world not tarnished by rules or social conventions. Within those limbs, she could do whatever she chose or become anyone she wished. It was a happy world where even the most unimaginable of things seemed possible. Harriett had raced horses, soared from treetop to treetop, and had even commanded the weather.

The reminder of her childhood imaginings brought a smile to her lips, and she couldn't help but wonder how it would feel to climb a tree now. Would she be able to find that almost forgotten world? Could she observe the surrounding countryside as Chris had once done? Or would all her years of learning how to be a proper young lady take the magic away?

Whether it was the wretched night's sleep or a fierce desire to escape, Harriett came to the conclusion that she very much wanted to climb that tree. The hour was still early, and if she hurried, she could probably do so without being noticed and be back before the others awakened.

As her mother had often told her, there was no time like the present.

Christopher sat on the edge of his bed after a sleepless night and raked his fingers through his hair. He had kissed his share of women in his time, but the memory of Harriett's touch, her softness, her curves, and her scent had kept him awake the entire night. Every time he'd closed his eyes, her image spun like a whirlpool in his mind, pulling him around and around. It felt like a mix between a dream and a nightmare because he did not know what lay at the bottom of it all.

Why did he feel so unsettled about her? Not only had

Harriett allowed him to kiss her, but she had kissed him in return. She'd pressed against him, and her fingers had threaded through his hair, wreaking all sorts of havoc on his emotions. With any other woman, he would have been confident where he stood, but with her, everything felt tenuous, like the rocky waves before a storm. At first, he attributed it to her unpredictability, but in the wee hours of the morning he realized the truth of it. When it came to Lady Harriett, there was too much at risk, too much to lose. It's what made opening up to her so blasted difficult. And now that he'd been given a glimpse of what he could have with her, the fear of her not returning his affections made him as skittish as a newborn kitten.

He combed his hair away from his face once more and pulled himself up. What he needed was a long and hard ride through the damp, brisk air. Perhaps that would clear his senses.

He poured cold water into the wash basin and splashed it over his face, not taking the time to shave. As he buttoned his shirt, he glanced out of his window and caught sight of a deep blue dress nearing the large oak tree. Intrigued, he approached the window and squinted. There was no mistaking Harriett's graceful gait, her dark curls, or her burgundy pelisse.

What was she doing out at this time of the morning?

Christopher quickly tugged on his boots and shoved his arms into his coat as he strode out the door. On his way to Jonathan's study, he dispatched a footman to the stables with a message to have Wicked readied. Then he rapped lightly on the door of the study, and when no one answered, slipped inside. On the top of the far bookcase rested a spyglass that Christopher grabbed before returning to his room. It was probably ungentlemanly to spy on her, but he could not leave the house without discovering what she was up to.

Looking through the small eyepiece, he focused on Harriett, who, much to his surprise, had climbed upon the lowest branch of the tree. At first, she tried to balance and walk along it, but when she wobbled, she dropped down on her hands and knees and began crawling, constantly tugging at her skirts to free them. She must have become frustrated by her slow progress because she finally pulled her skirts to her knees, revealing shapely calves. Christopher couldn't help but admire them for a moment before forcing his gaze elsewhere.

When she reached the trunk, she awkwardly pulled herself up, keeping her skirts tucked over her arm. Christopher had to grin at the sight. Apparently Lady Harriett was not so ladylike after all. He watched her struggle to climb up a few more branches before he tossed the spyglass on his bed and went to retrieve Wicked from the stables.

It didn't take long before he was cantering across the meadow, feeling the bite in the early morning air as he directed Wicked towards an area to the left of the large oak. When he arrived, he slowed his horse to a walk and looked around as though he found a sense of peace and enjoyment in his surroundings. Not far from the tree, he hopped down and allowed Wicked to graze.

With thoughts of Harriett high above him, Chris clasped his hands behind his back and wandered towards the tree, wondering what she might do. Would she call down to him and alert him of her presence, or would she remain silent, hoping he would go away before he saw her? Probably the latter. Knowing Harriet, she would not want to be reminded of her assertion that ladies did not climb trees.

He had to hold back a chuckle as he reached the base of the tree and casually leaned a shoulder against it, listening close for any sounds from above. But other than the chirping of birds and Wicked's munching, he heard nothing.

Christopher waited a little while longer before grabbing hold of a branch and swinging himself up. He settled in with his back against the trunk and one leg bent in front of him, as though he planned to stay a while. He began whistling and even broke off a young and tender limb, molding it into a circle.

Still no sounds. He had to give her credit for her ability to remain still. The higher one climbed a tree, the narrower the branches became, which made them far less comfortable to sit upon. Not many people could stay quiet for this long.

Another fifteen minutes passed before he heard a slight rustling, followed by the snap of a twig.

Chris looked up to find her sitting precariously on a branch with her feet dangling below her. She looked a bit wild and untamed, with several tendrils of hair flying about her face, but still beautiful. Always beautiful. Whether her cheeks were ruddy from the cold or embarrassment he could not say. Nor could he stop the grin that lifted his lips.

"Hello, Harriett."

Her eyes narrowed into a glare. "You knew I was up here, didn't you? You've known it the entire time."

He shrugged, not confirming or denying the accusation, and casually brushed some dust from his trousers. "I thought ladies did not climb trees."

He expected some sort of rejoinder or set down, but she said nothing. Instead, she began lowering herself down, using fast and deliberate movements as though he'd angered her. Christopher frowned and drew himself up, climbing up to another branch where he could assist her down. She ignored his proffered hand and continued on her own, moving around the tree and away from him.

"Harriett, won't you take my hand? There is not a pond below us to soften the ground should you fall," he said, trying to maneuver closer to her.

Her skirt snagged on a branch, and she yanked it free, tearing the fabric in the process.

Attempting to lighten the mood, Christopher clicked his tongue. "There goes another gown. Your trip to Tanglewood has not been good for your wardrobe, has it?"

Still no response. She didn't even glare at him again.

When she reached the last branch, she did not attempt to slide or crawl down it. Instead, she jumped from where she stood and landed with a small cry in the grass. Then she began limping forward in the direction of the manor.

Worried, Chris jumped down and was at her side a moment later, grabbing her elbow to keep her from injuring herself further. "You're hurt."

She stiffened, and her voice wobbled as she answered, "I am well."

She was crying, he realized, which meant that she was most certainly *not* well. Why was she so upset with him? "You're lying, Harriett. Please, allow me to put you up on Wicked and walk you home."

Harriett jerked her arm free and continued to limp towards the house. "I told you, I am well."

Christopher stared after her in confusion and frustration, trying to figure out what he had done to upset her.

"Why will you not let me assist you?" he finally called. "Harriett, please. Help me understand why you are so angry with me."

She spun around and winced at the pain the sudden movement must have cost her. Her eyes shone with tears as she glared at him. "Did it ever occur to you that while you were having your fun, pretending not to see me, that I might be growing quite frozen on an incredibly uncomfortable branch?"

He blinked at her, realizing that no, he had not considered the state of her comfort. "I'm sorry, Harriett. Truly, I am. I did not think . . ." He shook his head. "Why did you not say something?"

Her eyes widened as though she could not believe he could be so daft. "Why would I say something? What lady wants to be discovered in a tree, especially by someone who would tease her endlessly about doing something she'd claimed she'd never consider doing? The question is, why didn't *you* say something—you, who knew I was there? Instead you lay in wait like a child intent on a prank while my fingers and toes froze and my legs grew numb from sitting in the same position. All because you felt the need to amuse yourself at my expense."

"Harriett, I did not mean to—"

"I know. You never mean to, and yet you always do. It's as though my thoughts and feelings are nothing more than a continual joke to you." Tears fell from her eyes and trickled down her cheeks. "I'm tired of your teasing, Lieutenant, I'm tired of this ruse we're playing, and I'm tired of not being able to trust you. It all needs to end now. I cannot continue on like this anymore, I cannot."

At some point during her speech, Christopher came to the unhappy realization that her ankle was not entirely to blame for her tears. *He* was. He'd gone too far, and now she was pulling away from him. An awful feeling tore through him like a well-aimed ball in his gut, and he was quick to close the distance between them.

"Harriett," he breathed, taking hold of her hands. Even through their gloves he could feel how cold her fingers were. "I don't understand what I've done to hurt you so deeply— Heaven knows it wasn't intended—but please don't despise me."

She squeezed her eyes shut and dropped her head, shaking it as though she didn't want to even consider it.

A fear unlike any he had ever known filled him, and Christopher tightened his hold on her. When she winced and withdrew her hands, shaking them in an attempt to warm them, he knew this conversation would have to wait. He needed to get her to the warmth of the house and off that injured ankle.

"At least let me give you a ride back to the house."

After a moment, she finally nodded. He wasted no time collecting Wicked, who stood perfectly still while Christopher gently lifted Harriett into the saddle.

"It won't be as comfortable as a side saddle, but it will keep you off that foot," he said before taking the reins.

Under normal circumstances, Wicked would have never countenanced a casual walk through a wide open meadow, but the horse seemed to understand how precious his cargo was because he remained patient the entire way. Upon arrival, Christopher directed Charlie to give the animal an extra helping of oats as he lifted Harriett from the horse and carried her inside. In the great hall, he continued to hold her, despite her protests, as he asked the anxious butler to send for Tabby, and then he carried her up the stairs and to her room, where he deposited her carefully onto the bed.

"I need to remove your boot to make sure you have not broken anything," he said, moving to the foot of her bed. When she opened her mouth to protest, he added, "Or would you prefer that I send for the doctor?"

She closed her mouth and shook her head. "No doctor, please. The pain isn't nearly as intense anymore."

"Good. Then it shouldn't be too painful to remove your boot. Your ankle will probably swell, and the sooner we free your foot the better."

She sighed and nodded. "Very well."

Christopher began to loosen the laces, and Tabby rushed in, followed closely by Watts.

"Sir!" the maid cried in horror. "What are you doin'?"

"Calm yourself, Tabby," said Harriett, sounding more like herself. "I injured my ankle this morning, and the lieutenant is only freeing it from my boot to ascertain that it is nothing serious."

"Injured your ankle? How?" Tabby gasped. "Sir, perhaps I should be doin' that."

"If you'd like to be of assistance, Tabby, you can stoke the fire. Lady Harriett is chilled to the bone and this room feels drafty."

"Of course. Right away, sir." Tabby rushed to the fireplace as Christopher removed Harriett's stocking. There was a little swelling around her ankle, but no bruising as of yet, which was a good sign. He gently probed her foot to make sure nothing was out of order. When at last he was satisfied that the injury was a minor one, he stood and faced Watts.

The butler appeared unusually stern, as he had every right to be. He had undoubtedly noticed Harriett's rumpled appearance, her torn dress, the wildness of her hair, and her red-rimmed eyes. The scene they had made bursting into the house had not been a pretty one, and it probably didn't help that Harriett often returned from encounters with Christopher in a similar state.

But Christopher didn't care about that now. "Can your housekeeper make a poultice?" he asked.

"What sort of poultice?"

"One made with arnica, poppy-heads, and linseed will reduce the swelling."

"Very good, sir," the butler answered tightly. "I will see to it."

After he'd gone, Harriett watched Chris with a wariness he did not like at all. "You seem to know a great deal about medicine."

Christopher only wished he knew how to heal the damage he'd caused to her insides as well. "I learned a great deal during the war," was his only explanation.

"I'm grateful for your knowledge."

He swallowed, knowing he had no more excuses to remain. Propriety dictated that he leave her in the capable hands of her maid and the female staff. But oh, how he wanted to send everyone away, pull up a chair, clasp her hand in his, and stay until he convinced her to no longer despise him.

"Will you be all right?" he asked, referring to more than just her ankle and chilled body.

She nodded. "Thank you for your assistance, Lieutenant."

Lieutenant. The title had once meant a great deal to Christopher. It had forced him to leave his selfish ways behind and take on more responsibility. Over the years, he'd worked hard to earn the respect the title commanded, and by the end of the war, he'd felt as though he'd achieved it. The men under his command had not called him Lieutenant lightly. They had become brothers in arms with Christopher at the helm, and he'd always considered it a title of honor.

Now, however, he wished it to the devil.

AFTER A WARM BATH, a change of clothes, and a soothing poultice applied to her ankle, Harriett at last felt well again. Weariness finally took hold of her, and she was just drifting off to sleep when a quiet knock sounded on her door.

She pried her eyes open and called out, "Enter."

Cora slipped inside and smiled. "Tabby told me you were all fixed up and finally ready for visitors. I hope I am not intruding."

Anyone else and Harriett might have told them to go away, but not Cora. Never Cora. Harriett propped herself up, careful not to disturb the poultice, and patted the bed next to her. "It's about time you came to check on me. I was beginning to think you did not care."

Cora plopped down and tucked her legs beneath her. "I would have come sooner, but I wasn't allowed. Tabby can be quite forceful when she wishes to be. I was told that she had everything under control and my presence would only get in her way."

Harriett laughed, picturing her maid saying those very words. "Well, she was right. Between her and your competent housekeeper, I have never been more pampered in my life."

"Sally is a wonder," agreed Cora. "But I must know what happened to you. All Christopher would say was that you twisted your ankle on the far side of the meadow and needed Wicked's assistance to bring you home. I cannot imagine he would fib about such things, but I still find it difficult to believe. What were you doing out at such an early hour, and on your own, no less?"

Harriett had tried her best not to think about Christopher because it made her feel so befuddled and uncertain. How strange this morning had been. One moment, he had behaved thoughtlessly and she'd been convinced that he could never truly care for her, and the next he transformed into a concerned gentleman. He'd even instructed Watts about a certain poultice that would sooth her ache away. And it had, most beautifully.

Cora was watching her curiously, still waiting for an answer. What had she asked again? Oh, yes. She wished to know what had taken Harriett across the meadow at such an early hour. Goodness. How ludicrous this was going to sound.

Harriett could only turn her palms up and shrug. "I wanted to climb a tree."

"I beg your pardon?"

Harriett's thoughts exactly, but there was no undoing her irrational behavior now. She nodded in the direction of the window. "That large oak on the far side of the meadow. It looks so climbable, don't you agree? I awoke to that view and experienced a deep desire to see what the world would look like from the top."

Cora's forehead crinkled. She opened her mouth to say something, seemed to think better of it, and closed it. After a moment or two of silence, she said, "I see."

Harriett snickered. "Do you? Because I don't. I can honestly say that I have no idea what possessed me to do such a bird-witted and childish thing—other than a sleepless night, that is."

Cora smiled and looked down at her hands, smoothing her fingers across the silky bedding. "I did notice that you and Christopher were behaving a little odd at dinner last evening. Has something happened between you?"

Something had most definitely happened, thought Harriett. She had yet to tell her friend about the kiss because it had felt too intimate. But now, as Harriett questioned every word Chris spoke, every expression he made, and every action he undertook, her mind felt ready to burst from all the questions and uncertainty. She so badly wanted to let it all out, and if she could trust anyone, it was Cora.

"Yesterday morning," Harriett said, "after you left for the ruins, Chris led me to a spot beneath that large oak tree and kissed me. That is the reason I behaved oddly at dinner, the reason I could not sleep last night, and the reason I thought escaping into that tree this morning would somehow unburden me. But it only served to worsen the situation. He came upon me there and behaved in a boorish manner. In my frustration and inner turmoil, I leapt down from a higher branch and twisted my ankle before unleashing my fury on him. But then he was so kind and considerate and . . ." Harriett covered her face with her hands. "I don't know how to feel or what to think. He makes me so . . ." There was no one word to describe how she felt because it constantly changed. She was a mess—out of sorts one moment and weak at the knees the next.

Cora poked Harriett's arm with her finger and smiled. "I do believe Lady Harriett Cavendish has finally fallen in love."

Harriett's jaw fell open in shock. That was not at all what she'd expected—or wanted—to hear. "In love? With the lieutenant? Are you daft?"

"It would explain a great deal."

"No." Harriett shook her head vehemently. "Perhaps if he had always treated me in a thoughtful manner, but he does not. He prefers to taunt and tease and drive me mad. Do you know what he said after he kissed me? 'What, no slap?' There were no words of tenderness or warmth in his gaze. It had all been a lark to him. And this morning? He knew I was in that tree but pretended as though he did not see me, thinking it would be great fun to ferret me out while I grew colder and more miserable by the second. How, I ask you, could I ever be in love with such a man?"

Realizing she was working herself into a dither, Harriett forced her mouth to close. So much for drifting off into a peaceful slumber. But honestly, *love*? Surely not. She might care for the lieutenant in some aspects, but that was all. She would be an utter fool to fall in love with him.

Her stomach lurched as the toast and tea she had eaten earlier threatened to revolt. Could her friend not see the negative effect Chris had on her? Love, indeed.

Cora slowly traced one of the floral designs on the bedding, appearing perfectly composed. "Jonathan often teases me, you know, and I rather like it. It makes me feel as though he finds my oddities endearing."

"Yes, but he is also tender and sweet with you. I see the warmth and affection in his eyes when he looks upon you and the way he finds any excuse to touch or be near you. That man adores you, Cora, and is it so wrong for me to want the same? How could I ever love a man who does not love me in return?"

Cora pressed her lips together and nodded slowly. After

a moment or two, she said, "Christopher is not Jonathan, you know. He is his own person and will show affection in his own way. And perhaps he's wondering the same about you. Have you given him any indication about the extent of your feelings? Are you ever tender and sweet with *him*? Do you gaze upon *him* with warmth and affection? Do you find excuses to touch or be near *him*?"

Harriett opened her mouth to respond, only to close it and frown, realizing that she had not given the lieutenant much of anything in that quarter. Perhaps if she had . . . no, how could Cora even suggest such a thing? "It is not a woman's place to pursue a man, Cora."

"No, but a man does need encouragement every now and again. I'm willing to wager that Christopher's heart is every bit as vulnerable as yours."

Chris's heart? Vulnerable? Harriett could not fathom how that could be. He was so arrogant and self-assured. But then she remembered the fear she had spotted in his eyes following her outburst. Her angry words had subdued him, and from that point forward, he had seemed most regretful for his actions, not to mention genuinely concerned for her well being.

Did Chris care for her? Was he waiting for some sort of encouragement? Could she give it to him without knowing how he truly felt about her?

Harriett swallowed and pressed her hand into her still-queasy stomach. She remembered the first time she had taken a fall from a horse. Her body had ached for days, and she'd told her nursemaid she would never ride again. But one afternoon, as she walked past the stables, there was her father, leading out that same horse who had thrown her days earlier.

"Will you ride today?" he'd asked.

She'd shaken her head and quickened her steps, intent on getting away from the animal as soon as possible, but her father's words had stopped her.

"To have courage does not mean you won't feel fear. It means you are willing to face your fear."

Harriett had paused to look at him, thinking over his words.

"I'm going to ask again. Will you ride today, my pet?" he repeated.

Oh, how Harriett missed her father and his wise counsel. If he were here now, would he encourage her to be brave or would he think the lieutenant unworthy of her and tell her to stay away?

Somehow, Harriett knew her father would have liked Chris a great deal, just as everyone else did.

"You look tired," said Cora. "I should let you get some rest. With any luck, your ankle will mend and you will feel up to coming down to dinner later. The Biddings will be here, and we'll need you to round out our numbers."

Harriett did not know how she could ever face the lieutenant again, at least not before she had set some things straight in her mind, but she couldn't let her friend down. So she nodded. "Hurt ankle or not, I will be there."

Cora gave her hand a squeeze. "Not to worry. Everything will come out all right in the end."

"How do you know?" Harriett asked.

"Because it always does."

At some point during the afternoon, Tabby must have removed the poultice from Harriett's ankle. When she awoke, it was gone, as was the worst of the swelling. She cautiously put her foot on the floor and stood, testing it out. Much to her surprise, her ankle barely hurt. In fact, it felt almost as well as it had felt before she had twisted it.

She smiled, thinking of it as a sign of good things to come, and with that mild change of heart came hope. It was a lovely, invigorating feeling made brighter by the sun beaming through the windows.

When Tabby bustled into the room moments later, Harriett extended a cheery hello.

Tabby appeared pleasantly surprised. "You're lookin' a sight better, milady. Is your ankle on the mend?"

"Yes, though I can scarce believe it. Please convey my thanks to Sally for mixing up that poultice. It has worked miracles."

"Best be thankin' Lieutenant Jamison as well," said Tabby as she strode to the wardrobe. "'Twas his idea, after all."

"Yes, I'm aware of that, Tabby." Sometimes Harriett wondered if her maid forgot that she was the servant and Harriett the mistress. Tabby could be a little high-handed at times, not that Harriett minded overly much. She'd rather have a forthright maid than a timid one.

Harriett glanced at the clock across the room and stiffened. Was it truly almost half past five already? Goodness, she had slept late. No wonder Tabby was rifling through her wardrobe with swift movements. They would need to hurry if Harriett was to be ready for dinner in time.

"Would you like to wear the rose silk or the gold taffeta this evening?" Tabby pulled both dresses out for Harriett's inspection. It hadn't taken long for her maid to learn that Harriett did not like making decisions about what to wear, so she only ever suggested two options even though Harriett's answer was usually the same. *You decide, Tabby. I do not care in the least.*

Tonight, however, Harriett did care. She wanted to look her best, and since she had received more compliments on the gold taffeta than the rose silk, she offered an opinion. "The gold one."

Pleased surprise widened Tabby's eyes before she nodded and pulled the gown from the wardrobe. "'Twas my first choice as well, milady. This color looks lovely on you."

Harriett dressed quickly, and Tabby took extra care to coil her hair into the most beautiful knot with a waterfall of curls erupting from the center at the crown of her head.

Once complete, Harriett turned her head from side to side, examining the results. "Tabby, you have outdone yourself tonight. It's beautiful."

The maid blushed at the compliment. "You'll take Lieutenant Jamison's breath away tonight, make no mistake about that."

That was precisely what Harriett hoped to do, and she appreciated Tabby even more for perceiving her desire to impress him. "Let us hope he does not forget to breathe altogether. How will I impress him if he faints at the sight of me? Perhaps I should take some smelling salts with me just in case."

Tabby giggled and shook her head. "It's good ter see you've got your pluck back, milady. After this mornin', I worried it had gone missin' again."

Harriett didn't bother denying it. Tabby knew her too well. "It feels good to have it back, Tabby. Let us pray it remains intact because I am growing weary of it going missing."

Tabby grinned, added a gold ribbon to Harriett's hair, and pronounced her ready. "Enjoy yourself tonight, milady."

"Thank you, Tabby." Harriett walked out of the room but stopped abruptly when she spotted Lieutenant Jamison lingering not far away. She felt a mild twinge in her ankle but paid it no mind. He leaned casually against the wall, looking far too handsome in a deep blue coat, buff breeches, and brown boots.

Her heart stuttered to a stop before pounding at a furious pace. How long had he been standing there and why? Had he overheard her conversation with Tabby?

Please no.

His eyes were not twinkling nor his lips threatening a grin as they usually did, so it was impossible to guess what he might be thinking. Perhaps he'd come to tell her that he'd told his parents the truth, per her request, and would be leaving for London on the morrow to begin his search for a level-headed and not-so-lively woman.

Please don't be that either.

"Lieutenant." Harriett nodded in greeting, watching him warily. Why was he here and not downstairs with the others?

His gaze took her in, but she couldn't tell whether he liked what he saw or not. He seemed guarded and wary as well, as though he did not know which Harriett had greeted him—the one prone to outbursts or the lively one?

"You look beautiful," he finally said.

She tried not to let his somber mood affect hers and forced her lips into a teasing smile. "Not breathtaking?"

His moustache did not twitch in response, nor did his eyes crinkle at the edges. He merely studied her with that worrisome wariness. "Are you well?" he asked.

She lifted her skirts slightly and gave him a peek of her ankle. "Thanks to your intriguing knowledge of medicine, I am almost as good as new. Is that why you are here? To offer to carry me down in the event that my ankle is not better? Or were you worried I'd try to come down via the tree outside my window? If that is the case, you can rest assured that I have been cured of all inclinations to climb trees in the near future."

He smiled a little at that, but it only partially reached his eyes. "I came to offer my assistance in whichever capacity would help you the most."

"Then I shall gladly accept the offer of your arm, sir, along with your protection. It is a long walk to the drawing room, after all, and there's no telling what evil thing might be lurking in the shadows."

She held out her hand, waiting for him to extend his arm, but he stayed where he was and watched her with an expression of bemusement. When at last he pushed away from the wall, he approached with caution before extending his arm.

She linked her elbow through his, and they began sauntering down the hall at a slow pace. Harriett tried to think of something witty or lively to say, but nothing came to mind and by the time they reached the top of the stairs, the silence had become unbearable.

"Say something, please," she blurted. "You're making me anxious."

Chris turned and picked up one of her hands and then the other, gripping them firmly in his own. He drew in a deep breath and let it out slowly. "Before we go down, I must apologize. I am not a serious-minded person, and I often get caught up in the moment and don't pause to consider how my words or actions might affect another. I was in the wrong this morning and am deeply sorry. Can you forgive me?" He paused. "Again?"

A warm and delicious feeling spread through Harriett. She might have been brazen enough to wrap her arms around him if Watts was not stationed at the base of the stairs. Though she held the butler in high esteem, at the moment, she wished he would remove himself to another part of the house.

She straightened the lieutenant's cravat instead. "If I say no, will I be subjected to an evening filled with scripture on the virtues of forgiveness?"

The smile that prodded and tickled her heart at last emerged. "Most definitely."

She grinned in return. "Then I'm afraid that my forgiveness will have to wait. I'm far too curious to see how your parents will react to your stuffy sermons. With pride, perhaps? Your mother did say she thought you were better suited to the church than to war."

He smiled and shook his head. "Better suited? Hardly. She only hoped I'd choose the church as it would have encouraged me to mend my ways."

"Have you mended your ways, Lieutenant?"

"I hate it when you call me that." There was that seriousness again. It had a perplexing effect on her lungs, making them feel as though the room had suddenly become devoid of oxygen.

"Forgive me?" she whispered. "Again?"

"Forgiven."

She smiled, but it didn't go all the way to her eyes. "You forgive far more easily than I, it seems. Perhaps you *are* suited for the church after all."

"I'd much rather be suited for . . ." His eyes drifted to her lips. "Something else."

Harriett suddenly felt as though she'd just climbed the tallest staircase she had ever climbed. His fingers tightened around hers, and he leaned in close, sending a series of chills scuttling through her body.

A loud clearing of a throat sounded from below, causing

Chris to close his eyes and withdraw. With a sigh, he tucked her hand under his arm once more. "Shall we go down? Jonathan has some exciting news that you will be very glad to hear. He is probably wondering what is keeping us."

It took a moment for Harriett to make the transition from an almost kiss to Jonathan's news, but when the words at last registered, she brightened. "Has he heard from Mr. O'Rourke then?"

Christopher chuckled. "It is his news to share, not mine."

"Very well. I shall do my utmost to be patient."

"If it would help, I'm certain I could find a passage of scripture on the merits of patience."

"It would not help."

He chuckled again, and the deep, melodious sound wrapped around Harriett's body like an embrace. As they entered the drawing room together, she felt light, giddy, and full of optimism. Perhaps all she had needed this entire time was a change in perspective, some hope, and a little courage.

"You have come at last," said Mrs. Jamison with a broad smile. "We were beginning to think that Christopher had gone on a fool's errand to fetch you down here."

"As though I would allow Harriett to languish alone upstairs," said Chris with a wink at her. "She is fortunate her ankle is on the mend. Otherwise, I would have been forced to carry her down, and she would have been most displeased with me."

If he thought that, Harriett had certainly been much too sparing with her encouragement. Had he not noticed her shortness of breath or the pounding of her heart when he'd lifted her into his arms earlier? Or the way she'd clung to his neck, craving his nearness? All this time, she thought her attraction to him was so very obvious, but perhaps her attempts to conceal it had actually been effective.

Too effective, it seemed.

Harriett greeted the Biddings and inquired about Pippin's puppies. Mrs. Bidding was quick to reply. "According to the cow leech, they will be ready to leave their mama in another week or so. Mr. Bidding and I have decided that we are willing to part with one, Lieutenant, if you would like to take it with you."

"Or I could take it with *me*," said Harriett, realizing she had probably gone too far with her teasing about the puppy. The least she could do was offer him a way out.

But he surprised her by shaking his head. "Sorry, Harriett. I had first claim on that puppy, and so it shall be mine."

"Perhaps you can share," suggested Mr. Jamison with a twinkle in his eyes.

Harriett felt a blush heat her face, but she didn't bother glancing at Christopher for help. The man didn't seem to ever feel embarrassment and had probably paid his father no mind.

Thankfully, Jonathan was kind enough to direct the attention to him. "I have some news," he announced. "It will not mean much to most of you here, but it means a great deal to me."

"What is it?" asked Mr. Jamison.

"I have reached an agreement with the owner of the land to the west. He has finally consented to sell me a portion of his land for an agricultural venture that I plan to begin immediately." Jonathan slung his arm around Christopher's shoulders and gave him a hearty pat on the back. "Without the intervention of this man here, I would have emptied my purse and acquired more land than I could ever use. I cannot thank him enough."

Mrs. Jamison beamed at her son while Mr. Jamison

began to talk about how Christopher had always been a natural negotiator. Meanwhile, Harriett stood apart from the conversation and felt her magical evening pale a little. She should not care, but it pained her that Chris had kept her part in the plan to himself. She tried to be happy for Jonathan and not care that the spotlight did not extend to her—it was unchristian to seek for accolades, after all—but the truth of the matter was that she did care. She wanted Chris to notice her—not overlook her.

Chris lifted his hands to quiet all voices. "You are extending thanks to the wrong person. It was Harriett who suggested the idea to not back down. I merely realized the brilliance of the plan and took it upon myself to convince Jonathan of it as well."

Harriett's mouth parted in surprise, and she felt the greatest urge to throw her arms around him.

"Of course," Jonathan said. "You did mention Harriett's name when you first brought the idea to my attention, didn't you? Forgive me for not including you in my thanks, Harriett."

"'Tis no matter," she said dismissively, waving his thanks aside. She had eyes for only one man at that moment, and it was not Jonathan. It was the man listening to something Cora was now saying. A man who had also confided in Harriett, listened to her, and acted on a simple idea she'd had. A man whose pride did not get in the way of his integrity.

Oh, how much his simple confession had meant to her.

Harriett could deny it no longer. She was in love with Lieutenant Christopher Jamison. She loved his strengths, his sense of humor, and even his weaknesses. She loved the fact that he was imperfect like her and not afraid to admit it. She loved that he could tell her which bonnet looked well on her, allowed her to ride his horse, was well acquainted with the Bible, and knew precisely what to do with a twisted ankle.

Harriett had finally come to see what the Biddings, the Jamisons, and Cora had probably seen from the beginning. Chris complemented her in the way Jonathan complemented Cora and Colin complemented Lucy.

I adore you, she wanted to blurt.

Mrs. Jamison looked from her son to Harriett with a knowing smile and declared, "What a marvelous team the two of you make."

Mrs. Bidding nodded fondly. "I couldn't agree more."

Cora nudged Harriett playfully with her elbow. "It appears as though you've got quite the head for business—you who thought you had no talents."

"No ladylike ones, at any rate," answered Harriett with a grin.

"What are you talking about?" asked Chris. "You would never behave in an unladylike fashion."

"Under normal circumstances, no," she said. "But I have been known to make exceptions every now and again."

"What sort of exceptions?" asked Mrs. Bidding, her smile diminishing.

Harriett waved her hand in a flippant manner. "Oh, you know. Sneak down to the kitchen for a midnight assignation, swim in ponds, play in mud puddles, and of course, climb trees. But only on rare occasions when the mood strikes."

Mrs. Bidding's eyes widened while Cora burst out laughing, Jonathan grinned, and Chris pressed his lips together to keep from doing the same. Mr. and Mrs. Jamison and Mr. Bidding peered from one person to the next, obviously confused by the mixed reactions.

"You're joking, I presume," Mrs. Bidding finally said, her expression hopeful.

"Honestly, Mrs. Bidding, can you truly see me climbing a tree?" asked Harriett. "Ever since my unhappy encounter with the bird droppings, I have decided it is best to stay away from trees."

"Of course you have," said Mrs. Bidding with obvious relief. "You must forgive my doubtful nature when it comes to those residing at Tanglewood. I have often wondered if there is a mischievous spirit lurking about somewhere, encouraging all occupants to misbehave."

"Really?" said Mrs. Jamison. "I have heard of evil spirits inhabiting some houses. Do you think there could be such a spirit here? I certainly have not felt any such temptations. Have you, dearest? Christopher?"

Watts entered the room to announce dinner, much to Harriett's relief. She could only imagine what Chris's answer to that question might have been, and none of them brought her any comfort. He would have likely driven Mrs. Bidding into an apoplexy, the poor woman.

Chris offered Harriett his arm, which she accepted with pleasure, and the happy group removed to the dining room for a scrumptious meal of chateaubriand steak and roasted potatoes. Together, they laughed, talked, and lifted their glasses in a toast of good things to come. Harriett shared knowing, amused, and even flirtatious glances with Chris—*real* glances. As far as she was concerned, their ruse had come to an end.

Following dinner, Chris suggested an evening stroll through the gardens, much to Harriett's delight. Jonathan and Cora agreed to accompany them while the Biddings and Mr. and Mrs. Jamison opted to remain indoors. Harriett very much looked forward to a romantic stroll, hoping it would provide her and Chris with an opportunity to speak privately and perhaps sneak a kiss or two. She had it all planned out in her mind.

As soon as the foursome outfitted themselves in coats, hats, and gloves, they emerged into the beautiful, chilly night with hundreds of tiny stars sparkling above. A gust of wind caused Harriett to shiver, and she tightened her hold on Chris's arm, snuggling as close to him as she dared.

"Are you cold? Should we go back inside?" he asked.

"No. I love it out here. If it becomes unbearable, I will let you know, but for now I would like to remain." Harriett wouldn't dream of going inside now, not when she was certain this was the night that would change everything between them.

As though perceiving Harriett's wishes, Cora and Jonathan walked ahead. Like a good soldier, Chris slowed his steps and directed Harriett down a path to the left, into a small, shadowed garden surrounded by high hedges of evergreen shrubs with a dormant stone fountain at its center.

Harriett inspected the garden, wishing the air was a bit warmer and spring a little more advanced. "Only think of how beautiful this garden will look in a few weeks when all the leaves emerge."

Chris took hold of her hand and brought her around to face him. "Will you still be here when that happens?"

She wished she could say yes—it felt too magical to leave now—but after the letter she had received from her mother the day before, she had to shake her head. "I will leave at the end of next week for London. My mother has finally written to me with her plans, along with the happy news that Colin and Lucy are to accompany her with my new nephew. Lucy is in desperate need of a diversion, apparently, and seems to think that a month in London will be just the thing."

"Are you looking forward to seeing your family?"

"Oh, yes. Lucy has become like a sister to me, and I have always been fond of Colin. My sister, Charlotte, and my brother, James, will be there as well. It has been years since we have all been together, and I'm looking forward to spending time with them again. We used to taunt and torment one another mercilessly, but we have always been close, and for that, I am very grateful."

It seemed like a lifetime ago, so distant was the memory of those childhood years. How much the Cavendish family had changed of late—both for the better and for the worse. Colin had married Lucy, Harriett's other brother and sister had moved away to start families of their own, and their father had passed away. She missed him dearly, especially now, when she was hoping to introduce her family to a certain Lieutenant Christopher Jamison. He would fit in well and her father would have liked him very much.

"I'm certain they are grateful for you as well," said Chris, threading his fingers through hers and drawing her closer. "I know *I'm* grateful for you."

"Are you?" she asked breathlessly, her heart filled with anticipation.

"I shall prove it," he whispered as his lips covered hers. In an instant, all coherent thought flew from Harriett's mind and only her senses remained. She reveled in the softness of his lips, the tickling of his moustache, and the taste of cinnamon on his breath. A tidal wave of sensations engulfed her, and the chill in the air became an inferno. Oh, how she loved to kiss this man. He made her life feel full and complete, and when he drew back abruptly moments later, she longed for more.

She searched his face in confusion. They had only just begun the kiss. Had he not enjoyed it? Did she not affect him the way he affected her? He could have never pulled away so quickly if she had.

He drew in a deep breath and let it out slowly, peering down at her. "Harriett, there is something I must say to you."

She nodded, feeling anxious, hopeful, and ill at the same time. Would her stomach ever feel normal around him?

"This morning you said that my constant teasing was growing tiresome and that you were ready to put an end to our ruse, but now you seem to have changed your mind."

Harriett opened her mouth to explain, but he didn't give her the chance. "I'm not sure why or what you're thinking, but I agree that we should no longer pretend to feel something we do not. It was unfair of me to ask that of you, and I am sorry for it. I am also saddened that I went too far with my teasing and compromised whatever trust you had in me."

"It is forgotten, Chris. Truly," she said. "I said many things I did not mean either."

"Yes, but . . ." He seemed to grapple with the words he wanted to say, and Harriett silently pled with him to say what her heart yearned to hear—that he could not clear his mind of her and that he wanted to walk with her, talk to her, and kiss her every day from this point forward.

Tell me you love me, she silently begged. Those were all the words she needed to hear.

He cleared his throat and swallowed before beginning anew. "What my mother said tonight was true. We do make a good team, and for the most part we get on well together, wouldn't you say? I say that because . . . well, would you consider putting an end to our ruse and making it real?"

Harriett blinked at him. Make it real? A good team? They got on well together? Was this some sort of proposal? Her hopes deflated at the thought, leaving her aching with disappointment. He had said nothing about wanting or even needing her in his life, nor had he mentioned anything that led her to believe he truly cared for her. And he definitely had not said anything about love.

They simply made a good team. *Hurrah.*

"Perhaps I did not make myself clear," he said, his brows drawn together in worry. "What I mean to say is . . . Harriett, will you do me the honor of becoming my wife?"

Needing to hear something of substance, Harriett pressed, "Why?"

He frowned as though he did not understand the question. "I thought I had already explained. We are a good fit, are we not?"

"A good fit?" she asked. "The way a certain saddle or hat or boots is a good fit?" Did he not hear how ridiculous and unromantic he sounded?

He smiled a little as though he found her question humorous. "Perhaps, but a saddle, boots, or a hat cannot pull you out of a pond or carry you into the house, can they? And they could never work together to solve a problem the way we have done. Perhaps it would be better to compare us to . . . a fork and a plate—both useful in their own right, but definitely better together."

His eyes sparkled with mirth as though he'd made a clever joke, and Harriett felt a keen sense of disappointment settle over her. How many times had she dreamed of hearing a man she loved ask for her hand in marriage? So many times. But she had never pictured it as a humorous moment. She had pictured her heart thumping, her mind whirling, and her soul bursting with the most exquisite happiness imaginable.

And she had never once imagined herself on the verge of tears.

Harriett pulled her hands free and took a step back, hating that the beautiful evening she had envisioned had come to this. Every instinct told her to get away from him as quickly as possible, but she had determined to be honest with herself and him, and so she drew upon every ounce of courage she possessed and lifted her gaze to his. He deserved to know precisely why she would not be accepting his offer.

"You once told me," she said, "that if you cannot love or desire a woman, marriage to her would be an unhappy experience. I found the sentiment admirable because I have always thought the same. More than anything, I want to love and desire a man, but it cannot be one-sided for me. I need to be loved and desired in return and will not settle for someone who only thinks we get on well together or that we make a good team. Perhaps that is the sensible thing to want, but I do not want sensible. I want a man who finds my oddities endearing, a man who complements my weaknesses with his strengths, a man who is willing to make a fool of himself over me because he cannot help himself. I want to be loved deeply and passionately by someone I love deeply and passionately in return."

She glanced down at her trembling hands and clasped them together before lifting her gaze to his once more. "For a brief moment today, I thought I had finally found such a man, but I was wrong. So no, Lieutenant Jamison, I cannot marry you."

Harriett's tears remained unshed until that moment, when they began to leak out, falling down her cheeks like her own little rain shower. Feeling the last of her courage deplete, Harriett turned and fled, running as fast as she could. He called after her, but she did not stop. Nor did she pause to say goodnight to Cora or Jonathan as she rushed past. She ran directly to her room, where she closed her door on everything but her shattered heart.

Only then did she realize the pain in her ankle had returned with a vengeance.

CHRISTOPHER PAUSED AT THE top of the stairs, taking in the scene below him. Two footmen had just disappeared out the door carrying a trunk, and Harriett stood with Cora and Jonathan, wearing a rust-colored traveling dress with a matching bonnet. Christopher's stomach clenched, and his fingers tightened around the railing.

Harriett was leaving?

For the hundredth time, he cursed himself for being a fool. All of his life, he'd maintained the confident, fun-loving, and care-for-nothing persona that came so easily to him. He could even be serious on occasion. But when it came to opening his heart, it felt like trying to pry up a stone floor.

On the eve of the day he'd reported for war duty, his mother and sisters had cried tears of sorrow while he remained facetious and seemingly unaffected. But he had not been unaffected. Far from it. He'd been petrified by the possibility that he would never see his family again. But had he conveyed as much to them? No. They did not know he'd questioned his decision a great many times or that he'd left with a lump in his throat at the thought of missing them. He had not even told them he loved them. Why? Because to admit such things was a weakness—or so he'd once thought.

Last night, as Harriett stood before him, radiating beauty and dignity as she opened her heart to him, he realized that burying one's feelings wasn't a show of strength. It was cowardice. And now he had no one but himself to blame for the scene playing out below him.

Voices rose to where he stood.

"I wish we could convince you to stay," said Cora.

Harriett pulled her friend into a hug. "I shall never forget my time here. You have both been the most wonderful hosts, and I will always be grateful for the many kindnesses you have shown me. But it is time I stop delaying my life and move forward. The season is well underway, and Mother will be meeting me soon. I sent a note off to Charlotte this morning, telling her to expect me shortly."

Cora nodded. "I understand, but I will miss you so."

"And I you." Harriett held her hand out to Jonathan. "I wish you all the best with your agricultural venture. When I visit next, I expect to see fields and fields of crops."

"And so you shall. I cannot thank you enough for your timely advice."

"I'm just happy that it all worked out. Please convey my goodbyes to the Jamisons, along with the hope that our paths will cross at some point in London."

"Are you certain you do not wish to tell them yourself?" Cora hedged.

"I think it best if I don't."

Watts opened the door and bowed, and Harriett paused to give his hand a grateful squeeze as well. "It has been a pleasure to know you, Watts."

"And you, my lady."

Christopher could stay still no longer. Harriett couldn't

leave like this, not before he had a chance to explain. With quick steps, he descended the stairs, calling out, "Wait," as Harriett crossed over the threshold.

Her body stiffened, but she did not turn around. She did not even glance over her shoulder. She merely waited, as though being required to do something she was loath to do.

"About blasted time," Jonathan muttered as Christopher walked by.

He stepped past Harriett and stood before her, searching his head for something—anything to say that would keep her from getting in the coach.

Unfortunately, "You're leaving?" was the only thing that came to mind.

"Yes," she answered, fiddling with her gloves and refusing to look him in the eye.

"Harriett, I—" Christopher stopped, realizing how it would sound if he blurted out his love for her in that awkward moment. She would see it only as a desperate move on his part to win her back and would probably not realize he was in earnest. How could she at this point? He'd had his chance to reveal his feelings to her last night, and he'd taken the cowardly way out.

All this time, he had not understood her lack of trust in him, but as he stood before her ready to beg for it back once again, he realized it would not be enough. He had effectively destroyed it last night, and it would take a great deal more than desperate words and belated expressions of love to earn it back. It would take a miracle.

Christopher swallowed and forced himself to stand aside, leaving her with the only promise he could make. "I shall see you in London."

Without looking up, she nodded and descended to the waiting coach. The door opened, revealing Tabby already inside, and closed as soon as Harriett joined her. As the coach pulled away from the house, the last view he glimpsed of her was the brim of her traveling bonnet shielding her eyes.

16

HARRIETT WASTED NO TIME throwing herself into the London scene. She arrived at her sister's lavish townhouse two days later and insisted on accompanying Charlotte to a dinner party that very evening. Tabby dressed her in a peach silk gown, styled her hair beautifully, and Harriett breezed into the party with a winsome smile. She flirted outrageously, laughed at every opportunity she could, and pretended as though her heart had not been trampled upon.

The following morning, she entertained several callers, many of them gentlemen, paid a visit to her London modiste, and graciously accepted an invitation to drive with Mr. Hedgewick in the park. News quickly spread of her arrival, and within a day or two, invitations arrived with her name on them as well, albeit with only one T.

At the end of the week, her mother, Colin, and Lucy arrived, along with their new little son, Samuel. Harriett doted on the boy, stealing away to the nursery every spare moment she could. Who could resist a baby, after all? He snuggled into her arms without conditions or reservations, and oh, how she needed his sweet show of affection. The world would be a different place if everyone could love so openly.

Lucy happened upon Harriett in the nursery one afternoon and smiled. "I find you in here often and hear you have taken quite a liking to little Samuel."

"How could I not?" said Harriett, clutching the sweet baby to her bosom. "I do not understand how you can bear to leave him for even a moment."

Lucy dragged over a chair and took a seat next to Harriett, eyeing her friend with a look of concern. "You hide it well, but you cannot fool me. You seem sad, as though something—or more likely, *someone*—has disappointed or hurt you. What has happened?"

Harriett kissed Samuel's forehead, wishing she had done a better job of hiding her emotions. Only yesterday, her mother had made a similar observation, but Harriett had not been ready to talk about it then and had dismissed the claim as nonsensical. But now, holding a guileless infant in her arms, she could not fib so easily.

Harriett sighed and rested her head against the back of the rocker. "I've experienced a little heartbreak, is all. But you may rest assured that I am on the mend."

"Are you?" Lucy asked.

Samuel made a sound in his sleep, and Harriett smiled. "I hope so. This little man is helping me tremendously."

"I'm glad." Lucy played with the folds of her skirt, looking as though she wanted to say something more but wasn't sure if she should.

"What is on your mind, sister dear?" said Harriett. "You know I prefer frank speech."

Lucy continued to fiddle with her skirts, but after a few moments, she released the fabric and smoothed her palms across the top. "I'm only wondering if the cause for your heartbreak is the man you mentioned a time or two in your letters. Lieutenant . . . Jamison, wasn't it?"

Harriett nodded. "Yes, but I would prefer not to dwell on him any longer."

Lucy tapped a finger to her lower lip and gazed at the far corner of the room, her brow furrowed in thought. "Er . . . Suppose a rather interesting posy arrived for you with the lieutenant's name on the card. Would you prefer to be informed of it or would you rather it go away unnoticed?"

Harriett ceased rocking, and her heart thumped and bumped inside her chest, loud enough to wake the baby. "He sent me a posy?"

Lucy shifted in her seat, looking uncomfortable. "Yes. Was I right to tell you?"

"Of course," said Harriett, feeling nervous and clammy all of a sudden. "Was only his name on the card?"

"On the front, yes, but perhaps he added a message to the back? Would you like me to retrieve it for you?"

"No, I . . ." Harriett did not know what she wanted. Part of her desperately wished to see it and another part wanted to have it sent away. Simply hearing his name had undone what little peace she had struggled to find since coming to London. What would seeing a posy with his name attached do to her? Why had he sent it? Was it an apology or a farewell gift?

What did she want it to mean?

As though sensing her agitation, Samuel began to stir and fuss. Lucy held out her arms for her son and asked, "May I?"

Harriett nodded, but as soon as she'd relinquished her hold on the baby, she felt exposed and vulnerable. There was no attempting to hide her feelings now.

"I don't know what to do," she whispered. When she

had first come to London, she had held onto the hope that Christopher did love her in some way and would find a way to prove it to her. But almost a fortnight had come and gone with no word from him, and that hope had begun to fade. Was there something left to hope for, or was she doomed to experience even more disappointment and pain?

"Go," whispered Lucy. "Then tell me what he means by it. As I said before, the posy is quite . . . interesting."

Harriett rose slowly and went down, dragging her slippers the entire way. The side table in the great hall contained a small assortment of posies and bouquets, and she recognized the lieutenant's immediately. It appeared plain and pitiable next to the others, but the memories it brought to Harriett's mind were anything but plain or pitiable.

She walked over to it and gingerly touched the young and tender oak limbs that held a smattering of tiny, star-like leaves, all tied together with a gold ribbon. A calling card was tucked inside, revealing the printed name of Lieutenant Christopher Jamison. She flipped it over to find a short message on the back.

To new beginnings?
—Chris

New beginnings? Harriett's forehead crinkled, and she bit her lower lip. What did he mean by that? Was he wishing her a new beginning without him in her life, or was he saying he wanted a new beginning *with* her? Perhaps he was merely referring to the newly sprouted leaves and spring.

Goodness, could the man be any more cryptic?

Harriett sank down on a nearby chair and stared at the card. Perhaps she should not have left Tanglewood in such a rush, leaving things between them so unfinished. But how could she not have run at the time? Her heart had never experienced such pain, and she could not bear to stay.

Ever since her arrival in London, she had searched parlors, drawing rooms, parks, and ballrooms for a glimpse of the lieutenant. When the butler announced a caller, she would hold her breath, hoping to hear his name and then be disappointed when it was someone else. She had wanted him to follow her here and fight for her, but every day that had come and gone with no communication left her feeling less and less hopeful.

And now a sorry little posy arrives with the message, *To new beginnings?* What in the world was she supposed to think of that? She needed a reason to hope or a reason to let go—not a blasted riddle.

Harriett stood and walked up to her room, where she tossed the oak branches on her dressing table and frowned at them until the time came for her to dress for her afternoon drive with Sir William. From the moment he arrived and helped her into his dashing curricle, she could not concentrate on a word he spoke. Now that she knew the lieutenant was in London, her eyes darted about, searching for him, trying to think of what she would say if she saw him. She had to ask Sir William numerous times to repeat what he'd just said, and by the time he returned her to Curzon Street, his curt behavior told Harriett that she would not be invited to drive with him again anytime soon.

At the door, she wished him well and silently cursed the lieutenant's name.

On Tuesday, a peach parasol arrived for her in the afternoon—the same parasol Chris had given to her after her humiliating encounter with the bird droppings. She'd left it behind on purpose, not wanting the reminder of him, but now it was back in her possession, along with another note.

Birds are everywhere, even in London. You ought to hold on to this.
 —Chris

Good grief. Did he think she had left it behind on accident? That she would treasure its return? He'd initially given it to her as a joke, for goodness' sake. Why would she ever want to be reminded of that?

When Charlotte exclaimed, "What a lovely parasol," Harriett had answered, "You may have it," and left the room. Would it truly have been so difficult to write, *I cannot stop thinking about you. All my love, Chris*? Apparently so. Apparently he was incapable of feeling any tender emotions whatsoever. It was a good thing he was so handsome. Otherwise he would never have any hope of wooing a wife.

That evening, when Harriett said she would be unable to attend Almack's because her head ached, it was the truth. The others went ahead without her, and Harriett cursed the lieutenant's name yet again.

On Wednesday, a footman walked into the drawing room bearing a large cake slathered in cream frosting. All conversation paused when he stopped near Harriett. Not far away, the butler cleared his throat. "Forgive our intrusion, my lady, but I was told this needed to be presented to you right away."

If the lieutenant had wanted to cause a stir, he couldn't have timed the arrival of the cake with more precision. The Duchess of Chamberlain and her daughter had called, along with Lady Dawson, Sir Richard, Mr. Hedgewick, and Lord Weston. With her mother, Lucy and Colin, and Charlotte also in attendance, the room had never felt more crowded.

All eyes watched Harriett as she accepted the accompanying note from the butler.

This will always remind me of the night you pursued me of your own volition. And at midnight, no less.

—Chris

Harriett immediately closed her hand over the note and prayed no one had been peering over her shoulder as she read it. A furious blush heated her cheeks as she frantically tried to think of an explanation. Who gifts an entire cake to a woman? Not a person in their right mind, that was for certain. And now Harriett was left with the task of coming up with an explanation that would not be carried to every other drawing room in London by the day's end.

That man!

She forced a smile to her lips. "Thank you, Peters. It looks even lovelier than I expected, although it wasn't supposed to arrive until later this afternoon. I had planned to surprise, er . . . Charlotte with it tonight as a thank you gift for being such a gracious hostess."

"Truly?" Charlotte had the presence of mind to appear delighted, bless her soul. "What a wonderful surprise, and one that certainly cannot wait until this evening. Peters, please take the cake to the kitchen and direct cook to serve it with the tea."

"Very good, my lady."

"You are all in for a real treat," said Harriett. "That particular flavor of cake is nothing short of divine."

"Where did it come from?" asked Lady Dawson, eyeing Harriett's closed hand with speculation.

"Why, Mrs. Jamison's talented cook, of course. She is quite renowned for her cakes." Harriett could only hope the woman did indeed have a knack for baking. She was about to be inundated with requests for her recipes, and it was all the lieutenant's doing.

On Thursday, a large box arrived for Harriett. Inside was a new pelisse made from a rich, golden-brown that was lined with the softest fur. Her mother, Lucy, and Charlotte oohed and awed over it while Harriett read the accompanying note to herself.

I shall never not see you again.
—Chris

She had to read it twice to assure herself that she had not imagined or misinterpreted the words. As her eyes skimmed over it a third time, a delicious warmth radiated from the crown of her head to the tips of her toes. Why could Christopher not have started with *this* note? She would never have cursed his name if he had.

"I take it this gift pleased you?" said Lucy with a sly smile. "Or was it his note? When will we get to finally meet this lieutenant of yours?"

"Oh, he is not mine," Harriett said quickly, though she was beginning to wonder if he would ever appear instead of a gift and a card. How she craved to see his handsome face again.

"Nonsense," Charlotte said. "Any man who sends a posy, a parasol, a delicious cake, and a new pelisse is most certainly yours. At least he'd better be. If not, such gifts would be most unseemly."

Harriett refrained from informing them that the lieutenant was rarely seemly. It was a trait she both adored and despised.

On Friday, an invitation arrived addressed to *Lady Harriett Cavendish and Family*. She knew right away who'd sent it because her name had been spelled correctly. With trembling fingers, she broke the seal to find an invitation to

Lady Carlyle's musicale that very evening—the same invitation that Charlotte had declined the week prior because her husband had surprised everyone with coveted tickets to see Ambrogetti perform at The King's Theater. Did Christopher know Lady Carlyle? Why would he arrange to have another invitation sent? Surely, Lady Carlyle had received Charlotte's reply—or had she?

With a frown, Harriett turned the invitation over, surprised to see a few scribbled words on the other side.

Please come.
—Chris

Harriett's heart lurched as she traced the letters with her finger, feeling torn. While she yearned to see him again, her brother-in-law had gone to a great deal of trouble and expense to procure the opera tickets. Not only that, but her mother, Lucy, and Charlotte had talked of nothing else for days. Harriett could never ask them to forgo such an opportunity and accompany her to an amateur musicale. But Harriett could not bring herself to decline Chris's invitation either, not when her heart still held onto a sliver of hope. Perhaps she could attend with one of her friends instead?

With hesitation, Harriett showed the invitation to the rest of her family, hoping they would understand why she could no longer go with them to the opera. Much to her surprise, Charlotte grinned. "Of course you must go to the musicale, and of course we will accompany you. It's past time we meet this mysterious and romantic lieutenant of yours. How silly of you to even contemplate going without us."

The others nodded in agreement, and without any signs of regret or hesitation, Charlotte penned a message to Lady Carlyle, saying they would be able to attend after all. Another message was sent to a close friend, asking if she would be able to use eight tickets to the opera.

Tears dampened Harriett's eyes as her family rallied around her. She had never felt more touched, loved, or grateful for their support. The fact of the matter was that she had no desire to face Christopher alone, and now she wouldn't have to.

When the time came to dress for the musicale, Harriett slipped into a soft and silky blue gown chosen by her mother, Lucy, Charlotte, and Tabby, all of whom agreed that it matched her eyes perfectly. Once Tabby had finished with the buttons, Harriett smoothed her hands nervously across the fabric. "What do you think? Do I look ravishing enough to tempt the lieutenant?"

Her mother smiled. "You will tempt every man in attendance tonight, my dear."

"You look beautiful," added Charlotte and Lucy at the same time.

Harriett's fingers tangled in the folds of her skirts as she swallowed. "I'm so nervous."

"Why?" asked Charlotte. "The man has all but declared himself."

Little did any of them know that he *had* declared himself, just not in a way that Harriett could accept. Would tonight be any different, or would she come away disappointed and shattered once more? She did not think her heart could withstand any more pain.

"Why does he wish to meet me at a musicale, do you think?" asked Harriett, giving voice to some of her worries. "We will not be able to converse much, there will be no opportunities to speak privately, and with Lady Carlyle hosting, it is sure to be a crush. Surely a ball or calling on me here would have been a better plan."

"I'll admit to having the same thought, but it only adds to the mystery of it, don't you think?" said Lucy.

"Perhaps." Harriett didn't know why she still held onto any expectations with regard to the lieutenant. It wasn't as though he had ever done or said what she thought he ought to. She needed to come to terms with that and either accept him back in her life or walk away for good.

"I know why he chose the musicale," said Charlotte. "Don't you remember last season? Mrs. Jamison and Lady Carlyle are the closest of friends. The Jamisons always stay with her when they are in town, so it was an easy thing for the lieutenant to procure another invitation for you."

"That's right," agreed their mother. "I had forgotten about that."

Harriett nodded as well, but her mind had moved beyond speculation and to the musicale. What did the lieutenant plan to do or say? Would he greet her when she arrived? Sit by her during the performance? Would he make his intentions towards her known and possibly even whisk her away at some point for a few moments of privacy?

No, she could not think such thoughts or she would certainly be disappointed. He was probably only testing the waters to see if she would talk to him again.

Harriett picked up her wrap and swung it around her shoulders with renewed determination. She would go, she would speak to him again, and she would erase all expectations, opinions, and desires from her mind. It was the only thing she could do.

CHRISTOPHER STOOD ON THE outskirts of the crowd, conversing with a mother and her pretty young daughter with only half an ear. He had been in London for only a week, but he'd already met far too many painfully shy or flirtatious debutantes. This particular one happened to be the latter. Highly proficient in the art of fan waving and not much else, it didn't take long for Christopher to determine that she ought to have applied herself more to the improvement of her mind than fan acrobatics.

"You must be so very brave if you are a lieutenant," she said, batting her eyelashes above the ridges of her gold fan.

Christopher had no idea what his title had to do with bravery. "All those under my command were brave as well," he said.

"Of course," she simpered. "But you must have appeared so commanding atop your horse."

"I was a lieutenant in the *navy*, Miss Temple."

"Yes, I know." She frowned as though she did not know what that had to do with anything.

Her mother cleared her throat. "Naval officers command ships, not horses, dearest."

Miss Temple's cheeks took on a rosy hue, and the waving of her fan became more rapid. "I see."

Christopher wasn't sure that she did. Perhaps he should leave her to be coached a little more by her mother. He opened his mouth to make his excuses, but closed it abruptly when he caught sight of Harriett stopping to greet his parents and the Carlyles in her graceful way. She wore a shimmering azure dress that hugged her figure in the most alluring way, and he could almost smell the scent of orange blossoms from where he stood.

Harriett said something that made all those around her smile, and Christopher suddenly wished that she was at his side instead of Miss Temple. Harriett knew the difference between the army and the navy, she understood that all men who fought were brave, and she did not need a fan to secure his attention. She drew it from everyone around her simply by being the multi-faceted woman he'd come to love and admire. She could be witty, silly, courageous, strong, determined, prideful, vulnerable, and kind. It's what made her so interesting, so complex, so . . . captivating. Add to that her beauty, and Christopher wondered if he could ever be deserving of her affections.

Could any man?

She turned from her hosts, and her intelligent eyes scanned the room, stopping when they found his. Her body stilled, and her mouth fell open ever so slightly. An almost palpable connection passed between them, tugging on Christopher with a very real force. How had he ever let her slip away?

"Excuse me," he said to Mrs. Temple, realizing belatedly that he had interrupted her. She would probably think him quite rude, but he didn't care at the moment. He moved forward, dodging and eluding people until he stood before Harriett.

She watched him, saying nothing.

"Thank you for coming," he said, feeling like a dolt for not coming up with something better than that.

She nodded and gestured to the woman at her side. "Lieutenant Jamison, I would like you to meet my mother, the dowager Countess of Drayson."

Her mother's dark hair was beginning to gray, but she was still quite beautiful with Harriett's same defined cheekbones and blue eyes. He bowed low over her hand. "It is good to meet you, my lady. Harriett has spoken of you often."

"All good things, I hope," she replied.

"Of course."

Harriett turned to her left and began more introductions. "This is my brother and his wife, Lord and Lady Drayson, my sister, Lady Charlotte and her husband, Mr. Baxter, and my other brother, the Honorable James Cavendish and his wife, Lady Arabella."

Christopher bowed to each in turn. "How wonderful. You've brought your entire family."

"How could I not?" she asked. "It is not every day one receives two invitations for the same event."

"Yes. Well, you declined the first one."

"Only because Mr. Baxter had procured tickets for us to see Ambrogetti tonight."

Christopher's eyes widened at this news. She had to be jesting, surely. He glanced over the many faces of her family for hints of a smile, but they all watched him expectantly, as though waiting for him to pull a tropical bird from his sleeve—one that could sing better than Ambrogetti.

Sadly, he was no magician. "Please tell me you did not give up those tickets to come here tonight." he said at last.

Harriett leaned forward and placed a hand on his arm. "That is precisely what we did, Lieutenant. Now, if you'll excuse us, we should like to secure our seats here before there are none left to be had."

A feeling of unease filled Christopher's stomach. Devil take it. This was merely an amateur musicale with only one group of professionals hired to perform the final number—none of whom could come close to competing with Ambrogetti.

As Harriett glided away with her mother, Christopher touched a finger to his forehead, feeling a sudden headache coming on. Good gads. The family he hoped to one day call his own would never forgive him for this.

Lord Drayson patted him on the shoulder as he passed. "Not to worry, Lieutenant. I'm certain you will see to it that we are delighted by this evening's performances."

"Agreed," said Lady Charlotte as she walked by on the arm of her husband.

The Honorable James chortled, stopping next to Christopher and lowering his voice. "If it is any consolation, I was glad for the excuse to avoid the theater tonight. I do so hate the opera. All that wailing gives me a headache."

"How can you say such things?" chided Lady Arabella. "Ambrogetti is a wonder."

"*You* are the wonder, my love, and the only reason I was willing to attend the opera tonight."

Such a comment earned him a pleased smile from his wife, along with a charming tap of her fan on his arm. As they moved to join the rest of their family, Christopher wished he would have met James sooner and taken a lesson or two from him. Perhaps if he had, he would not feel it necessary to do what he was about to do tonight.

With one last lingering glance at Harriett's back, he went to join his parents and the Carlyles.

By the time intermission arrived, Harriett felt weak and lightheaded. She should have forced herself to eat something earlier, but the mere thought of food had set her stomach on edge. She rubbed her clammy hands against the cool silk of her skirts, wondering where Chris had gone and why he hadn't taken the vacant seat at her side. Surely, he did not plan to say only a few words to her and leave it at that, did he?

Drat the man.

Harriett refused to search the room for him, but that did not stop her from eyeing the double doors leading out to a balcony with increasing desperation. She had been able to keep a cool head when she'd spoken to him earlier, but she had felt anything but cool. It didn't take long before she felt her composure begin to slip and so she had quickly made her excuses, needing a moment to catch her breath.

She needed another one of those moments now. The balcony called to her, and Harriett stood, knowing that if she did not step outside at once she might faint.

"I'll be back in a moment," she said to her mother before dodging several people and making her escape. She soon learned that she wasn't the only guest in need of fresh air—several others were already scattered around, talking and laughing. Harriett quickly located an empty spot along the balustrade and went there, leaning against it as she gulped in air. Despite her determination to come with no expectations, she knew precisely what she wanted most, and she was frightened to death of leaving without it.

Heavy footsteps sounded behind her, and Harriett froze. Had Chris followed her out here? Was she ready to speak to him alone? Would he see the fear in her eyes and the trembling of her limbs?

"You look as though you could use a drink," said Colin, appearing at her side. He held out a glass to her, which she accepted gratefully and drank all at once, hoping it would settle her stomach and ease her anxiousness.

Her brother took the empty glass from her and set it on one of the pillars. "Are you well?" he asked.

"No," Harriett answered honestly. "I feel as though I have wagered all of my funds on a man who is bound to disappoint me. Why? Why have I come tonight? I feel ill." Queasiness took hold of her stomach, and she placed her hand over it in an attempt to calm it. "I should have sipped that drink and not guzzled it."

Colin leaned forward, resting his elbows on the balustrade, and looked out over the gardens. "I don't know exactly what has occurred between you and Lieutenant Jamison, but I cannot imagine he'd go to such great lengths to see that you came tonight if he intended to disappoint you."

"I don't think he ever *intends* to do it," she said. "I think it's just the way of things with him."

"He must have some redeemable qualities or we would be at the opera right now and not at an amateur musicale."

"Oh, he does," she agreed. "It's just . . ." Words failed her, and she shook her head, imploring her brother to understand her confusion and say something to comfort her.

He straightened and leaned his hip against the railing and cocked his head at her. "Perhaps you are the problem."

She blinked at him, wide-eyed, thinking his words not at all comforting. "I beg your pardon."

He laughed. "That came out wrong, didn't it? I only meant to say that love can turn a level-headed man into a bumbling fool. Let us wait and see what the remainder of the evening brings before we judge him too harshly, shall we? It appears as though everyone is taking their seats. Will you join me?"

He held out his arm, but Harriett did not accept it right away. "Only on one condition. If tonight proves to be a disappointment, will you promise to challenge Lieutenant Jamison to a duel? It is a brother's duty to stand up for his sister, after all."

He snickered. "You're asking me to call out a former lieutenant in the navy? He's probably a crack shot."

"Judging by his skill at archery, I would say you are correct."

His snicker became a chuckle. "How about I plant him a facer instead? Would that suffice?"

"I suppose."

"Good." He tucked her arm into his. "Now let us take our seats before we are forced to interrupt."

She nodded, and as she accompanied her brother through the doors and back to the ballroom, she noticed that her stomach did not feel quite so queasy any longer. She gave his arm a grateful squeeze, thankful to have such a brother. He'd given her a reason to smile when she needed it most. She could only hope that Chris would give her another.

A quick perusal of the room showed no sign of him, and as Harriett took her seat, she experienced a small surge of irritation. It actually felt good and even calmed some of her fears. Why had Chris asked her to come tonight if he did not intend to speak with her? She and her family had missed the opportunity to hear Ambrogetti sing, and for what? To hear a series of mediocre performances? It didn't take long before

Harriett decided that it might be *she* who planted Chris that facer and not her brother.

The second half of the musicale soon began, and with each passing performance, time slowed to an excruciating pace. Had her state of mind been different, Harriett might have found something to like in each performance—the musicians were all accomplished—but her frustration held her captive, stealing all pleasantness from the evening. By the time Lord Carlyle stood to announce what she prayed would be the final performance, her head pounded. Though she had tried her best not to expect anything from Chris tonight, she *had* expected *something*.

"Before I introduce the talented musicians who will play our concluding number," said Lord Carlyle, "I would like to give a few moments to someone I have come to think of as my own son. He has written a sonnet he would like to share, and I hope you will indulge us with this slight deviation from the program. Please extend a warm welcome to Lieutenant Christopher Jamison."

Applause sounded in Harriett's ears, but it seemed to come from somewhere faraway. Had she heard correctly? Chris was to read a sonnet that *he'd* written?

She twisted in her chair to see him walking from the back of the room, clutching a piece of paper in his hand and looking for all the world like a man on his way to the guillotine.

Harriett's own words echoed in her mind. *I want a man who finds my quirks endearing, a man who complements my weaknesses with his strengths, a man who is willing to make a fool of himself over me.*

Oh dear. Was that the reason he'd invited her here tonight—to make a fool of himself over her? If so, what did he plan to say? She could only imagine what words he'd written, and none of her imaginings brought her any peace of mind. Surely he would not claim affection for a certain Harry, would he? Harriett closed her eyes briefly, attempting to shut out worrisome thoughts about midnight assignations, climbing trees, mud puddles, or bird droppings.

Surely he wouldn't make her appear the fool as well. That would defeat the whole point of it.

Christopher took the center of the stage with his confident stance and offered the crowd his heart-stopping smile. From the curious glances her family sent her way, Harriett knew they were very much interested in what he had to say. She, on the other hand, was petrified.

His smiled landed on her for a brief moment before he addressed the audience. "In keeping with the theme for this evening's entertainment, I have asked the talented Miss Taylor to accompany my reading with the lovely sounds of her harp. While we wait for her to take her place, I feel it necessary to inform those of you who are skeptical of my poetic abilities"—his gaze landed briefly on Harriett—"that every word of this sonnet is mine and mine alone. If you are impressed, feel free to shower me with praise." Laughter sounded throughout the room, and he had to wait a moment for it to die down. "But if you are not impressed, which may very well be the case, all I can offer is my promise to never write another poem as long as I live." More chuckles sounded as he nodded towards the harpist. "Miss Taylor? Whenever you are ready."

The woman lifted her fingers to the harp's strings and began to play while Chris unfolded the piece of paper he carried. The slight tremors in his hands were the only indication that he was at all nervous.

You don't need to do this, Harriett thought, willing him to leave the stage at once.

A hush fell over the room as his rich tones filled the air.

"What's in a Name?
by Lieutenant Christopher Jamison

"I encountered a lady one spring day
Who surprised me. With liveliness and grace
And mud on her face, she swept me away
To an enchanting and luminous place.
Clever and strong with a flair all her own
She's as unpredictable as the sea.
Scaling trees, plopping in ponds, she is prone
To entertain, and I love her hopelessly.
She walks with grace, radiant and stately.
My eyes linger on her. I contemplate
And conclude: She is too much above me.
But dunce that I am, I cannot negate
The power she wields over my poor soul.
Without her, I'm but a sad, wretched fool."

Silence reigned for a moment before applause echoed through the room. Harriett could only stare at Chris while her heart pounded loudly in her ears.

I love her hopelessly.

The words echoed in her mind, overwhelming her emotions. In fourteen short lines, Chris had done the unimaginable. He'd proven to her that he saw more in Harriett than her beauty. He saw her strengths, her weaknesses, her quirks. He saw her for who she truly was. What's more, he loved her for them.

She ought to be upset that he'd exposed many of her humiliations to a room filled with people, but she wasn't. She didn't care a whit what others might think or say if they were to discover that she was the subject of that sonnet. On the contrary, warmth, tenderness, giddiness, and joy swept through her like a burst of wind, somehow warming and chilling her at the same time.

Oh, how she loved that man.

The applause died down, and Chris bowed briefly before exiting the stage. He glanced at Harriett as he passed, then disappeared through a door at the side of the ballroom. Harriett would have leapt from her chair and followed him had her mother not squeezed her hand, reminding her that there was still one more performance to endure.

As the musicians took the stage and began to play, Harriett's foot tapped impatiently against the marble. It was a lovely tune, truly, but it seemed to go on and on and on. Did they intend to play all night? Would she be able to find Chris when it was all over?

When at last the song came to an end, she lifted her hands to join in the applause, grateful for its conclusion. Before she could leave, however, Charlotte, Arabella, and Lucy clustered around her.

"Scaling trees? Plopping in ponds?" Lucy whispered. "What did he mean by that?"

"And mud on your face?" added Arabella. "Was that true?"

Harriett smiled, feeling deliciously happy. "He neglected to mention the bird droppings as well."

"What *have* you been doing at Tanglewood?" asked her mother.

A light tap on her shoulder caused Harriett to look up and find Mrs. Jamison at her side. "Forgive my intrusion, my dear, but my son would very much like a private word with you at your convenience. He is awaiting you in the library."

Harriett immediately stood, more than ready to see him.

"Where is the library?"

"Come with me."

Mrs. Jamison led her to the same door Chris had disappeared through earlier and down a long hallway, finally stopping before a pair of mahogany doors. As Harriett drew in a deep breath, Mrs. Jamison took one of her hands between both of hers and squeezed it firmly. "Before I leave you, my dear, I want you to know that you have been a godsend to my son. Regardless of your answer, I shall always think of you with great fondness."

Tears filled Harriett's eyes, and she threw her arms around Chris's mother. "I do not know why I am crying. I must look a fright."

"You look lovely," Mrs. Jamison assured her. "Now go and put my poor son out of his misery."

Harriett nodded and faced the doors. After taking another deep breath, she pushed one open and slipped inside, closing it softly behind her. Compared to the brightness of the ballroom, the library was dark and shadowy. The fire crackling in the hearth was the only source of light. Chris drew himself up from a large, wingback chair and turned to face her.

How handsome and mysterious he looked with firelight flickering across his face. A few locks of hair had fallen across his forehead, and Harriett felt the strongest urge to tuck them back into place. She moved forward to meet him, stopping a few feet away to study every crease and line etched into his face, the most pronounced being those that crinkled when he smiled.

She had missed seeing that smile and hearing his laughter. She had missed him.

"Apparently I can add 'poet' to your extensive list of talents," she said.

He stepped forward and cautiously reached for her hand. "You liked it then?"

She nodded. "I think your sonnet may very well have taken the place of Mr. Chant's as one of my most treasured possessions, assuming you will make me a copy of it."

"Only *may have* taken the place of it?" he asked. "Because I'm fairly certain his so-called sonnet was not technically a sonnet."

"Then yours will definitely be my most treasured."

"I'm glad we sorted that out." He cautiously threaded his fingers through hers and pulled her closer with wariness in his eyes. He swallowed nervously. "My family doesn't have much, you know. It is going to take years to build our estate back to what it once was, and until then I cannot offer you the comforts you are used to having."

"I know," she said.

"I hope you also know that whatever dowry you possess will be yours and yours alone. I do not intend to touch it."

"Then you are a fool."

He smiled slightly and captured her face with his hands. "Agreed. I was a fool to propose to you the way I did and an even bigger fool to let you walk away. Will you forgive me yet again?"

She leaned into his touch and sighed with pleasure. "I suppose I must if I am to be a good Christian."

He grinned. "I am glad to hear that all of my biblical readings did not fall on deaf ears."

"No, only annoyed ones."

His rich laughter echoed through the room as he pulled her into his strong and capable arms. She reveled in the feel of him as she breathed in the scents of cinnamon and leather, perfectly content to remain tucked up next to him forever.

"You do know that I adore you, don't you?" he

murmured into her hair, sending a flurry of chills down her spine.

"Do you?" she breathed.

He lifted his head and pressed his forehead to hers. "I have always had a difficult time sharing what is in my heart, but from this point forward, I intend to do a better job of that." He paused for a moment before continuing. "Harriett, you have invaded my mind and heart and now hold them captive. When I contemplate a life without you, it is unacceptable to me. I want to see you every day, kiss you whenever I wish, and wake up to your beautiful face each and every morning. I want to run my family's estate with you at my side and continue to best you at archery and shuttlecock and cards. I want to share cake with you at midnight and love you to my heart's content."

He lifted his head from hers and searched her eyes. "Will you please consent to becoming my wife?"

Tears fell freely down her cheeks, and Harriett didn't bother wiping them away. She nodded. "Of course I will marry you. It could never be anyone but you."

His mouth found hers in an instant, and Harriett was swept into a glorious world of dazzling sensations and indescribable joy. He kissed her long and hard with a passion she didn't know existed. It intoxicated her, making her feel dizzy and lightheaded and so very loved.

Something prodded and nipped at her slipper, and with a squeal of fright, Harriett jumped back and looked down, expecting to find a rodent of some kind. But as soon as she spotted a familiar brown and white puppy sniffing at the floor, her squeal became one of delight. She dropped to her knees and gently lifted it to her face, nuzzling it with her nose.

"You brought it with you," she said.

He crouched beside her and gave the puppy a playful rub. "Apparently, he's the naughtiest of the bunch. He was supposed to stay in his basket until I retrieved him."

"Him?" Harriett asked with a smile, tucking the wriggling puppy against her chest.

"I made sure it was a male so you wouldn't be tempted to place a ghastly pink bow on its head. I was thinking we could call him Mischief."

She laughed. "This little fellow? Mischief? I don't think so."

"Come now, after his behavior just now, you must admit the name suits him. He and Wicked have already become the best of friends."

The puppy squirmed from Harriett's hold and scrambled to the floor, nipping at her slipper yet again.

She laughed. "Very well. Mischief it is. But should we ever have children, Chris, you are not allowed to name them. Otherwise, we will have a Lucifer, Iniquity, and Trouble running about, and how would we explain such names to our neighbors? Every disaster would be blamed on one of them, and how fair would that be?"

"If our children take after me, it would probably be more than fair."

She laughed again and kissed him on the cheek. "In that case, I will see to it that they take after me."

"How do you plan to do that, exactly?" He grinned, taking her hand and pulling her up. "By adding a duplicate letter to the end of each of their names? Are we to have a Francess, Hannahh, and Phillipp running about?" he asked, adding an extra sound to each.

She took hold of his lapels and grinned up at him. "Even you must admit that would be the preferable option."

"We will be accused of being nitwits."

"Better nitwits than unchristian, wouldn't you say?" she countered. "Or do you plan to do away with your sermons?"

He chuckled and wrapped his arms around her, dropping a kiss on her lips, "You always have to have the last word, don't you?"

"Hmm . . ." she murmured, feeling giddy and scattered and so very happy. "Perhaps you should start kissing me before I speak. I will likely lose all train of thought and forget any and all last words."

He kissed her again. "Have I ever told you that you're brilliant?"

"No."

"You're brilliant."

"Thank you."

With one last kiss, he loosened his hold on her and cast a pained glance at the door. "I suppose we ought to find the others and share our happy news. At least my parents and the Carlyles will think it happy. I cannot say as much for your family. I'm probably in their black books for denying them Ambrogetti and subjecting them to an inferior night of music. Do you think they'll be inclined to forgive me, or should I bring my Bible along?"

The puppy nipped at one of Harriett's slippers again, so she scooped it up, nuzzling it against her neck. "Once we show my sisters this adorable little face, I'm quite certain they'll forgive you anything."

"Are you implying that my face will not do the trick? Because I am far more handsome than Ambrogetti, you know."

She nodded in agreement. "That you are, my love. But I still think we'll need the puppy."

"If you insist." He gently extracted Mischief from her

arms, tucked it against his coat, and held out his free arm for her to take. Together, they rejoined the others in the ballroom.

As her mother and his parents exclaimed over the news of their betrothal, and her sisters doted on the puppy, Harriett's thoughts drifted back to her visit to Tanglewood and all the events that had led her to this one blissful moment.

For years and years, Tanglewood had sat vacant, serving no purpose whatsoever. Then, like a trickle of rain before a summer storm, things began to change. Life was introduced to the estate once more, granting it a purpose, a reason for being built. And with that life came love. It was at Tanglewood that Lucy had found Colin, Cora discovered Jonathan, and Harriett had somehow managed to snare Chris.

And this was only the beginning.

Across the world, a great many homes sat empty and purposeless. What would happen if a little rain happened by and breathed new life into them? The transition wouldn't be seamless—change never was. There would undoubtedly be plenty of mischief, mayhem, and misunderstandings. But Harriett had learned that if a person chose to weather the storm, the rainbow that followed would be nothing short of miraculous.

That first day when she'd encountered Chris, Harriett had seen a rainbow, and she was seeing another one now. Only this time, instead of a hazy, unexceptional thing, it was vibrant and breathtaking, arching over her world with beauty and majesty.

And it had all begun with only one little raindrop of change.

Dear Reader,

Thank you so much for reading and supporting my efforts! I hope this series provided you with a break from the daily grind and rejuvenated you in some way. Tanglewood was a fun world to get lost in these past few years, and although I'm sad to say goodbye to these characters, I'm excited to embark on a new regency series (stay tuned for more news concerning that).

If you're interested in being notified of new releases, you can sign up for my New Release mailing list on my website at RachaelReneeAnderson.com. I will happily notify you when books and audiobooks are available and keep you in the loop of what to expect in the future.

Also, if you can spare a few minutes, I'd be incredibly grateful for a review from you on Goodreads and/or Amazon. They make a huge difference in every aspect of publishing, and I'm always so thankful when readers take a few minutes to review a book.

Thanks again for your support. I wish you all the best!

Rachael

TANGLEWOOD SERIES

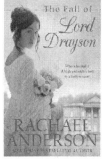

BOOK 1   BOOK 2   BOOK 3

ACKNOWLEDGEMENTS

I always feel so overwhelmed and grateful when I write this section. It's at the end of a book as I reflect back on the entire process that I realize how I could never go at this alone, and I'm so grateful I don't have to.

My fabulous sister, Letha, is always my go-to person for helping me plot and outline. She's one of the most happy and selfless people I know, and my books are so much better because of her input. My good friend and walking buddy, Alison Blackburn, also helped me work through several sticky patches, and I'm so grateful for her in my life.

I wouldn't dare to publish this book without the help of Braden Bell, Andrea Pearson, Karey White, Karen Porter, Megan Jacobson, and my sweet mother, Linda Marks. I can't even tell you how many errors and mistakes they've helped me see and fix. I used to think that I would someday get to the point where I could write a story that didn't need a million corrections, but I've come to realize that will never happen. Thank goodness for smarter people than me who are able (and willing) to fix my stories.

My least favorite part of this business is marketing, and I have no idea what I'd do without my awesome friend, Kathy Habel. Not only does she read all my books, but she's invaluable when it comes to helping me promote them. She's the best kind of person there is.

I also want to thank my newfound friend in the UK, Helen Taylor, for her input and for narrating the audiobook so beautifully. She's a genius, in my opinion.

Kathy Hart, thank you for nudging me to write this series and cheering me on along the way.

Last of all, I must express my deepest appreciation to my husband and kids for their continued encouragement, to my readers for their support, and to my Heavenly Father, for challenging and blessing me throughout this journey.

ABOUT THE AUTHOR

RACHAEL ANDERSON is a *USA Today* bestselling author and mother of four crazy and awesome kids. Over the years she's gotten pretty good at breaking up fights or at least sending guilty parties to their rooms. She can't sing, doesn't dance, and despises tragedies, but she recently figured out how yeast works and can now make homemade bread, which she is really good at eating. You can read more about her and her books online at RachaelReneeAnderson.com.

Made in the USA
Middletown, DE
07 April 2018